THE VAULT

JETTIE NECOLE

To: Brandon & Jill

Enjoy my radioactive love triangle!

Thank you for all your support & love.

xoxo

Jettie Necole

JETTIE NECOLE

The Vault
By Jettie Necole

Copyright © 2012 Jettie Necole

Jettie Necole
www.jettienecole.com

First Paperback Edition: May 2014

ISBN 978-0-9887469-0-9

Cover design by Robby Davis
www.robbydavis.com

Mom ~ for always believing in me

Todd ~ my wonderful "hus-bud"

THE VAULT

Chapter 1

Silence had finally come. The heavy draw to close her eyes on a day not easily forgotten was too alluring. Olivia Parker could only hear her own breaths now, a steady rate, not deep panting sobs as before. No, they'd dissolved along with the tears on her cheek, leaving a crusty trail that reflected her loss—everyone's loss. A pain had welled up in her throat until it finally couldn't be contained any longer at the thought of saying goodnight to her mother and her brother, and this had triggered it all again. She'd cried until her eyes felt as if they'd explode out of their sockets, until her mouth had dried out so badly it reminded her of cardboard. She'd mourned harder than before, the last time being her father's death, but that was natural, that was supposed to happen. This wasn't!

She laid curled up on a tiny bed, tightly gripping her pillow in a hug. She imagined it was her mother instead of a feathery carcass. It helped, for she began to drift off into sleep, but not because she wanted to; no, she wanted to continue crying, cry until she too were dead, because she didn't belong here. She was meant to be with them, with the dead. Then it happened, she couldn't fight it any longer, she gave in with one shuddering thought: The world is gone…

Olivia awoke abruptly to a knock at the door followed by a short command from a husky male voice, "Grand Hall, ten minutes!"

Olivia rubbed her eyes, wondering for a brief moment if Jack was playing some sort of game, but then she noticed the room, a metal dresser, a desk—neither were hers. Where was she? It happened in a flash, the entire previous day came racing back to her mind and she cringed, half believing it must have been a dream. A second scan of the room and male voice fading as it announced to the next door and the next, "Grand Hall in ten minutes," confirmed this was her nightmare. Everyone's nightmare.

She brought her hands to her face, rubbing out the thoughts that seemed unreal. She opened her eyes to see her fingers shaking. Her eyes glided to the gold bracelet that hung on her wrist, her mother's bracelet, a gift she'd given her only a few days ago when she'd still been alive. Olivia shook the thought of her mother, knowing that she'd not make it if she allowed the memory to come back. Instead, her bladder reminded her that she had to get up and out of bed, that a natural need couldn't be ignored, and so she found the bathroom promptly.

When she'd relieved herself, she thought how silly it was for her to think of lining the seat with tissue, the toilet probably had never been used. It appeared brand new. Everything around her was brand spanking new. She screamed in her head. Where was she?

When she finally glanced at herself in the mirror, she cringed at her appearance, especially under her eyes. She felt the tiny red veins wave at her, declaring themselves as a tattoo of her pain—the truth displayed for everyone to see. Vanity wasn't her worry. That she could see her reflection was unsettling because it announced that she was with the living, no matter how much she wanted to die. It scared her.

"Am I real?" she whispered to her reflection, confirming her answer with a wince of pain as she touched her swollen eyelid. *So, everything* did *happen?* she thought to herself. The person in the mirror now appeared more like an older woman than a girl of seventeen. She forced a smile at herself, seeing for the first time the person, not the girl. "You should be dead," she whispered. Then she raised her voice to a shout, "Why do you get to live?" She laughed without knowing why. She suddenly became disgusted with the person looking back at her. She drew her fingers into a fist and punched the mirror. A small grinding sound followed her scream as a crack formed in the center of the mirror. She grabbed her fist, caressing it as she watched the mirror hold inside its casing. She shook her head at herself, her reflection now slightly distorted, but not enough to matter. She exhaled deeply as she forced her eyes to look away and down at her wounded knuckles. They appeared fine, no bleeding, only sore.

She huffed. "We'll that hurt, idiot," she stated sarcastically to her reflection. She shook her head and mumbled, "I'm alone," sinking down to the floor, defeated. Drawing her knees to her chest she didn't know what to do next. Staring at the concrete floor, she noticed the tiny pores found in what seemed to be a perfectly cemented bathroom floor. Quickly, she was reminded of her father, who had once tried laying concrete for the backyard patio, how he'd spent so much time trying to make it level and smooth. The thought that her father could have done better on his weekend project brought with it a slight glimmer of Olivia's previous recovery. *Moving forward*, her mother had said to her all those years ago after his death, *moving forward is what your father wanted*. She'd said it as more of an order he'd given than an insight about what to do next. Olivia sighed at this thought, knowing those words had worked, but only because she'd been able to say goodbye to him. She'd not been able to say goodbye to her mom, to Jack. How could she move forward?

At that moment, a male voice shouted from the other room, "Olivia!"

Olivia looked at the bathroom door, knowing exactly who was beyond it. She couldn't believe that she'd forgotten about him, but he was there, standing on the other side of that door, and she hated him for what he'd done.

The Los Angeles airport was gigantic. Olivia couldn't believe how it seemed to go on forever. Her arm had actually started to hurt. Her mom had told her she'd packed too much, enough for a month when the trip was only for two days. Looking down at the large purple luggage on wheels made her second guess her choices. Did she really need five dresses and four pairs of pants? Her arm at the moment said no! She smiled though, not really caring that her mom had been right again—she was just thrilled to be on her own. She'd never dreamed that her overly sheltering mom would actually allow her to travel by plane to another city alone.

She was seventeen, the smartest student in her senior class, employee of the week twice, regional debate team winner, and the only one who could fix any and all electronic problems at home. Her confidence level was above ordinary, at least in the intellectual department. Her self-assuredness was still lacking in her social interaction when dealing with the opposite sex, at least the good-looking ones. She figured them to be more of a distraction than anything else, having never been on a date. Not that she couldn't get one if she wanted, considering that in the last year she'd bloomed into her full woman's body, and guys couldn't seem

4

to take their eyes off her. She'd noticed too. Still shy, instead of being swept away by the new attention, she'd convinced herself that getting into a good college was her number one goal—being social came last. Besides, after her father's funeral her priorities had changed. She'd changed. Her biggest desire was to prove to her mom that all her sacrifices in raising her as a single mother were well worth it. She was basically an adult now, at least that's what she'd petitioned to her mom on more than one occasion. Each time, her mother insisted that she'd never be convinced, always stating that she was *her little girl*. How Olivia hated that response. However, being a little girl forever didn't keep her from being accepted to Berkeley!

Olivia had been invited for a last interview as a condition for being accepted into the fall semester at Berkeley. Her mother couldn't say no, but she couldn't afford the second plane ticket to accompany her, since bills had to be paid. Olivia, using her talent at convincing almost anyone to agree with her, won this battle, and was permitted to fly alone to California for the interview. Luckily, a chaperon was provided upon her arrival, and the trip had gone as she'd hoped, ending with the Dean of Engineering extending a congratulations and welcome.

It had been a beautifully designed campus that leaked sophistication at every turn, especially the open air of possibility that seemed to surround it. The trip had blown Olivia away, in no small part due to her capable chaperon, who'd given her one eye-opening tour that left Olivia in a jaw-dropping daze. She'd been sure she'd not have gotten that exposure if her mom had been there. Excitement boiled under her skin at her first step as an adult. It only sucked that she still had a month left in her final high school semester and an entire summer before she would be on her way to college.

Olivia spotted Gate 22, her connecting flight home. She pulled out her cell phone and checked the time, eleven thirty. She had an hour before departure. She'd already called her mom and told her the good news. She'd been thrilled and wanted to wait to tell Jack, Olivia's twenty-year-old brother, together. Then her mom had immediately gone into her nagging about safety and watching out for strangers and not leaving her luggage unattended. A few reassuring *yeahs* later, as it usually took with her mom, and she finally had her off the phone. With no one to call or text, Olivia decided to read something and darted off to the first shop she could find.

She scanned the walls quickly and stopped at a romance novel, one that she would have to hide from her mom. The cover screamed hot and steamy, especially the guy they'd chosen for the picture, revealing his defined chest. About six months ago, Olivia had found an old stash of romance novels in the attic. She knew they were her mother's from long ago, and her interest started out as only curiosity. She'd even made fun of them, especially the covers, yet after secretly reading one, just one, she'd become hooked. It had been that handsome warrior who saved a young beauty around her own age that drew her in. The romance, the passion, the descriptions of everything, not just the past medieval era, but the love scenes, things she couldn't have ever imagined, that she'd never done! She'd assumed that since she wasn't active with the guys at her school like most of the other girls were, she'd at least read about it in a love story—there wasn't any harm in that! She was only learning more about the unknown, and it was pretty amazing, certainly nothing she'd ever willingly discuss with her mom.

Olivia's eyes glanced side to side, checking to see if anyone noticed her. Alone for the moment, she decided to pick it up, turning it over she read, *A Viking prince is forced to wed Shana, a foreign princess who he vows never to love because of the hatred he has for his father, yet Shana is different from any woman in his lands. Before he can deny her, she denies him...* Sold. Olivia clasped the book tightly to her chest with a giggle, wondering how this hero would win the lady's hand. Thirsty, she hurried down the aisle to find a Coke. With a soda and book in one hand and an uncooperative piece of luggage in the other, she made way for the checkout. She kept her eyes on the luggage's wheels, trying to stop them from veering into shelves, and then it happened. She collided into something... someone!

"Uh," Olivia grunted as she fell to the floor, dropping her Coke and book, her palms smacking hard against the tiled floor as she landed. A hand extended before her. Stinging hands and knees made Olivia groan again as she slowly followed the length of the arm to its owner's face. Her mouth dropped open, slightly.

"Sorry, I didn't see you," he said, his deep voice smooth and sincere.

Olivia's breath caught in her throat and the guy before her had everything to do with it. His dark features were stunning as he towered over her in a simple pair of jeans and a T-shirt that fit snuggly against his strong form. His blue eyes and dark hair were amazingly unlike anything she'd ever seen.

"Here, let me help you," he insisted, not waiting for her to reply. He grabbed her by the shoulders and lifted her up to her feet effortlessly. His touch sent a jolt to her stomach, then their eyes locked, causing a tiny gasp to catch in Olivia's throat. He stared down at her, his features mesmerizing, his presence closer than she could believe. "Are you okay?" he asked with concern, taking a step back and dropping his hands from her, his eyes scanning her body for damage.

She nodded, unbelieving that his touch had made her stomach flip. He was older than her, she could tell, she guessed twenty-one. "Yeah, I'm fine," she managed to mumble as she noticed his gorgeous smile that accented his eyes. Who was this guy? He must be a movie star she quickly figured, considering she was in Los Angeles, but she couldn't place him in anything. His five o'clock shadow made him appear as rugged as the warriors Olivia read about.

He looked down at the ground and picked something up in one fast motion. "Is this yours?" he asked, pushing the object into

Olivia's hand.

Olivia slowly looked down at the item he'd given her, the half-naked Viking prince jumped out at her. *Oh no*, she silently groaned to herself. The book! All she could think about was how she wanted to die of embarrassment. Quickly recovering her voice, her eyes hidden from his, she mumbled, "No," shaking her head as she pushed the book back to him. "No," she reaffirmed while searching the ground until she found her Coke nestled against a rack of neck pillows. "That's mine," she said, her voice raised in a desperate attempt to change the subject as she bent down to pick it up. Rising with a little hop, she held the Coke in her hand, shaking it in front of him, hoping it would distract him from the book.

His eyes fixed on her for a brief moment before darting from the Viking prince to her red face. "You sure?" he asked with a half grin that said he wasn't buying it. He turned the book over and began reading from the back: "A Viking prince is forced to wed…"

"No, it's not," Olivia squeaked, interrupting him before he could finish. She quickly grabbed the handle to her luggage and turned away, trying to put as much distance between her and the man as she could.

"Hey!" he shouted after her.

Olivia gripped the luggage handle tighter at the sound of his voice. *What now?* Gradually, she turned around, trying not to stare directly into his eyes; however, it was proving to be difficult.

"You might want a different Coke, that one's all shaken up," he stated nonchalantly.

"Oh, yeah." She hesitated, wondering if he noticed that she was ready to fizzle even more than the Coke in question.

"I'll get it," he offered, turning toward the cooler and giving Olivia an excellent view of his totally fit physique. *Oh my God*, she thought to herself. In no time, he was back around to her with a fresh Coke in hand. "Here you go." His friendly eyes beamed.

"Oh, thanks," she said. Without thinking, she extended the

old Coke toward him and cast her eyes down.

He took the ruined can from her and gave her the new one. His eyes scanned her face, her lips. His stare changed to a curious mode, and Olivia could feel it.

She peeked up at him and found a charming smile form on his face. She wanted to move away as fast as possible. She lifted her head, meeting his smile with a quick one of her own and then turned, held her breath, and hurried down another aisle, pretending to continue her shopping. She stopped in the candy aisle where she locked eyes on a bag of chocolate covered pecans, scolding herself for her ridiculous behavior and how lame she'd been. An above average, way above average guy talked to her, and what does she do, she runs! He could have been a model, she thought, and she'd come off as some kind of freak who reads dirty books.

She wanted to see him though, one more look-see, she thought. She sighed. Grabbing the bag of chocolate covered pecans she raised her eyes above the shelf. He wasn't there. She scanned the entire store, finding only the cashier and an older woman checking out. He was gone. She sighed again, wondering who he could have been. When she was sure that no one else was nearby, she quickly walked back over to where he'd laid her Viking prince book and snatched it up. She was determined to buy it now more than ever. She'd suffered for it, that was for sure.

She casually slid the book, cover down, toward the twenty-something-year-old cashier, who didn't pay it or her any attention, just another customer and another product to ring up, which eased Olivia's mind. In less than a minute, she'd purchased her Coke, chocolates, and her first own romance novel.

Upon exiting the shop, she stretched her neck from side to side wondering if maybe… but he wasn't there, the blue-eyed star was gone. She shrugged her shoulders and decided it would probably be best if she went back to her gate. She was lucky to have returned, because Gate 22 was packed, every seat. Some people had even gone so far as to put their luggage and personal belongings in the seat beside them. She glanced to her right. Gate 21 seemed to have one open. She glided through the passengers' legs and bags, fighting her own luggage the entire way. She really needed to get that wheel fixed, she thought to herself.

When she came around a bend of passengers, she saw the open seat and came to an abrupt halt. There he was, the blue-eyed movie star sitting before her, beside the one open seat! She didn't budge, not knowing if she should sit down or if she should bolt. She stared at the empty chair wanting to sit, but she was scared of something she couldn't put her finger on. Before she could make up her mind, he glanced up.

She stared back.

He recognized her. "Hey, we meet again."

"Yeah," she said with a slight smile, feeling unable to breathe as her heart rate increased.

"Need a seat?" he asked as his phone beeped.

"Yeah," she said, taking the seat.

He turned his attention to his phone, checking the newly arrived message. "Great," he sarcastically mumbled to himself. Olivia watched as he responded to the text, unable to tear her eyes away from his handsome profile. Once her heart settled to a semi-normal pace, he turned his eyes to her. "You're going to Vegas?" he asked as if he couldn't believe it.

"No," she said, noticing how close his face was to hers.

He glanced to his right, checking the gate. "Huh, you must be at the wrong gate."

"No."

"This is gate 21 to Las Vegas," he said with a wry grin, as if trying to figure her out.

That expression instantly made her understand that he believed she sat next to him on purpose, maybe? "Oh, no. I'm flying out of gate 22 to Louisville," she gestured with a flick of her hand, "It's completely packed on that side."

"I see. So, where's that soda?" he asked eyeing the bag Olivia held.

Not again, Olivia thought. The bag not only contained the soda but also the book! "I'm going to save it for the flight," she said, opening her purse and stuffing the entire bag into it. Luckily she'd brought her biggest purse for the journey.

"What else did you get?" he asked with a raise of his brow.

"Some snacks." Trying to sound casual as she zipped her purse closed. She wondered if he knew about the book.

"I bring my own too," he said, pointing to his bag.

Olivia looked down to see a small black duffel bag at his feet. "Travel light?"

"Yeah, always. I hate checking anything. You know how it is." His phone beeped again and he checked it.

"Yeah, I know," she lied, not really knowing from her limited amount of travel experience.

When he'd finished his message, he leaned back in the chair as if aggravated. Olivia turned her head in another direction, thinking that perhaps he wanted privacy.

"So, what's a kid like you doing here alone?" he asked seriously.

She couldn't believe he'd just called her a kid. She did not look like a kid! She was an adult, couldn't he tell? She was five-six with long auburn hair, athletically toned, and had curves, very good ones too. She'd even had to buy a bigger bra last week.

"I'm coming home from UC Berkeley. I'm far from a kid," she pointed out.

He grinned. "Sorry, didn't mean to presume, you seem young is all. College student, huh?"

"Yeah." *It's basically official*, she thought.

"That's nice. What are you studying?"

"Engineering."

"That's good. I have some buddies that do that."

"Yeah, well, it's a hard program. A kid couldn't get in."

He flinched. "Sorry about calling you a kid. It's just that you remind me of my sister, she's seventeen."

Seventeen! He thinks that's a kid, she thought, disappointed.

"Yeah, she's pretty smart too. That's who I'm going to see in Vegas, my family."

"That's nice," she mumbled.

His phone rang. "Well, if work will ever leave me alone." He hit ignore and turned that charming smile on her.

She couldn't help but enjoy staring at him. Even if he did think she was a kid, he sure was handsome. "What's your work?" *The first question an adult would ask*, she thought.

"Management."

"In Hollywood?"

He smirked. "No, far from it."

"Oh." *Disappointed again*, she thought. *Not a movie star*. "Ever met a celebrity?"

"Yeah, once, some television guy, can't remember his name right now."

"Lots of celebrity hangouts though?"

"Sure, I've gone down on sunset strip and done the clubs," he said.

Olivia's ears perked up. "Really, how are they?"

"Well, they have girls on blocks in some and then sometimes you'll see…" He broke off as his eyes softened at her eager expression. "It's fun, a few times," he said, shrugging his shoulders.

"I'd love to go and see everything. Walk those sidewalks with the stars and check out the beach. I bet there's plenty to do," she said with a big smile.

He laughed as if what she'd said amused him deeply. "Yeah, that's how my sister is."

"She is?"

"Oh, yeah, ready to see the world, that one is."

"Shouldn't she?"

"Couldn't imagine Jessie going off to college alone, like you." He'd spoken more to himself than to her.

Olivia sank back in her chair, wondering if her flight would be boarding soon. Then his phone rang. He exhaled, annoyed, reluctantly picking it up. Olivia couldn't help but eavesdrop, he was only a few inches away from her own ear. "Yes... I've been granted this time off. It's already been approved. Changed? Why?" He rose from his seat and began to pace. He stopped. "Get someone else," he said with authority in his tone.

Olivia watched him, wondering why his job wouldn't leave him alone. She decided to just enjoy staring at him, because soon her plane would board and she'd never see him again. This time tomorrow she'd be back in high school and he'd be visiting his family and *kid* sister in Las Vegas. If only he'd taken one look at her and seen that they were soul mates, swept her off her feet and taken her to Las Vegas to be married in the same little chapel where Britney Spears had been. She laughed to herself. It would probably have lasted just as long, once her mother found out.

Suddenly, her daydream was cut short when she heard the tone of his voice change from being annoyed to being concerned, the kind that accompanies bad news, and suddenly an eerie expression covered his face. He looked at Olivia. The brightness in his blue eyes had disappeared. His jaw clenched, while his free hand ran through his black hair with several frustrating motions. Something was wrong.

"Yes." His voice cracked and he took a deep breath. "Yes. I understand. On my way." He ended the call, staring at the phone in his hand for a lengthy moment.

Olivia wanted to ask, but she felt it wasn't her place. His troubled eyes made contact with hers briefly. She shivered. He turned away. Olivia figured she'd better say something. "Is everything okay?"

He wouldn't look at her. "Yeah." He bent over and grabbed his bag, hooking it over his shoulder. "Gotta go," he said, his back to her.

His job, she thought. "Nice meeting you," Olivia called out.

"Hope you have fun visiting your sister."

He stopped mid-pace. She thought she heard him mumble, "My sister," but couldn't be sure. He turned to face her then, his gaze intently focused on her. She froze. In two steps, he stood towering above her, glaring down. "Get up," he said smoothly.

Olivia didn't understand and her expression relayed such.

"I need you to get up and come with me."

"What?" she muttered shocked by his words.

He bent down, placing his mouth beside her ear, and she gasped. "Get up and come with me now," he whispered.

She jerked at the warm breath that delivered the strange request, considering this must be a joke. "Uh, no, I have a flight," she reminded him.

His lips brushed her ear, causing goose bumps to ignite along her body. "It's cancelled. Get up and come with me now. That's an order." His voice was stern.

Olivia panicked. He wasn't kidding. He was crazy. She summoned all her courage, silently cursing his looks for luring her. "I'm not going anywhere with you."

He pulled away, taking a step back. Olivia figured it was over at that point and waited for him to turn and leave, but he didn't. In one fast motion, he bent over, grabbed her by the waist and threw her over his shoulder with ease, carrying her through the airport. She tried to scream, but the sudden impact of his shoulder in her ribs blew the air out of her lungs. She tossed her head from side to side, sending pleading stares at the surprised passengers, but no one moved to help. It was as if this were a regular occurrence to them. She tried to kick her feet, but he gripped them tightly. Air returned to her lungs and with it her voice. She released a scream, but it wasn't delivered with the force she anticipated; instead, it came out as a tiny squeak.

"Be quiet," he instructed under his breath, entering a security door.

She couldn't believe it. In only a few moments, he had taken her from the public eye. Surely someone would stop him. She began to swing her arms, pounding on his back, finding that it hurt her fist more than him. She was about to get another scream out when he broke into a sprint, causing her to bob up and down, each time knocking the wind out of her lungs. She could only hold on, trying to stop each impact from sending another sting to her ribs. When she thought she'd black out, he finally came to a stop.

"Halt there," a masculine voice ordered.

Thank God, Olivia thought as she gasped for air.

"National Security Threat," the guy holding her yelled back. He shifted her on his shoulder as he pulled something out of his pocket, throwing it to the other man. She strained to see, but his arm was in the way.

"Go ahead," the masculine voice ordered, tossing back the item.

What! She couldn't believe it! Olivia began to scream, raw and weak. She twisted and turned but he took off running again. Olivia began to scratch, tear, pull at anything and everything on him that she could grab.

"Stop it, be still," he yelled. "You want to die?" He asked in a deep voice.

Olivia froze. He'd kill her? She became horrified and before she could make another move she was thrown into the back seat of a car, flipped around, and forced face down.

"Please don't," she whimpered.

He loosened his grip on her wrist, but only for the time he needed to lock a pair of handcuffs on her. "I'm not going to hurt you."

She wanted to cry. Her ribs were beyond bruised and she knew when kidnappers say they're not going to hurt you they do just that. Every horrible movie or documentary she'd watched of what happens to girls when kidnapped flashed through her mind. *Oh God*, she kept repeating silently to herself. *He's going to… oh God, what is he going to do?*

Chapter 2

Gavin Grant wanted to regret his actions. He knew that he should. It went against everything he'd sworn to, everything he stood for, and still he didn't regret it—even if he would probably be locked up. It had been a moment of weakness on his part. He wouldn't argue that point. Deep inside he was satisfied with his hasty choice, but he had no time to question it or dissect it. He couldn't. Not now. There was no turning back.

He caught himself staring at her in the rearview mirror, curled up in that self-preservation sort of way. Her eyes transfixed on some irrelevant point, glazed over like a frightened deer. His words could not soothe her and he'd tried, but of course she had no reason to believe him. It was written all over her face, she was terrified. *And she should be*, he thought. A beautiful girl full of life, and he'd not been able to walk away.

Something deep inside his gut churned with the thought of her. Her smile and those amazingly green eyes, *so pure*, he thought, *so innocent.* He made himself look away from her. He needed to concentrate on his next move.

In a flash, his thoughts turned to his father, the man with all the answers, all the orders. He wondered if he would pat him on the back or renounce him for his choice. It didn't really matter at this point, yet he couldn't help but consider his father's face, his expression at this very moment. Would he know what to do? Would he hold his composure like the many times he had in the past, the way a strong man would do, or would he for once cry like a baby? The idea of tears finally hitting his father's cheeks did not sit well with Gavin, even though he'd wished so many times to see them in the past. No, not today. The image made him ill.

He imagined that his mother was in the kitchen at that very moment, cooking her infamous chocolate pecan cake, wearing that silly palm tree apron he'd given her, a stupid gift he'd bought at some airport because he'd missed her birthday two years ago. And Jessie. She'd be there too, her books scattered around her in an attempt to complete some random essay that was due the next day, procrastinating because her nails needed to be painted. He smiled. Where there were chocolate-covered spoons and bowls to lick, there would be Jessie, joking and laughing in her distinct high-pitched giggle. The warm image of his two favorite women in the world made him want to throw up.

He shook his head as a mad man might. He didn't want to think of them, his family. They were too far away. His hand itched to call them. He couldn't. What would he say? Would they want him to? He rubbed his face with two rough pulls, groaned, and slammed his fist into the dashboard. Quickly, he wished he had not. One look in the rearview mirror and he saw her tears explode from hiding. He searched for words to ease her, but her attempt to muffle a sob broke him.

"Stop, stop it!" he shouted, instantly realizing he'd been too loud, too harsh. "It's okay. I promise it's going to be okay." He shouted that too. He was breaking!

He watched as she turned her face into the seat as more sobs emerged. *Great, just freaking great.* He'd never been good with females. He turned the mirror away with one fast yank. *Concentrate,* he told himself. *You're almost there.* Then what?

He'd been called an honorable man. "A hero with a lion's heart," his mother had said. "A good start," his father once slurred. "A leader of good men" was all Gavin would ever admit to. Still, receiving two medals of distinction at the age of twenty-two had proven nothing to the one person who mattered more than anyone, his idol, his mentor, his father. He loved that man, and the rest didn't matter. Not anymore.

Born into a military family, Gavin was predestined to follow his father's and grandfather's footsteps, and if the thought had ever occurred to him to do differently, his father's conviction had erased any doubt in his mind. Engulfed in any and everything to do with his father, the colonel, a highly decorated officer of the army and a war hero, he'd been guided straight to his future, the Army.

Being groomed from birth by an elite officer had not been the only benefit he'd received but his connections opened many doors. The biggest start to his career had been attending West Point, the most prestigious of military academies, which required a congressional nomination just to be considered. As connections would have it, the colonel, his dad, was friends with the secretary of the Army as well as one U.S. Senator he'd served three tours with. Two recommendations had been more than enough, and the rest had fallen to Gavin. Since he'd been privately tutored since age five as an extra "one up," as his father liked to call it, there were no surprises when Gavin's academic abilities surpassed that of his fellow cadets. He boasted an early graduation from West Point and was immediately assigned as a second lieutenant in the army at the young age of twenty.

Commanding a platoon size of twenty-five men validated the rare leadership ability in his blood, his *legacy.* "A natural," Gavin had heard the term more than once from his superiors. "The boss" was what he'd been nicknamed by his own men. Everyone seemed impressed by his skills, and before a year was up he'd found himself pinned with several awards and promoted to first lieutenant, leading his own specialty platoon.

Yet Gavin's unsatisfied father had wanted to see him lead a platoon of fifty to sixty men, saying it was the way he'd done it to gain his own regiment. That had been the first time Gavin had said no to his father. Instead, he'd chosen the specialty platoon, made up of twenty men, snipers and heavy machinery techs that led in defense and provided support, his own desire, which wasn't a bad choice, only not his father's.

Gavin had learned more about himself during his first year of service than all his years at West Point, discovering that his interest lay in defensive protocols and strategic analysis of preventing casualties, not in leading the most men. He'd imagined that the work would save lives. He'd been wrong. Experiencing several close encounters with death and witnessing men he'd laughed with die before his eyes had been enough to change his path. He didn't want to be an executioner. So he'd taken a transfer out of the line of action and into a California military base. This second choice all his own had been the killer to his relationship with his father. Though he couldn't speak of his current position, his father had ways of knowing things, and Gavin's career move wasn't anything close to the standards the colonel had for his son. The thought of it all seemed so ridiculous now.

Gavin forced himself to look at her. Their eyes met. He turned away, gritting his teeth. Concentrate on the plan, he told himself. He dug for his cell phone and pulled it out. He held it in his hand considering if he should make the call.

He'd spoken to his mother yesterday, reminding her that he would be on the afternoon flight. She'd had the dishwasher on in the background, apparently cleaning the house and getting it ready for him, as she always did. She'd been so excited, reciting the events for the next few days she'd planned for them to do together as a family. Even Jessie had shouted joyfully in the background. He'd not heard his father. He was there, though. Probably sitting by the pool, reading one of his mystery novels, nodding silently as his mother looked at him while she spoke on the phone.

He looked at his cell phone and decided to dial. It rang twice. His mom answered, "Hello."

Her voice struck him hard. He could feel the knot form in his throat instantly.

"Hello," she repeated.

He found his voice. "Mom."

"Hey, honey. Are you about to board?"

He coughed. "No…"

"Is something wrong?"

He didn't speak. Should he tell her?

"What's wrong?" Her tone rattled with concern. "Don't tell me you missed your flight? You're not coming, are you? I can't believe this—"

"No, Mom, no." He managed to interrupt her before she became upset, and he wasn't going to upset her. He wasn't. "I wanted to see, uh, where's dad?"

"Oh. Why?"

"Mom, can you just put him on the phone."

"Honey, he's not here."

"Okay, I'll call him on his cell."

"He left it here. He went golfing."

"When?"

"A few hours ago. What's wrong?"

He couldn't believe it. "Is Jessie there?"

"Yeah. Gavin Grant, what is wrong?"

He considered telling her, then decided not to. "Nothing. I just need dad to call me. When he gets home tell him to call me immediately."

"Okay. Is that all?"

"Yes. Just nervous about this flight."

"You, nervous? I can't believe that."

He forced a laugh for her. "You know me well."

"I would think so. And I know there's something wrong, and you'd better tell me when you get here."

"I will." He paused. "I love you, Mom." He could feel the tears pushing for release.

"I love you too, Honey." Her familiar motherly tone was almost too much for him.

He hesitated for a few seconds, finding his voice. "Do you think Dad—" He broke off.

"Do I think what?"

He sighed. "Nevermind," he said stubbornly.

"Hmm, I know what it is. You don't have to worry about him. He's been sober for six months now."

"I know." He nodded as if she could see him.

"Oh, Honey, I have to go, your chocolate cake is going to burn."

He smiled weakly. The knot in his throat tightened. "That would be tragic."

"Bye, Honey."

"Bye," he mumbled hoarsely.

He waited for her to hang up. She did. He gripped his phone in rage, the tears welling up, but he refused to allow them to spill as he shoved the phone back into his pocket. Why couldn't he have told her? It wouldn't help? He'd already done more than he should.

He fixed the rearview mirror and saw her staring at him, realizing suddenly that he'd had an audience to his conversation. What must she be thinking? He guessed he better try and talk to her, now was the best time.

"We're almost there," he said, watching to see if she moved. "I didn't mean to scare you at the airport. I had no choice." He waited, but she lay there silently. "We only have a few minutes. When you get out of the car you must do as I say. Do not speak. Do not try and run. If you don't listen to me…"

"I'll die," she squeaked out.

He cringed. Had he really made her think that? "Look. You and I. There's no other option for us. You do as I say or we both die."

She gasped.

"I'm not going to let anything happen to you. I promise."

She pleaded. "Just let me go. Stop the car and let me out. I won't say anything."

He shook his head. "I wish it were that easy. I can't imagine what you're thinking, but I didn't have time to explain."

"Then explain now," she said in a panic.

"I don't have time. Just do as I say and you'll be safe." He stopped the car and turned around to face her. "We're here."

She began to shake her head in a crazed fit. He grabbed her and lifted her to a sitting position.

"Look at me," he ordered.

Her wide eyes locked with his and he could see her fear. He knew he had to say more or it wouldn't work, his plan wouldn't work.

"Listen to me. Listen to me carefully. My name is Gavin Grant. I'm a lieutenant in the United States Army. At the airport, I received a command to be recalled to base. We're at war. New York, Chicago, D.C., everything is being hit." He turned her head, forcing her to look outside at the military helicopters that had just arrived. Two men in fatigues were rushing toward them. "You see. We move now, and we move fast, or we die!"

Chapter 3

From the other side of the bathroom door, she heard him say her name twice.

"I have to talk with you," he said, his urgency not hidden.

Olivia ignored him. She hated him for bringing her here. It was his fault.

"Olivia, we have to get a few things straight before the meeting."

She wiped her eyes. He sounded worried, she thought, like yesterday when he'd told her everything in a rush. She'd been unable to say one word as he'd pulled her out of the car. She hadn't believed him at first, but when they arrived, two soldiers near his car and then three more at the helicopter had all taken orders from him without question. Each soldier had called him Lieutenant Grant. She could have been invisible.

For a split second, she had thought of screaming for her life, but her voice had failed, and she'd allowed him to guide her as one might a child. The surrounding men were large soldiers dressed in full fatigues with shaved heads, further intimidating her as she was still haunted by his words, that they'd both die. They had rung in her mind like a headache, and before she knew it she'd been shoved into the helicopter, silently watching as Lieutenant Grant shouted out several commands to the pilot. Somehow she'd slowly begun to believe his crazy story, and then in the air it had happened.

A flash of light! At first, she thought she'd been blinded, struck, dead in an instant, but then the light had drawn back and revealed the source, the true occurrence, and as if she were on a roller coaster ride her gut had pivoted. *Unreal, it has to be unreal*, she'd first thought, yet the gasps and groans and *Oh my Gods* confirmed that time had not stopped. The mushroom cloud had loomed in the distance, soaring high against the sky. She'd grabbed his hand and he'd held it. Her eyes locked with his truth and she'd known. He'd saved her.

She remembered her entire body shaking to the core as they'd flown on in an unsettling stillness, leaving the nuclear stamp behind. That's what someone had called it when trying to calm one of the soldiers. "Man's nuclear stamp," a childlike voice had come out of one of the men as he'd begun to pray. She hadn't turned to see who, but then more followed. In their anguish, they'd all started mumbling their disbelief, and she had quickly agreed. How and why and where was it? Were they next? She'd looked into the sky wondering if she would see it coming. Everyone and every word had turned from shock to panic.

Lieutenant Grant had been the one to rein them into compliance. "It's over! It's over. Stay focused. We have a mission." Strangely they'd fallen back into their uniforms, alert and ready as before.

Gavin tightened his grip on Olivia's hand as he leaned in. "It's not a war. It's an annihilation," he'd mumbled low for her ears only. She'd been unable to respond, only focusing on her own breath and marveling that she in fact was still breathing.

Gavin knocked on the bathroom door again. "Olivia, you have to come out. Remember what I told you. We must take care—Olivia."

Olivia glanced up at the doorknob, wanting to unlock it, but her legs wouldn't move.

Yesterday, he'd said to her, "There will be a time, a place for grief, but now you must be strong and survive."

She'd been caught up in that image, that flash, *man's nuclear stamp*, and had not really understood what happened after. The helicopter had landed, and she'd been ushered out in one fast motion, with Gavin pulling her along until her feet wouldn't move any further, for what she saw was unimaginable. A crowd of people was before her, regular people mixed in with the military uniforms, outnumbering the military, it seemed, scurrying about carrying suitcases, garbage bags, and kids. It was as if a concert of campers had let out and they had no idea where to go. She'd had no idea where to go. Her legs wouldn't move.

Gavin had not hesitated for one second, he'd picked her up in one fast motion, carrying her in his arms and whispering those words of survival. She'd responded, "We're going to die!"

"No, we'll live. I promise you that." He'd said it in a way that she couldn't doubt, the same way he'd snapped his soldiers back into their rank on the helicopter. His words had been soft yet firm, and she wanted to believe in him as his men had, with confidence.

When she'd asked, "How?" and he'd said, "I'll take care of everything. I'll take care of you," she'd believed him and trusted him to take her through what was before them.

She'd found that holding on to him was the easiest and simplest thing to do, not thinking about the bomb, not thinking about the people it killed, not thinking about her family, and not thinking about whether or not she would die. Instead, she'd held tightly around his neck, burying her face in his shoulder. She'd thought the entire world was coming to an end and holding on to him seemed to be the only thing she wanted to acknowledge as real.

She'd tried not to listen to the chaotic frenzy that surrounded them, to the men and women yelling and crying as they pushed and shoved their way to hopeful shelter, to safety. Olivia had blocked out the people and their faces, holding her eyes tightly shut against Gavin's shoulder, hoping that he'd be able to protect them both as he'd said.

Eventually they'd parted from the crowds of people. Olivia first noticed the noise level drop off, then the sudden rush of cool air. She had opened her eyes to find they were inside of a building. Gavin had run, holding her tightly against his chest. Olivia noticed the dark hallways first, then the lights, how they'd magically come on as they moved toward them. She'd wanted to ask him where they were and where all the people had gone, but he'd stopped abruptly outside a door and before she could get a word out, he'd deposited her onto a bed.

He'd said everything in a rush. "Stay here and you'll be safe. Don't go out that door. I have to go now, but I'll be back. Promise me you'll stay here." She'd nodded. "What's your name?" He'd asked as if needing her name would bind her in that promise. She'd told him and he'd repeated it back twice, "Olivia. Olivia Parker." Then he'd left.

Hours passed as she watched the door, waiting for it to open. When she had finally glanced down, she found her purse, the strap still hanging around her torso. Immediately she dug for her cell phone, but no service could be found. She wondered if staying in this room was the right decision, considering she didn't have a clue as to what was happening outside of it. Within those few hours, she'd caught herself in a silent trance several times, not remembering what she'd been thinking. Then he had returned.

He rushed in, closing the door softly behind him and she'd stared up, waiting. He had seemed relieved to see her there, perhaps thinking that she hadn't listened to him. When he'd sunk down beside her, she finally found her voice and asked about them, her family, if they'd be alive.

He'd not been able to respond until she'd cried. That's when he'd held her, softly chanting, "It's going to be okay Olivia. It's going to be okay." He'd laid her down when she'd finally stopped crying and said, "I've brought you here and you're safe; however, I've gone against protocol, and we're going to need to make sure you answer questions correctly or we'll both be in trouble."

She'd not cared about the protocol and had asked again about her family. Still he'd not been able to answer, but she'd known, they were dead. In the helicopter, one soldier had said it, half the United States had been wiped out already, and they were next. Then he had left her again, stating that he'd give her some time alone.

Now he was back. The heavy knock came again, and Olivia knew she should unlock the door, but she didn't want to face him or any of it.

"Olivia, I have a key and am going to use it."

She continued to watch the knob, silently cursing him.

"I'm unlocking it," he warned.

The knob turned and the door opened. Gavin appeared in the entrance. He'd changed. He wore a dark shirt with fatigue pants and upon seeing her his expression grew to concern. He noticed the mirror and rushed to kneel beside her. "Are you okay?" he asked, scanning her face, then suddenly grabbing her hands. He flipped them over, examining each one until he came to the fresh bruise on her knuckles. He sighed and spoke softly, "Olivia, don't hurt yourself."

She watched his fingers gently stroke her knuckles. It soothed her, and that made her angry. "I hate you," she mumbled. She had thought it, and now she'd said it out loud and she didn't care. Why should she?

He narrowed his eyes, his face inches from her own. "What?" he asked, as if he wanted to clarify what she'd said.

She yanked her hand away from his and met his gentle glance with her own rage. "I. Hate. You!" she said, raising her voice, making sure that he heard every word clearly.

He arched one eyebrow. "You do?" he asked, calmly, not moving an inch away.

"Yes." She tore her eyes from his, glancing at her wounded hand. "You brought me here." She didn't even know where here was. She felt empty.

"I did." He admitted it as a fact.

"You shouldn't have." She wanted to make sure he was aware of his mistake. He shouldn't have made a choice for her. It wasn't fair.

He frowned. "Maybe not."

His words surprised her. Had he just agreed with her? She glanced up for a second, noting the seriousness on his face and quickly glanced away. "My family is dead." That was all she could think about, and she should be with them.

"Mine too," he quickly added, not hiding his own pain.

She felt as if she'd been hit in the gut, remembering his earlier call in the car. He'd spoken to his mom, he'd said goodbye. She hadn't. She stared at the floor for a brief moment. She could feel his eyes still on her. "I should be with them," she confessed.

He huffed, shaking his head. "Dead. You want to be dead, is that it?" His anger grew more apparent with each word.

"Yes," she whispered in a tiny voice. What was left?

He jumped to his feet as if her yes had punched him away. He thrust his hand through his hair, surveying her. "You don't even know for sure, and you want to be dead," he said in disbelief.

She looked up. "They might be alive?" she asked with hope.

He shook his head. "I can't be sure."

She growled. "Yeah, if not, they're being irradiated right about now," she said in her own sarcastic tone. She hated herself immediately for saying such a thing, because the image of her family in pain popped in her head, making her feel even worse.

"Been thinking a lot in here have you?"

"I have." She couldn't stop thinking.

"Thinking a lot about your poor self?" he asked, fully laying on his own thick sarcasm.

She gave him an angry scowl. She wasn't thinking of herself, that wasn't true. She wanted her family to be alive, but they weren't. How dare he say that! She wanted her family not to suffer. She hoped they hadn't.

"Might think you're lucky to be alive."

"I don't care," she groaned, wanting him to leave her alone. She wasn't lucky. Her family was dead.

"Well, doesn't matter now. Does it? You're alive and you're going to join the living," he said in a matter-of-fact fashion, picking her up and placing her under the shower effortlessly.

"Let me go," she yelled as she noticed his hands going straight for the knobs. She tried to move but he'd already turned on the water. "It's cold! It's cold!" she screamed, her wet clothing plastered against her.

He grinned. "Feels good to be alive though, right?" He didn't wait for a response. "There's a change of clothes in the closet. Be dressed in five minutes or I'll dress you myself," he ordered in his military tone.

He was gone by the time Olivia found the knob and turned off the water. "Jerk!" She felt utter rage at the way he'd just spoken to her and funny enough, it felt good. Great, actually. Feeling something other than sadness made her smile. It was as if the cold water had switched her back on, and she was thankful for that. Five minutes! She wasn't going to give him any excuse to dress her. She found a towel and ran to the dresser. Within four minutes, she'd found a T-shirt and oversized jogging shorts.

A quick knock came just as she'd slipped on the shirt. "Uh, hold on."

The door opened. She pulled up the shorts as he came through the door.

"Well, don't need any help I see," he said smugly.

"No," she stated firmly. She wondered if he really would have dressed her. He seemed a man of his word.

He shut the door behind him. "Ready to talk?"

She groaned, running her hands through her hair in an attempt to pull it back. She wanted to slap him for throwing her in the shower.

He stood with military poise, back straight, hands behind his back. "Okay. Well, as I was saying earlier. It was against protocol for me to bring you here, and we're going to need to get our story straight."

"If it's against protocol, why'd you bring me?"

He frowned. "Let me guess, you wished I hadn't."

"I—"

"Ungrateful brat!"

"Brat?"

"Yes, brat. I risked everything to bring you here, and you don't even give me a thank you or anything. Instead you're going to act like a typical brat and whine about it."

Olivia glared at him. "I'm not."

"Not a brat or not a whiner, because all you've done is cry that you want to die."

Olivia could feel the rage return. She didn't ask him to risk everything to bring her here, and what else could he expect of her in these circumstances. She defended her actions. "That's what normal people do when the world's ending." It took every ounce of control for her not to scream.

"They lay around wishing for death?" he asked. He hadn't moved from his stance, and in some way it annoyed her that he appeared to be judging her as some crazy, childish brat who couldn't stop crying. How could he be so cold?

"Yeah," she defended, unable to think of anything else to say.

"Well, I'm wanting to live, and you're stuck doing the same, so deal."

"Deal? We'll probably be dead in a few days, once the radiation has set in."

"Oh, so radiation is it? Well, you'd rather sit here moping while you might have several days of life left?"

His insults reached one too many and she was plain tired of his stupidity. He seemed emotionally removed from the reality of what was going on around him and she couldn't contain herself any longer. "What else should I be doing? What else is there to do? You think I'm going to meet with a bunch of people who want to cry and pray while we all radiate? Or better yet let's think up a story to cover you for protocol when you'll probably be dead in two or three days. Who freaking cares about protocol? The world is ending. This is it. I don't care. What are you going to do? Stand around and take orders?"

He walked up to her in three full strides and stared down at her raging expression. "I give orders, and I'd do this," he said, grabbing her and planting a kiss.

She'd not expected that, and when he pulled away she stumbled, grabbing his firm chest. Confused by the sudden urge to pull him back, she tightened her hand on his shirt, gasping as she stared at him in shock. No one had ever kissed her, not like that, not ever. The warmth of his lips lingered.

"Besides, good news, we're going to live safely from bombs and radiation."

"Huh?" She didn't know if she was confused by his kiss, that it had only lasted a brief second, or that he said they'd live, but he stepped away from her, causing her hand to fall from him. Alert, she found her own balance. "How? Is it over, the bombs? Did we win?"

He turned. "No. We didn't win."

"But you said?"

He turned slightly, revealing his profile. "I said we're safe."

"How?"

"We're in an underground vault, and here's my first order: You're going to do everything I tell you to do."

31

Chapter 4

Understanding people's emotional responses and triggering them with motivational words was one of Gavin's many skills that contributed to his position as a leader. Sure, he'd learned plenty of the psychological reasons for a person's actions; however, a true leader can transfer his unique style into a variety of situations, conforming to and understanding the needs of others to inspire them. It came naturally to him. He didn't manipulate others. He had no intention of doing so. He simply reacted to others and led by what he believed in.

Gavin's sudden reaction to kiss Olivia had left the both of them standing in utter silence.

Seeing Olivia angry with herself for living had not been something he'd expected. Her harsh words about hating him had been nothing, but that she wished she were dead pulled at his heart. He didn't have much skill for talking with females, unless they were soldiers and under his command. So, naturally, he'd fallen into his own familiarity and decided that he would make her face the truth, that living was the only option he was giving her. He'd almost lost it when he had to mention his own family being dead too. He had understood her completely; he even thought of what she said, of how she should be with her family instead of being safe—this was a reasonable reaction. Though he wouldn't admit it, he needed her to snap out of it, and throwing her in the shower had been the only way.

He hadn't wanted to come off as a brute, but he was sure that's what she was thinking. She'd not given him much choice. Then, he'd kissed her. He didn't know why he'd done it, except for a heat of the moment thing. He'd been so angry that he'd been unable to save his family, and he had wanted to join her on that bathroom floor, hold her.

He'd understood everything she'd said with a heavy heart, but he didn't want her to wish for death. He'd saved her and needed her at the same time. Kissing her had made the blood rush inside of him once again, declaring that he lived. He hoped that she, at that moment, had felt the same. He shouldn't have, but she was beautiful to him, and he couldn't think of her wanting to die. As soon as he'd done it, he'd regretted it. She was a kid! He was twenty-two years old and she was like his sister, young, too young. He wouldn't go there. But then she had looked at him as if she wanted more! How could he blame the kid, though, she didn't have a clue what was happening.

He stared hard at her now watching for relief to come at his mention of them being safe.

Olivia was overwhelmed with a need to punch him. He'd kissed her, then ordered her to follow his every command! The fact that the kiss still tingled on her lips, that it had literally taken her breath away, that it was the very first kiss to do so, that it was a kiss she was sure would go down as the best ever only fueled her anger. She'd gathered the information that they were safe and that had begun to register, but then he'd added that she was to do as he ordered. She really wanted to punch him.

"Your first order? What makes you think I'm going to take orders?" she asked boldly.

He tightened his lips for an instant. "You have no choice. We're in an underground vault, and you're not supposed to be here."

Olivia shook her head, finally registering that they were below ground. *A vault?* She'd heard him say it, yet she really hadn't understood. Could it be? Instantly, she imagined the people in the black and white movies building bomb shelters during World War II. "This isn't a building?"

Gavin didn't hide his impatience. "No. We're in an underground fallout shelter designed for 200 chosen people, not one of whom is you. I have to be at the meeting. So let's go, and do as I say. By the way, your uncle is Harold Kramer, a wealthy oil man who willed you a ticket."

"What?"

"No time. Harold Kramer died and left you the ticket to be here, that's all you say." He opened the door and walked out to the hall. "Follow me."

Olivia did as directed and matched his fast pace. "A ticket? I don't understand," she said catching up with him.

He sighed. "Lower your voice. Yes, everyone besides military has to have one to be here."

"And if they find out I don't?" she asked in a whisper, even though no one was around, she hadn't seen another person since they'd first arrived.

He shook his head. "I don't know, but I don't want to find out. Not with these people."

Olivia scrunched her brow. *What kind of people are they? Would they really kick me out?* Olivia kept up with his fast steps. "I don't understand."

He grabbed her arm and pulled her toward him so that he could whisper in her ear. "Olivia, no more questions. When we go through this door, you listen and say nothing." He waited for her to nod before he released her.

He scanned his badge at the door. It slid open. They walked a few more feet down a corridor, then met a flight of stairs. At the bottom, they opened another door. Gradually they began to hear people in the distance, voices mingling, reminding Olivia of a crowded lunch cafeteria. When they entered what must have been the Grand Hall, Olivia gasped. The room was full of people, alive and talking. It made her heart leap with gratitude. Everyone wasn't dead!

Gavin tapped her. "Wait here," he said as he jetted off through the crowd.

Olivia tried to watch him, but he disappeared. She glanced around. A prickle of excitement confirmed her safety and suddenly a stab of guilt formed deep in her chest. She pushed the thought away, reminding herself that she wasn't going to have self-pity, that she'd prove him wrong, but she still didn't feel normal. The entire room weighed heavily with the soft murmurs between people, the tiny sobs breaking out destroying her image of a pleasant cafeteria. It was, in fact, a funeral. The air around her reminded her of her father's. Squeezed together in a room of mourners and people half out of their minds highlighted the morbid reality of their situation.

Again, she reminded herself to push it away. She concentrated on something else, the room that she stood in instead of the people within it. The Grand Hall, as they'd called it, seemed larger than she would have imagined for a room underground. It was oval in shape, with a high ceiling. It almost seemed like they were in an actual building that had natural light. She took a closer look at the oval ceiling that matched the room. The light was not natural. It was fake. Why wouldn't it be? They were underground. How long would they be in here?

A crying child caught her attention and she looked over at a mother holding a toddler. Olivia felt her heart drop. The sight of a living child should make her happy, but it only reminded her of the Randall's three children she was supposed to be babysitting this weekend. She wondered if they… She forced herself not to think about it. She didn't want to be back on that bathroom floor again.

The crowd hushed as a military person stood up on a table. Olivia followed their view. A white-haired man dressed in a military uniform, with pressed pants and blue shirt, waved his hands in the air as he asked everyone to be seated. His presence leaked out every stereotype of a high-ranking military officer, encouraging the civilians to stand at rapt attention. The room responded quickly, filling with the sound of chairs rustling back and forth. Olivia grabbed the closest seat between an older woman and man, probably in their forties. Neither one seemed upset, which she found unusual.

"Everyone, quiet please," the older man's voice boomed again. Everyone fell silent and turned their full attention to him, including Olivia, who was surprised to see Gavin standing beside him. The white-haired military man cleared his throat. "I am Major Sullivan of the United States Army. I have an update on our current situation. As you know by now, the United States was attacked by a number of nuclear bombs at 11:52 a.m. Pacific Time. Washington D.C, New York, and Chicago were the first to receive impact. Other cities followed soon after… we'll have a complete list in the days to come, uh, but I must tell you now, it isn't good."

"What about San Francisco?" a man shouted.

"Phoenix?" a woman yelled.

"Las Vegas?" another man shouted.

Olivia wanted to shout Louisville too!

Major Sullivan held up his hands and cleared his throat once again. "I know everyone has family scattered. I will have a list posted." He appeared to be holding himself together.

"Tell us, please," a man shouted, which ignited a sudden roar of agreement from the entire room.

Major Sullivan nodded while raising one hand, and the room fell silent once again. "Las Vegas was hit."

Several people moaned. Olivia cringed as she stared at Gavin's face, realizing from his reaction that he hadn't known.

Major Sullivan continued. "A tragedy has fallen on us today. We will take several days to mourn, and I will update you—,"

"The radiation?" a man interrupted with a shout.

"Please, everyone. There is no need to worry about radiation. We are safe here. As you know, when you purchased your ticket, this vault was designed to last until the radiation levels are safe. We must all stay calm at this time. We will begin by issuing each division military personnel. You will report to and obtain information from them.

"The vault was designed to hold 200 people. Unfortunately, we were unable to wait for everyone, due to the close proximity of the last bomb. We are currently at 159. As of now keep to your assigned room and take another look at the instruction packet provided. We will be going into the first step immediately. You should all be aware of the standard protocol as these rules and regulations were given to you upon signing the contract.

"We are now engaged in the first step, be aware. We will begin by asking you to return to your rooms, where one of our soldiers will greet you. I am in command of this vault, and I assure you that everyone will be made aware of information as I receive it.

"Lastly, I want to introduce you to Captain Gavin Grant. He will be in charge of all the soldiers in each division." He motioned toward Gavin, who responded with a simple nod. Then the major continued. "The next few days are going to be rough, but we have designed this vault to give every amenity that a small city would allow. Again, read your packets and wait to be greeted by your assigned soldier. My deepest regrets to all of you for our losses this day. Let us bow our head in respect for our loved ones." He bowed his head and everyone followed.

After several silent minutes, he adjourned the hall and everyone began to spill out, returning to their own rooms. Olivia continued to sit at the table, remembering that Gavin had told her to wait there. Her thoughts were full of questions as she wondered what other cities had been hit or had even survived. Her instinct told her she was wrong to hope. She tried to think of what the major had said about a packet and a contract. What were they? Step one?

She needed to speak with Gavin. She thought he had said he was a lieutenant; however, she had no idea about military rankings or protocol. She scanned the room, noticing Major Sullivan speaking with Gavin for several minutes. Though Gavin had brought her here, ordered her around, called her a brat, and then kissed her, she couldn't help but feel sad for him as she recalled his slight flinch when Las Vegas had been announced as hit. The mysterious stranger she'd met at the airport had been just as affected as her, losing everything, but somehow still managed to save her. She stared at her personal hero. His name turned in her mind as she thought about how he'd done so much without even knowing hers. She wondered why he'd done it.

A man interrupted her thoughts. "Are you okay?"

She glanced over to see a thirty-something-year-old man seated across from her. She nodded.

"I'm Jeremy."

Before she could answer, Gavin interrupted. "Miss Parker, you must come with me." He glanced over to Jeremy, then back to Olivia.

Olivia didn't hesitate, she knew she shouldn't be talking to anyone, and she hadn't.

"Follow me," Gavin said in his official tone.

Olivia nodded and followed him out the doors they'd come in. "Where are we going?"

"You're going back to the room."

"My room?"

"For now."

She didn't understand his response, but she wanted to console him. She felt that she needed to. "I'm…" she hesitated, "sorry about your family."

He took two more strides before responding. "I'm sorry about yours."

She walked with him, but nothing else was said. When they arrived at the room she'd previously been in, he opened the door but didn't go in. He spoke again in that military tone of his. "Stay here, and try to get some rest."

She didn't want him to go, not until he'd told her what he'd gotten her into. "Will I see you?"

Her question caught him off guard. "Of course."

"Can't you tell me more now?" she asked.

"I will, but as you heard, I'm now second in command. I have a lot of work."

"I thought you were a lieutenant?"

"I was. The captain didn't make it, so I was promoted." No happiness or contentment in that new fact.

"Oh."

"Everything has changed, Olivia. People must step up and do what they have to. You'll have to do the same." He stared at her with those blue eyes that seemed suddenly to intimidate her again.

"I can try." She wanted to, she thought.

His lip curved up, almost into a smile. "Read The Packet in the desk. It should answer some of your questions."

"Will you come back and tell me who I'm supposed to be?"

He nodded. "I will. Get some rest. I'll see you later."

"Where's your room?" she asked, not believing it came out of her own mouth. She quickly added, "in case I need you."

"You're in it."

Chapter 5

When Gavin had said that this was his room, for a microsecond Olivia had imagined him returning later to share the tiny bed. Before she could express her shock or wonder if that would even be something she would want, he'd settled the entire mishap by mentioning he'd be back later to escort her to her own. He'd even seemed uncomfortable when he'd blurted out that information, apparently anticipating exactly what she'd been thinking and wanting to make sure she wasn't getting the wrong idea. He'd even said, "Get some rest, kid," as he left.

She hated that he called her a kid again, and when he shut the door she had stomped her foot in anger, wanting to punch him again. Her temper quickly fizzled out as she began to register that she was alone. Alone.

She lay down on the bed and thought of what was to come, but all she could imagine was that this was his bed, and she was lying in it. She jumped up in one fast motion, deciding to try and keep her mind off of him, yet that's where it was as she studied his room. She looked at the bed in the center, at the closet and desk against the left wall, and then finally at the dresser against the right. Had he actually stayed in this room? She assumed so, because of the clothes she'd seen in the closet. They'd been worn, she was sure of it. She was wearing his shirt, his shorts, both swallowing her up.

I need to sleep, she told herself, but she already had. She'd slept and he'd come and gotten her. The entire room had no clock to check the time and she assumed it was now late into the night. She was aware that she was emotionally drained and figured that her mind kept wandering back to him as a way of coping with her loss. Why else couldn't she stop thinking about him and wondering if he would keep his promise and take care of her? She was in an underground vault with 158 other people who were all strangers except for one: Him.

She was going to have to rely on him. She wondered what was to come and who were these people who'd made plans to live underground? It was an information overload for her mind. She had the same fuzzy thoughts and tired eyes as someone who had stayed up the entire night to see the sunrise.

She looked at the bathroom door and decided not to go in. That's where she'd lost it, that's where she'd told him she would like to die. She'd known that she must have sounded like a crazy loon and knew that this was not the road her mother would have wanted her to take. He'd saved her in the airport, and she'd told him she hated him for it. Shame sunk in as she remembered his solemn expression, that he might have agreed that helping her was wrong. She didn't want to seem ungrateful. Truly, she didn't. She wanted to thank him, and she would, she thought.

When she finally lay back down on the bed, he returned.

"Get your things together," he said in a rush as soon as he opened the door. "I'm taking you to your room."

She could tell that now wasn't the time to discuss anything. She grabbed her purse and wet clothes, the only items that she owned now. She followed him down several halls, watching his straight back and wondering why it felt like a bizarre march into the unknown, instead of a walk from point A to point B.

When he stopped in front of her new door, he finally looked at her, his emotions hidden as his blue eyes scanned hers.

"This is yours. You're in Division Four."

She didn't hide her confusion. "Division Four?"

"Didn't you read The Packet?"

"No," she admitted.

He nodded. "That's okay. Get some rest, but make sure you read it before you leave this room." The serious nature of reading it was conveyed.

She nodded. "I promise." She wanted to apologize, to tell him she didn't hate him. The way he stared at her made her uncomfortable. Was he wondering if she was going to go crazy and mess up their entire lie, that she didn't belong here? "I will. I'll do as you say."

"Glad to hear it. Get some sleep then."

The casual remark didn't ease Olivia's guilt. She wanted to tell him she had acted crazy, but she couldn't find the words.

He narrowed his eyes on her face. "You'll be fine in here." He tried to comfort her nerves.

She couldn't find the courage to apologize, so she said in a rush, "I don't want to be alone."

His expression softened at her words as if he too didn't want to be alone. "I have to get back to my post. They're waiting for me. There's a lot to do tonight since—,"

She interrupted, embarrassed that she'd asked. "Oh, I understand. I'll be fine." She tried to pretend, unaffected by his denial, but she was sure he'd noticed.

He attempted a smile, but only a slight tug of his lips showed through. "Tomorrow we can discuss everything. Okay?"

She nodded.

He leaned in to whisper. "There's one thing I forgot to ask you, but it's too late. You'll have to remember October 3rd is your new eighteenth birthday. I had to make something up and..." He trailed off for a second. "I didn't know."

She nodded, unable to answer him. *He was close*, she thought, and right about her age. Her eighteenth birthday was in September. September 30th.

He turned abruptly and left her to enter the room alone.

He hadn't wanted to leave her alone, though. He could see it in her face, her confusion and fear. The girl had been pulled and dragged into the ground by a complete stranger. He'd forced her to exist, and she hated him for it. He didn't blame her. He had no idea what kind of life awaited all of them. Was it better? When he'd found out Las Vegas had in fact been one of the impact zones, he'd held his emotions in, forcing those images of his loved ones to remain locked away, only concentrating on the vault that had saved his life, her life. He didn't dare think about his family. He couldn't.

His mind wasn't one to dwell. Perhaps he could blame the military training he'd received or *the legacy* that coursed through his veins. No matter the source of his endurance or his ability to persist onward with tactical proficiency, he only thought of his new problem. A pressing issue had revealed itself tonight. On more than one occasion he'd thought the entire vault project was for a bunch of rich fools. He never imagined that he'd be in it. *Who would want to live in the ground for years? So many unknown variables, so many things that could go wrong*, he thought.

That's why the army had been given the duty of designing the vault. Rich men in suits had partnered up with the government to make a profit. The cost of building the vault was well worth the money the tickets brought in. The project did touch the hands of people with good intentions, though, and several government leaders had hired on some of the finest intellectuals to design and implement a plan that excited numerous scientists in what they deemed a wonderful experiment, an underground community that could potentially exist for years, whether two or fifty. These men had used this particular vault as an opportunity to design the next society if the apocalypse did occur.

Next The Packet was conceived. Many different variations were made in hopes of figuring out the most effective government and formula that would sustain a happy and productive life underground, allowing the last of the human race success in surviving. Of course, none had actually been fully tested. The most current packet that had accompanied the contracts had been the most successful, tested for a two-week trial period with a group of college kids who had volunteered as subjects. The current plan had been included in the contract, and a clause was written in to allow for changes, in the event that the head scientist, Dr. Alfred Smothers, made changes. Unfortunately, Dr. Alfred Smothers was not one of the 159 survivors currently in the vault. The current packet would be law.

Gavin had read The Packet himself, several times, finding several interesting aspects he agreed with, but also discovering major issues that he didn't see lasting long term. That is what worried Gavin the most. He'd been made aware of the scientists and their experiments and had believed that would be all it ever would be, but now the idea of The Packet being law worried him.

Out of the 159 survivors, several scientists, doctors, engineers, and political heads had made it to the vault, all seeming safe in that regard. The major's passion to follow The Packet had been where the alarms had gone off. The Packet had only been an experiment, not law, and if they should follow any government rules and regulations, it should be the standard that they'd lived by, sworn to.

The major, however, felt differently. Gavin found this out when the major quickly briefed him on his promotion, explaining the unfortunate circumstance of the other officers not arriving on time. After he'd been informed that he was to be captain and second in command, Gavin had been cautioned on the importance of going by The Packet, with the major explaining that it had been created for this situation and that they were lucky to have it.

Gavin's first thought had been to protest this, but his first words to the major couldn't be insubordinate. When he'd stood beside the major in the Grand Hall as he'd informed everyone to follow The Packet, he'd cringed inside. *God help us*, he had thought.

The civilians in the vault were wealthy men and women who didn't have a clue as to what they'd signed off on. They'd probably never read it themselves, and those that had, well, survival was probably the only thing on their minds at the moment. Gavin couldn't argue with that. He'd come straight here himself. He'd not thought that they'd actually turn to The Packet. He still didn't think it would last long. The major would probably see this soon enough. *He has to*, Gavin thought. There was no other logical assessment when considering the foreseeable problems that would arise.

When Gavin had been assigned this position, he'd seen it as vacation from war. He'd never thought for one second he'd be trapped in it. He'd arrived several months ago as the lead officer to run drills and various scenarios inside the vault, testing to see if it performed, and it did. The entire experience for him had been a futuristic, space-age fantasy that seemed cool. In reality, it wasn't anything but a large tomb, trying to preserve the past, trying to outlast the inevitable. He, like everyone else, fought to live. Now here he was, another antiquity if things turned wrong. The air, the water, and the food were all unpredictable. Presently, he didn't like considering himself a lab rat that had just been promoted into the experiment of a lifetime.

It was all out of his hands. He'd made several choices that had brought him here, and he had to accept that. He also had to accept that he brought Olivia along for the ride and had promised to take care of her. He would keep his word. He always did. *Will she be happy*, he wondered, *once she knows the truth?*

He'd done everything in his power to protect her. When they'd first arrived and he'd dropped her off in his room, he'd immediately fallen into his own drills, assisting his team in ushering in the survivors. All ran as smoothly as one could hope, considering all they'd done to prepare themselves for this very moment. He didn't want to imagine the faces of the people he had shut out. He would have held the door open longer—he'd wanted to. He'd seen in the distance another helicopter arriving, but the major had made the order, "Too dangerous, son," he'd said, making the call for the doors to be locked.

He couldn't cause a rift or refuse orders because he'd snuck Olivia into the vault, and he couldn't risk her being discovered. For her, he'd broken the rules. He'd found an unassigned ticket, due to the death of Harold Kramer, who'd willed it to his niece. His luck had come through on that one; he'd feared at first that she would have to take an original ticket-holder's identity. That would have been more complicated, especially if tests were run.

Each and every vault resident had to supply their blood for analysis. Every person had been screened, not only for their money but also their genes. Weaknesses had been filtered out. Everything was taken into consideration: intelligence scores, physical ability, age, and career.

A salesman from Ohio wouldn't make the cut. If the dentist quota had been filled, the next dentist's application would be denied. If a celebrity didn't have the skill needed to fill the labor slots, sorry, unless they qualified for the young generation slot. Some parents were lucky enough to apply as a family, but they were compared to other eager families, and only those with the highest scores were accepted. Each and every person had been picked for the vault in hopes of making a new life run more smoothly. The missing forty-one could considerably hurt the plan, and Gavin held that as a definite counter to the major's argument behind using The Packet.

Gavin would have to explain all this to Olivia, especially the fact that she had been willed a ticket from her fake uncle. In the contract, it states that every resident is allowed to will their ticket to another, but they must fit successfully into their slot, passing several tests. Gavin had the clearance and had gone into the system. Apparently, Harold Kramer's true niece had passed her tests successfully and had been allowed to take his place. His death had occurred recently, though, and the official record had not been updated or changed. The niece's blood was not yet on file. Also, this would be the first ticket to be willed, so it was reasonable to assume that mistakes might happen. It was Gavin's only shot at not being caught. He'd put Olivia's name and her fake age in easily. He'd not known her real age. She could have been eighteen or nineteen; she'd pressed the fact of being a college student, but he'd made a conscious choice to give her the same age as his sister, her birthday. If she didn't like it, that was too bad. She seemed too young for what would come.

He didn't want to imagine what would happen if the major found out about this lie. A normal person on this day would applaud Gavin for his effort. Major Sullivan was not a normal person. Gavin had interacted with him few times, but the stories he'd heard had been pretty insane. Major Sullivan had a tendency not to bend any rule, no matter the reason. He was a tyrant when it came to meeting regulations. He thrived on them, to the point of one inappropriate greeting or question and he'd be calling the MP's, or worse, stripping an officer's command from them. Power hungry or simply nuts from old age, Gavin didn't know what made the man tick. He just knew not to cross any lines. Olivia would be safe only if she blended in.

Gavin thought of the vault's prison. They had one, and he was sure they'd use it. The vault had been designed with everything a small town would need. Eight divisions had been created, each holding twenty-five people and segregated by age range. Military members were assigned to Division One, with one soldier assigned to each of the other divisions to act as a guard or assist with needs. They were referred to as the guidance counselor of each division. The Grand Hall, at the center of the vault, was designed for meals, community meetings, and gatherings. The first level, as it had been named, also contained several rooms for scientists, engineers, doctors, and workers to conduct their procedures, examinations, or services for the vault residents. Additional rooms had been created for entertainment and games, exercise, school, and an undesignated house of worship, based on no single religion—a place where everyone could go. A large kitchen connected to the Grand Hall on one end and an annex for food on the other. The largest of the rooms on the first level, the garden, where foods were grown under natural heating lamps, was fully guarded at all hours.

The second level, where Division One was located, was restricted from all civilians. It contained an intelligence room for all military communications, a prison, an armory, a main storage facility for equipment and repair, food and water storage, and the control center that operated all functions for the vault, including cameras, water, and air.

Gavin had toured the vault on his first day, realizing that, strategically, the military division was placed above the civilian divisions to enable watching them. The Packet described the military presence as an honorable security guard, ready to please and assist, when in truth the military was designed to control the vault and the people within it.

Chapter 6

It had been a week since Olivia arrived at the vault. Nightmares had come every night. She was unable to remember the dreams completely, only that she ran from something—continuously running. When she'd wake, she'd cry. Until recently, she had welcomed a miracle. She'd dreamed of her mom and brother. They'd been on a picnic at their favorite park, and her mom had spoken softly, soothingly explaining to Olivia that everything was fine because they were all together. She'd risen from that dream with a new outlook.

They might still be alive. She'd somehow convinced her worried mind to settle on the idea that no one knew 100 percent if they were dead. She'd spent most of the week finally at ease, encouraging herself to live, live so she could find them, live so she could prove—prove to herself—that she would never give up, not on them.

Olivia stretched out on her tiny bed, doing what she found herself doing most evenings—thinking not of death, not of the radioactive land above her head, but of him, Gavin. Captain Grant, who'd saved her life, who'd risked everything so that she'd be safe. Did he regret what he'd done? Did he truly care about her? These questions rattled through her mind along with the thought of him each night, each day. *How could he have done this to me*, she thought again and again.

Gavin had returned the second day as promised, checking in and making sure she'd read The Packet. When he showed up, Olivia was so happy to see a familiar face, someone she could trust. He seemed genuinely concerned. "Did you understand it?" he asked, appearing to be uncomfortable for the slightest second. Then he corrected himself—his stance, his expression—turning into the model soldier who conveyed no emotion as he spoke again, "Did you?" His voice had changed, abrasive, a slight impatience to it.

Olivia was taken aback by his strange behavior but excused it, since he showed signs of being sleep deprived. The clothes he was wearing were from the previous day. Below his eyes, dark circles had formed and his whiskers had thickened, giving him a sinister appearance. The thought crossed her mind that if she'd seen this person at the airport, she would have been too scared to think of his remarkable looks. She concentrated on his questions, answering them instead of staring at him as she wanted to.

She'd understood most of The Packet, at least what she read, and she went over it with him. The layout of the vault had been the most interesting to her, seeing that there was ample space to move around underground assured her that a hidden claustrophobic trigger somewhere inside of her wouldn't go off. She didn't tell him this. Instead, she skimmed over the steps. Step one was called *The Divisions*, and it briefly summarized what Major Sullivan had explained to everyone earlier.

Olivia had met her guidance counselor that first night. She told Gavin about her, how she'd given two fast knocks and opened the door without a word. Olivia had been startled. She'd been reading The Packet from her desk. Her eyes had shot up toward the unannounced intruder in surprise, and the woman had quickly introduced herself in military fashion, "Miss Olivia Parker, I'm Private Dillard, the guidance counselor assigned to Division Four. You will get all information and vault duties from me. We'll conduct our first division meeting tomorrow evening. Goodnight." She'd left as fast as she'd come, closing the door before Olivia could question her.

When Olivia asked Gavin about Private Dillard, he mentioned her being a good solider. Then he told her that neither the private nor anyone else should know what he was about to tell her. Olivia agreed, finding out the length to which Gavin had gone to cover her identity. He had changed Kramer's niece's name to her own, explaining that Olivia could never tell because of the type of people who ran the vault. Olivia was amazed when he explained that the vault's dynamics had been planned by several scientists, all of whom had picked residents from applications and blood draws. The idea of a designed community underground that had been formed with such calculated intent seemed somewhat unreal.

She started to feel fear when Gavin's stern voice explained the seriousness of keeping their secret. She couldn't understand how anyone could hold it against her for wanting to live, for Gavin wanting her to live, but he explained that he knew the men in charge and assured her they would not see it her way. She agreed to keep the secret. He questioned her on the rest of The Packet, asking if she understood it completely. He didn't once move from his soldier position, keeping several feet of distance from her while she sat at her desk with The Packet in hand.

Olivia hadn't understood it all. It was rather difficult considering the many addenda, changes, and lawyer talk, as she'd called it, when trying to decipher it in its entirety. There were five steps in all. *Step One: The Divisions, Step Two: Career Growth, Step Three: The Reviews, Step Four: Established, Step Five: Mature.* She repeated all of them to Gavin, reading each one followed by a single, summarizing sentence. *The Divisions*: Military guidance counselor assigned to guide each division and duties. *Career Growth*: Assigned guidance counselor guides their division residents to correct career path in the vault. *The Reviews*: Assigned guidance counselor submits reports on their division residents and makes adjustments to each career path in the vault as needed. *Established*: Residents are comfortably adjusted to daily lifestyles and needs. *Mature*: The vault's residents will be fully ready and prepared for the next generation.

Gavin seemed troubled when she merely read the steps of The Packet. "You haven't read the detailed portion in the back?" he asked carefully.

She shrugged, not knowing who could have understood it. "No, it reads like a contract, confusing," she said.

He had the hardest time finding his words. "Olivia," he said softly. For the first time since he'd entered her room, he showed his softer side. "You understand that the military is running this vault and that they've made these rules based on what scientists figure is the best?"

She said, "Yes, I see that." She thought that it sounded well prepared. She didn't give much thought to his reaction to her not reading it more fully.

Then he almost said something, but he stopped himself. She tried to ask him what was wrong, but he suddenly went back into his military posture and tone as he said, "Things are different here. There will be rules and regulations that you are not used to. You will have to follow them. All of them."

Olivia was touched by his concern. She believed that he wanted to make sure she was aware of everything, and if not, he'd show her. She even thought he tried to hide that softer side behind his uniform. Olivia responded with confidence, "You're the military. You're in charge. Why would I be scared?"

He stared at her for the longest time after that response. When he did speak, he seemed to think of each word carefully. "You're right, but there are 157 other people in here. Living differently, like here in the vault, has its stresses. Just be careful who you trust. Follow the rules."

"I trust you, that's enough," she said simply.

He inhaled a deep breath at her confession and quickly added. "I'm part of the military leadership here. I won't be the only person you talk to."

"I know," she said nervously. She considered giving him her apology for her words the previous day, but he spoke first.

"I must go. Make sure you follow your assigned guidance counselor."

"Gavin," she dared to speak his name for the first time, "when will I see you again?"

He seemed shocked, then almost angry that she'd addressed him by his first name. When he answered her question, he spoke in such haste that she was blown away. As the official soldier, he delivered his words harshly. "I'm second in command, Captain Grant to you. We should not be on a first name basis, we cannot be. We won't. I have my duties, and you will have yours." He stared at her for a second before taking a deep breath and then saying, "Follow all of Private Dillard's orders. Remember, there are no choices down here." Then he left.

Olivia stared at the door, thinking of his words, about how she had no choices here and that the only person she knew had spoken to her as if she were a child. The apology that had been on her lips quickly dissolved. She was hurt by his words and worried about them at the same time.

The rest of the week went by slowly. Mostly because Captain Grant had kept his word and continued to do his duty, which included ignoring her, confirming her opinion that he believed her to be a child. Perhaps, she thought, he even regretted his decision to save her and didn't want to have any reason to be reminded of his choice. She even attempted to wave at him during one breakfast in the Grand Hall, and he pretended not to see her. That had made her feel stupid for trying.

He'd been right too. Her guidance counselor, Dillard, shot out orders faster than her mother ever could. Olivia found out exactly what was expected of her that week, the day to mourn everyone's loss had been background noise as each division began to run. Dillard turned out to be an authority to dread, not at all the delicate blonde she seemed to be. In those first few days, Olivia discovered the easiest way to stay under her radar, and that was not to question her. Olivia kept her nose down and listened and learned as her father had taught.

First, she learned everything she needed to know about the divisions. Eight divisions were ready and prepared to house twenty-five people each, however, the anticipated total of 200 had not arrived. Only 132 civilians, or residents as The Packet referred to them, had made it inside before the doors had been ordered shut. Twenty-seven soldiers managed to get safely behind the walls too, probably due to most of them already being stationed at the vault, something else Olivia had read in The Packet. The biggest fact to surprise Olivia was that each division was based on age, except for Division One, which was all military. The other seven divisions included twenty-four civilians and one military representative. Division Two was for families with children between pregnancy and seven years old. Division Three was for families with children between ages eight and twelve. Division Four, Olivia's, was for teens between the ages of thirteen and nineteen. Division Five was for adults ages twenty to twenty-nine. Division Six was for ages thirty to thirty-four. Division Seven was for ages thirty-five to forty. Division Eight was for ages forty-one to fifty-two.

What stood out most to Olivia was that the age range stopped at fifty-two. No one above that age had been allowed to apply to the vault. The oldest person alive was only fifty-two and that's only if they'd been one of the 159 survivors who made it inside. It made everything seem so surreal. She would not see anyone over that age again; at least not until the years began to roll around and they all began to age, together, but that particular thought was one she refused to dwell on.

Since the vault wasn't at the full capacity of 200 people, each division would have rooms and duty positions vacant. Everything would be adjusted accordingly and some people would actually be trained or shifted to cover those slots. Of course, the guidance counselor would be the one to decide. Everything seemed to run like a ship, and Olivia, out of fear of being discovered, had become very compliant.

Each day had a specific routine, which aided in taking her mind off the world above. Rising by seven o'clock was an order. Everyone needed to start the day at the same time so that vault life would begin to run smoothly. Between breakfast, lunch, and dinner in the Grand Hall, each person was required to check in at their designated duty or training, which included school for age-appropriate residents. After all duties were completed, each resident was allowed to use the rest of their day for entertainment, homework, or exercise, the latter of which was required at least five days a week.

Everyone seemed to fall right into their positions, which were understood when they had signed the contract. While everyone else was becoming acquainted with a career path, Olivia wasn't. Information on the person she was supposed to be had not been filled in, or maybe it had been accidently deleted thanks to Captain Grant. When Dillard came across the oddity, she had to sit down with Olivia to find out all of her basic information, her interests, and her degree, if any. Olivia had given her the data very carefully, stating that she'd been admitted into the engineering department at Berkeley, hoping that information would keep her chosen career path alive. Instead, she'd been assigned to the childcare service as a glorified babysitter. Once everyone else had settled into their positions, Dillard told her she'd be moved to a training program; until then, she was stuck covering for one of the empty slots that never arrived.

Babysitting never bothered her, but crying kids too upset to play because they missed their mommies at work made her wish she'd been able to go to school, yet even if she wanted to, it wasn't an option. The Packet stated that at age sixteen residents would be assigned to a training program for their particular career path. She accepted her days of changing diapers and drying tears with a positive outlook and even started to enjoy playing games and entertaining each and every one of her charges.

Olivia almost welcomed the orders to a certain extent. Each command was a direction to move on, as her mother would have said to her. When she finally finished reading The Packet thoroughly, though, the orders suddenly became too much. Inside The Packet, it stated: *Residents are only allowed to socialize with other residents. Military personnel are only allowed to socialize with other members of the military, unless assigned otherwise. Military personnel and residents are NOT allowed to socialize or fraternize.* After reading this warning of military members and residents not being allowed any kind of friendship, Olivia understood Captain Grant's distance and her heart sank. She couldn't understand why such a restriction had been placed. They all lived together, yet they were separated by this rule. Why?

Olivia also realized another dark truth. In *Step Five: Mature*, she had to read the detailed description again and again to understand. *In preparing for the next generation, female residents are expected to bear one child at age twenty and continue up to age twenty-nine. The regrowth of population will be dependent on the female residents.*

Chapter 7

Curled up in bed, Olivia could only think of him. He'd brought her here. He'd known what her future would be and even if they were forbidden to socialize, he could still acknowledge her. Why didn't he? Did he fear his own military? She remembered how he'd acted when she told him she hadn't read The Packet, how he'd seemed uneasy. Had he been thinking of it too? He must have known she didn't have a clue. She hated herself for telling him she trusted him. How stupid she must have sounded, she thought. He'd probably thought she was stupid too.

Olivia squeezed her eyes shut, wishing she would forget his lying face, his eyes. She couldn't stop herself and that made her angry. Why would she still look for him everyday? She asked herself that single question again and again. She didn't want to see him though, *not today*, she thought, not after what she'd figured out the night before.

Olivia had resigned herself to her room for the entire day, claiming to be ill. That night marked her eighth in the vault.

Yesterday had been when she'd finally understood the entire impact of living there, inside a community that was run like a prison. She'd begun to figure out why Gavin had become so distant. He'd known what would be expected of her, and he didn't care. In a little over two years, she would be expected to bear a child for the good of repopulation! Were they mad? How could anyone be told to do such a thing? Commanded!

She didn't want to spend her day or evening mingling with the other residents. She'd come to dislike them. They'd signed the stupid Packet, agreeing with its terms. She glanced over to the metal nightstand that held the *Viking Prince*, her book. The one thing she owned besides her purse and her one pair of clothes, besides the new ones that had been issued to her. She'd been unable to read the romance novel, completely obsessed with reading The Packet over and over again, each time finding out it was the truth. She was stuck under their rule—the military—and Gavin was one of them.

She'd tried to imagine that the idea of breeding girls in a vault wasn't going to happen, but today Dillard had announced the success of step two going into effect: career growth and education. It should have made Olivia excited, but it only confirmed that they were going by each one of The Packet's steps. She'd wanted to ask Dillard if step five was seriously going to happen. Instead, she'd asked, "Is the vault going to hold every part of The Packet as standard rules."

Dillard had given a tight smile as she'd said, "Of course, Major Sullivan has already announced that. It's our regulation guide." Dillard hadn't even hesitated in her answer, making Olivia feel dumb for asking. Then, Olivia had claimed a stomach pain and shut herself in her room.

All day she'd stared at the metal desk and dresser that were exactly like the ones in Gavin's room and wondered if he would ever speak to her again. Today she'd seen him for a brief moment, cleanly shaven and leading a couple of military men through the

Grand Hall. She'd dared to stare straight at him, but he hadn't even noticed her.

She had lain in bed staring up at the light fixture most of the day, thinking some of the time about The Packet and her horrible future, then about the person who'd brought her there, which made her sick, especially when she kept falling to the distant memory of that kiss he'd given her. Somehow she'd go into a daydream of believing that everything around her was a dream and soon she'd wake up to the sound of her mom's voice urging her to get out of bed. Even now she wanted to pinch herself and she did. "Ouch," she moaned, "Still real, still here."

She flopped to her side, staring at the *Viking Prince*, wondering if he would allow harm to his princess. She laughed at herself, remembering that most romance stories she'd read had involved the girl being ordered around and not being given many choices, except for one: to love whom she wanted in her heart. *You can't make someone love you*, she thought, *and if you don't love the guy you end up with, he won't be able to make you love him either.* She quickly thought that if she were to be with someone, it would have to be with someone she loved, and who would that be in two years?

She thought about the people she'd met so far. In her division, the ages ranged from thirteen to nineteen. She hadn't seen much of the people in her hall, other than during the short meetings Dillard conducted before breakfast hours. They'd all seemed so frightened the first few days, especially the younger ones, not being allowed to sleep without their parents nearby. At age thirteen, children were required to live alone, making growing up faster and easier on them. The older ones seemed to enjoy the newfound freedom, though, smiling and laughing with one another, an interaction she'd been jealous of, seeing others laugh, content with being alive.

She'd met a few boys and girls around her age, polite enough, but in their eyes she could see them judging or even guessing that she didn't belong. They'd hardly said a word to her, too busy with their own assignments to really get the chance to talk, and at night, she hadn't taken anyone up on their offer to meet them for a game or watch a movie. She didn't care to. She'd rather come to her room to think.

The older people seemed delighted to be kept busy, not paying her much mind since she was included in the kids' division. She had watched others during meal times, conversing with one another, making new acquaintances. She'd overheard several conversations about where these people had lived and what they had done for work. It seemed in some instances as if they tried to outdo each other with the sort of lifestyle that had existed for them. A joke, because now most everyone was in the same situation, or at least it seemed so to Olivia.

No, Olivia didn't care to meet anyone. She rather enjoyed being alone. That's how she would keep it for now, she thought. She found herself wondering about the world above ground and if they were trying to find her. Dillard's information sessions were minimal and not as informative as Olivia would have liked. The above ground situation was always the same, unknown. Communication to the outside world was down. Dillard had said they would probably know more soon enough. And so everyone had turned their full attention to the vault and kept themselves busy.

Olivia picked up her book and stared down at the cover of the *Viking Prince*. With a deep sigh, she opened it to the first page. As she was beginning to imagine the prince's homeland described in painfully slow detail, a knock at the door interrupted her. She glanced at the door just as it opened.

Gavin stepped in, causing Olivia to flip her book over and sit up in one fast motion. Her eyes were widely staring at the guy she never thought would talk to her again.

He stood at the door, wearing a grey T-shirt and jogging pants. He gave her a slight nod. "Miss Parker, may I come in?"

Olivia bit her lip at his formal announcement and didn't say a word. She'd waited days for him to just look at her and now he stood before her, addressing her as Miss Parker! She didn't know whether she wanted to smile or yell at him to get the hell out.

He closed the door behind him and in two fast steps was sitting beside her on the bed. She froze. "Are you okay?" he asked. The concern that she thought didn't exist clearly burst through his voice, surprising her. "You didn't report to your duties," he stated, as if that explained everything.

Olivia watched his blue eyes scan her, checking for any sign of illness. She could feel her lungs tightening; she hadn't taken a breath since he'd arrived. She gasped. His hand touched her face as if to feel for heat, but she was sure she wasn't the only one feeling a sudden warmth, noting it as quite an odd rush. He pulled his hand away and narrowed his eyes at her.

"You're fine," he said with a hint of annoyance. "Why didn't you attend to your duties?"

Olivia took a breath and reminded herself that he'd ignored her for a week, and now he seemed concerned about her skipping out on a single day of work. "It matters to you?" she asked defensively.

"Of course. You can get in trouble if you don't report for work."

She stared at him confused. "In trouble?" She wanted to tell him that he hadn't spoken one word to her in days, a week. That he didn't even glance her way when she was in a room. That she must be nothing to him. How could he ask her about her duties? She couldn't find the words, and then the pleasant scent of a woodsy cologne caught her attention, and she could barely get her words out, "What kind... of trouble?" she asked, trying not to stare at his smooth face as she realized it must be his aftershave.

He exhaled in frustration. "You still haven't read The Packet have you?"

That did it. That set her off and she bounced to her feet. "Of course, I have. I've read every detail."

His eyes widened at her sudden attack. "You have?"

She held his eye, staring down at him. "Yes. I've read it all."

He glanced away. "Then you should know that you're only allowed to miss work if you have a doctor's statement and that if you don't present it to Dillard tomorrow, you'll be punished."

"Punished?" Olivia repeated with surprise. "I thought that it meant two days in a row."

He shook his head. "Two days or more if the doctor allows it. One day per month can be granted, but you have to get the doctor's note indicating that you've taken your day for the month. If you don't have the note, then your socializing for the evenings will be replaced by a cell for a week."

"What?"

"Here," he said, throwing her a folded piece of paper. "Next one you have to get."

Olivia stared at the tiny note he'd dropped on her bed in disbelief. She'd be punished for not getting that note? She couldn't believe it.

He moved closer, and she immediately shifted her gaze to him. His hot breath hit her cheek.

He didn't budge as his face hovered inches from hers. "Read it again. The Packet," he stated in his military tone.

Olivia flinched at his order. She tightened her fist at her sides. "I have, several times, and I didn't see that."

"Read it. I can't come back here again," he said, turning away from her and taking a step for the door.

Olivia hadn't said everything she wanted to yet, and her anger had started to rise. Before she could stop herself, she blurted out, "But you promised."

He turned, revealing an intense stare. "I did, and I just took care of you."

She shook her head trying to find the words to tell him that he'd hurt her more this week than anything by ignoring her. "How can you do it? How can you live here with these rules? What they ask of everyone? What they order?" For the first time, she felt scared.

His eyes glazed over with a dark emotion. "Who?"

"The people that signed that ridiculous contract, The Packet. The rules that everyone is going by."

"To stay here, everyone must follow it."

"But how can anyone in their right mind follow it. It's insane to ask people to live like this. It's a prison, and you're telling me I should be happy to be in it."

He took a breath before speaking. "Olivia, I know what it looks like, but stick with it and follow the rules. There's nothing else I can do or say."

"Because you're the military."

"I am."

"But you're the one who enforces the rules of The Packet." She paused for a brief moment. "Don't," she whispered, more of a plea than the solid demand she wanted it to be.

He clinched his jaw. "You're correct, but I can't break any more rules. The major is in charge, and he deems The Packet necessary, so we go by it."

"And military can't socialize with residents."

He shook his head. "No, no they can't," he confirmed.

She noticed his perfect posture slowly hunch as if the weight had been too much. She dared to ask him. "Is that why you won't talk to me? You brought me here, but you won't even speak to me." Her hands unclenched as she began to believe that she had struck a nerve.

"I can't." He shifted his weight. "Follow the rules Olivia," he said as he turned toward the door.

She hadn't convinced him of anything, and she didn't want him to leave. She didn't want him to go on ignoring her. So she said the first thing that popped into her mind. "But you kissed me!" Instantly, she regretted the words as utter horror crossed her face in the form of red inflammation, yet she still stared at him, waiting for his response. Her heart pounded in her throat as he stopped and his back straightened.

"That will never happen again." His tone was sharp and deep, and the words registered with Olivia only after the door shut against his back. She stared at it, feeling truly alone.

Chapter 8

G avin walked down Division Four's corridors with guilt plagu-
ing his thoughts. He couldn't believe he'd been so cold to her,
yet what other choice did he have? It was for the best. Both of
them had their roles to fill, and as she'd reminded him, military
and residents were not allowed to socialize. Being in her room,
speaking to her—it wouldn't take much for someone to get the
wrong impression. He hated himself for leaving her like that.

She'd mentioned that kiss. A kiss that had been on his mind
for a week, a kiss that he regretted ever taking. It was just to prove
a point, he'd told himself on several restless nights. She was a kid!
He shouldn't be thinking of her in that way. But he did and the
fact that she mentioned it again drove him crazy. "Never again,"
he'd said, and he meant it. His reality was the vault, and the vault
had rules.

He quickened his step, wanting to make it out of Division Four
before someone spotted him. He gritted his teeth at her image. It
had made him sick being that close to her and seeing her green

eyes flicker with anger. *That was it,* he thought. If she hadn't disliked him before, she sure as hell did now. He grunted when he clipped the edge of a door.

A week had gone by and he'd thrown himself into the full operation of the vault, day and night sometimes, not getting any sleep. The entire system had to be monitored. He was second in command, and he wasn't allowed the comfort of taking evenings off. Besides, the only thing that crept into his thoughts when he wasn't working was her and those green eyes. He'd been unable to forget them, to forget her. She'd been right. He'd been ignoring her not only for their safety, but because of the urges he had when he saw her, since when he'd first seen her.

He smiled remembering her face at the airport, at how she was completely mortified when he'd read from the back of that romance novel. It had been hers. He knew it then, but he had just seen it on her bed a few minutes ago. She was absolutely adorable, shy or mad. He'd compared her to his sister at the airport, and maybe he had saved her because he'd wished someone, if given the chance, would have done the same for Jessie. But he didn't see his sister in her at all, nor were his feelings brotherly. Not after that kiss.

He'd kept an eye on her throughout the week, making sure she was attending her meals, her duties, taking care of herself. He thought that she'd try and make friends closer to her own age, but she went back to her room every night. Then, when she hadn't showed up to work today, he'd risked speaking to the doctor on shift about a resident that he hadn't even seen. Gavin had confirmed that she was sick to get the note. Luckily, being the second in command didn't warrant any questions.

Gavin was thankful that he'd found her well, but the idea that she'd skipped out on her duties and hadn't truly understood each and every rule within The Packet worried him. Sure he'd been angry and frustrated that he had to take on the responsibility, he had enough already, but she'd become the most important of them all, and the most dangerous.

He shook his head, trying to get rid of the image of her betrayed expression. What else was he supposed to do? He'd saved her, brought her here, broken rules—something he'd never done before. What else did he owe her? He would continue to check on her, but he couldn't speak to her, he couldn't think of her as anything else but a resident. He must not, he told himself again, the same as he'd told himself every night since they'd arrived. He had sworn to uphold these regulations. It was his duty. His father wouldn't have broken the rules, and he wasn't going to break anymore.

"Captain." A woman's voice echoed through the corridor, causing Gavin to turn.

He recognized her instantly, Alison Dillard, one of the soldiers that had been assigned to him since he'd accepted his post at the vault. She was a woman who seemed to be on the mind of every man in his platoon, including his own on more than one occasion. It seemed only natural, since she was a woman with exquisite good looks. She had been compared to a younger version of Charlize Theron to the point that she was secretly nicknamed, *Charlize* by all of his men. Not that he condoned it or ever called her that, but he'd agreed in his own thoughts—she was a beauty. His men had salivated alongside one another the moment they'd first seen her, until they'd found out her soft, feminine appearance did not reflect the inner soldier. Dillard was highly capable of reminding love struck soldiers that she hadn't been named champion of the kickboxing ring twice because of her looks. Gavin hadn't been shocked though, not when she sent one solider to the infirmary after a slight graze of the hand to her rear, and he hadn't disciplined her for it either. He knew her file and that she had to prove a point. She was a fellow soldier, not a woman to lust.

Gavin was impressed with her as a soldier. Women were common phenomena in the Army and should be treated as such. Any consideration for womanly characteristics would be ignored. He concluded that most of his men had acquired the same thought after several incidents with her, none of which he ever heard resulted in a successful move on their part. Gavin had no issues with any of his soldiers including her. They all respected him; however, he had the impression that she'd been a sort of apple polisher when it came to him. Alison Dillard had more than a crush, he was certain then, and he was certain now—her eyes told him.

Dillard's lip curved up slightly on one side as if seeing him pleased her. He wanted to make it through the division without being noticed, and he tried to hide any of his displeasure. "Dillard," he formally announced to acknowledge her.

She stepped out of her room to stand at full attention, wearing her fatigues and her hair down as if she'd begun to get ready for bed. Her eyes quickly scanned Gavin, confirming his uneasy feelings as she did so. "Is something needed sir?" Dillard asked.

"No. Continue with your evening," he said, abruptly turning to leave.

"Sir?" she asked.

Gavin gritted his teeth as he faced her and was surprised to see her smiling. "Yes, Dillard."

"You need me for anything?" she asked, not hiding her hope that he did need something from her.

Her insinuation could not be ignored. It was plain as day. She'd never been so blunt before, there had only been slight hints in her expression when he came near. "No." he said quickly, and then realizing his fast response had made her lose her smile, he quickly added, "Keep up the good work, your division is performing."

"Thank you, Sir," she said with a nod.

He nodded back, then turned and left, hoping that she never asked that of him again.

When he made it to the control center, he was finally able to shift his thoughts from Olivia's hurt expression and Dillard's tempting offer to the operation checks that he was responsible for.

The tiny room that controlled the entire vault buzzed with a low hum and three short beeps as the solider on duty made alterations to the control panel. A light blinked above, cascading a red glow every minute on the dot, a confirmation that the oxygen system was still online. The monitors that lined the room were links from observation cameras throughout various areas in the vault. There weren't many, not all of them had been installed, but there were enough to keep eyes on the storage units and the second-level entranceway. The room had always surprised Gavin, how small for all that it was meant to do, with off and on switches for water, air, electricity, and communications.

Gavin interrupted the soldier who seemed to be placing several commands into the main computer. "How are things?" he asked.

The soldier turned in surprise. "Sir." He straightened his back at seeing Gavin present. "Everything is good, Sir."

"What are you updating?" Gavin asked.

"Changing temperature, Sir. To conserve power at night."

Gavin nodded, remembering the alterations that were made to get optimal usage for every resource. "Everyone in position?"

The soldier nodded. "Yes, all division soldiers have reported. Residents are all accounted for."

"Good. Anything else?"

"No, Sir. Everything is normal."

Gavin couldn't help but grunt at the word normal. "Good. Continue on Davis. Let me know if anything is out of the ordinary."

"Yes, Sir," he said.

Gavin turned and left. He continued on in what had become his usual routine. First, he would walk the vault, checking in on every soldier and their post, making sure that things were going *normal*, or according to The Packet. Major Sullivan wanted to be watchful of the residents, keeping an eye out for any number of inevitable issues that was predicted to arise. The moment a resident or soldier went into a claustrophobic fit, they'd have to step in immediately so that there was minimal exposure to the other residents. Containing such reactions helped prevent a domino effect from igniting. Once an individual had been charged with such an offense, they would be locked up and tended to by a physician. If the physician didn't see any hope for readmitting them to resident life, they would be permanently removed, an order that was within the military's own Packet, a Packet that had been designed specifically for the soldiers. It predicted certain situations and outcomes and how the military should react. The military had protocols and procedures for noncompliant residents, and Gavin didn't look forward to those predicted situations, even though he knew that more than likely they would occur, and he would be ready as directed.

After Gavin had ensured that the first level was locked down for the night and the control center had no concerning issues, he made one more round on the entire second level to check that all rooms: the prison, the armory, and the main storage facility were undisturbed. Even though Gavin had several soldiers reporting to him that all these things had been done, he had always been one to make sure. It wasn't that he doubted his men, it was just a habit he never could break.

He'd never been considered a micromanager or a power hungry leader. He'd seen a lot and experienced more than enough to set his mind straight. A leader is responsible for guiding people to meet their full potential, not for forcing them or degrading them for his or her own pleasure. This was an ideal he resolved long ago to hold himself to, especially during his years at West Point. He assumed the academy was much like any organization, with a few bullies or wannabe dictators fighting to be the best smart ass around. He hadn't played into their game, and he'd gone on to survive his first post in the Army, where he'd served directly under a massively arrogant officer.

Lieutenant Avery was the biggest prick Gavin had ever met. He'd survived that egotistical slimebag by being tactful. Lieutenant Avery was the type of man who believed that a truly great soldier must be made with an iron fist, not only of military values but also his own twisted thoughts of breaking a man beyond his point of endurance and confidence. Gavin had seen more than one guy destroyed, leaving an unwanted shell of a soldier to be turned into the M.P's.

Gavin had learned to keep the appearance of an agreeable Second Assistant Lieutenant while secretly bonding with his own men by listening and communicating, relatively easy concepts that came naturally to him. These actions helped smooth things over and yielded the most productive unit in the squad for that particular year. Of course, Lieutenant Avery had patted himself on the back, but the soldiers all knew why, and that was all that mattered to Gavin. Doing the right thing had always led him to success.

Gavin hoped he would be able to do the right thing this time inside the vault. He knocked on Major Sullivan's quarters wondering if he could prove his point. He'd try.

The door opened, revealing Major Sullivan's tired eyes. He wasn't in bed yet, but he wore a blue robe that suggested he'd recently taken a shower. Gavin silently scolded himself for coming by too late.

Major Sullivan scanned Gavin with squinty eyes. "What is it, Grant? Is there a problem?"

Gavin stood with his shoulders squared and his hands behind his back. "No, Sir, no problems. All is locked down. I wanted a word, if possible."

Major Sullivan grunted as if this suggestion surprised him. "Well, come in then." He walked away from the door. Gavin watched as he walked across his room to a television playing a movie. Gavin couldn't tell what it was, but it appeared to be an action flick. Major Sullivan turned it off and the screen went black.

Gavin made a quick assessment of the room, noticing that Major Sullivan didn't have the standard-issue furniture that all of the soldiers and most of the residents had. Instead, he had a large wooden bed and matching furniture that seemed highly detailed, perhaps hand carved, way above any budget he'd seen. Beside the bed were a comfy couch and reclining chair that faced the flat screen television. The room was bigger than his by far, though he'd opted not to take the room upgrade with his promotion, wanting instead to be among his men. Gavin thought the phrase *luxury suite* would best describe the major's quarters as his eyes fell to an inlayed bar directly behind the oak dining table.

Major Sullivan noticed Gavin's gaze and smiled. "Would you like a drink, Captain?"

Gavin turned back to Major Sullivan. "If you're having one, Major."

"Well. Why not? We should. Make us two scotches then, Captain."

"Yes, Major."

Major Sullivan chuckled. "Come in and close the door."

Gavin did as instructed, shutting the door softly behind him. He watched from the corner of his eye as the major took a seat on the large plush sofa. The major appeared more like an elderly man in his robe than a top-ranking officer filled with overwhelming power issues. The major was only fifty-one years old, yet his white hair gave him an elderly look. When Gavin had finished making the drinks, he handed the major his drink first and stood waiting.

"Please have a seat Captain, and relax, no need to be uncomfortable while having a drink with your commanding officer," he said with a pleasant grin.

Gavin swallowed, unsure of the offer as he reminded himself that the major had sent several good men to jail for being at ease. He did as directed, though, and took the seat at the other end of the sofa. He held the scotch in his hand, already planning on making himself drink it no matter how much he disliked scotch. If he didn't, it would be an insult. He waited for the major to take the first sip. When he did, Gavin followed.

The major sighed in delight. "Goes down smooth. My favorite. A young man like you probably doesn't know the value of what's just passed through your lips. Well, I'm telling you it's quality—the best—or I wouldn't have it around."

Gavin nodded as he forced another sip, not feeling any smoothness. The liquid shot down his throat, trailing a slight burn.

"As are most things I acquire. The best."

Gavin was waiting for a moment to speak to agree with the major, yet he didn't see an opportunity. The major, he was learning, seemed to be more of a talker than he expected, so Gavin continued to listen.

Major Sullivan twirled the drink in his hand, causing the ice to jingle. "I've always been one to keep an eye out for things of value. My furniture, you must have noticed, isn't standard issue. It's my own, shipped from England. It belonged to a welsh Duke of Powis in the late 17th century, and I decided this would be one luxury I would have if I were to be encased in this concrete box for years to come. Oh, well, you might ask why I'd go to the trouble? Who would ever think we'd use this vault? I don't deliberate on maybes. I'm prepared for all things that are possible, and being prepared has given us this wonderful scotch. You do like?"

Gavin raised an eyebrow. "It would be a sin not to, would it not?"

Major Sullivan chuckled. "Yes. That's very true." Major Sullivan took another gulp of his scotch on that note. When he'd swallowed it down, he licked his lips for any remaining drops before turning his attention back to Gavin. "As I was saying, I'm a collector of quality in every aspect, especially in my regiment. I knew that a colonel's son would be a good choice."

This confession wasn't much, since Gavin was sure the major already knew everything there was to know about him; it could easily be found in his file.

"Yes, I knew you would make a great addition and so you have. Though, there aren't any gallantries needed here." Major Sullivan paused for a moment, his eyes seeming to center on Gavin as if he were about to challenge him. Gavin immediately felt the threat and held himself back from making any sudden moves that would alert the major to his own disagreement to the man's opinion.

Major Sullivan waved his arm with scotch in hand, causing some to tip over the side of his glass as he spoke again. "All those awards you won may have gotten you promoted, but you weren't ordered to do it." Sullivan's voice changed to a deeper and more challenging tone. "In my regiment, if you're not ordered, you don't do anything. Is that understood?" One side of his lips curved up as if mocking.

Gavin saw the delight in Major Sullivan's face. He'd seen it before—the pleasure of being in control danced across the man's expression. It wasn't a warning but an order of what he expected out of his captain, a basic lap dog who did as told, no thinking. Immediately, Gavin knew that he could not go through with the real reason behind his coming to the major's room. He couldn't ask him not to use The Packet. It would be considered out of his duty to do so. *Olivia*, he thought at his first sign of defeat. He didn't want her to be subjected to those rules. They were barbaric.

Gavin tilted his head in a sign of respect, continuing to make eye contact with the major. "Yes, Sir. Understood."

Major Sullivan sat back with a smile and a nod of acceptance to Gavin's response. "So, what brings my second in command?"

Gavin knew he had to come up with something quickly. Something that would be considered important enough for the major's ears, and in a way that didn't appear as if Gavin himself was asking but that the major was solving a problem by himself. After a brief hesitation, Gavin began, "As you know, I've been surveying the residents for any sign of noncompliance. There's been one issue."

Major Sullivan's interest perked. "Go on."

"Major, as you know, we are missing forty-one people in the vault's original plan for The Packet." Gavin watched for any sign of intolerance for his mention of an apparent fact. The major didn't give any, so Gavin continued. "The missing people have left certain jobs open."

Major Sullivan nodded quickly, showing his first sign of being agitated by the direction of Gavin's topic. "Yes, yes, that has already been solved. People will have to be cross-trained or redirected as needed."

Gavin nodded. "Yes, Sir. The problem isn't the redirecting, but the missing people that would be involved with everyday life."

"I don't see this as being relevant. Get to the point, Captain."

Gavin nodded. "The current residents are socializing with each other. Some have been witnessed as perhaps beginning relationships."

"Relationships? Captain Grant, please explain."

"I wanted to report that residents have been coupling with each other outside of the designed protocol."

Major Sullivan's eyebrow lifted as if he finally understood. "Uh, so the residents are dating one another. That's interesting. I didn't... hmm." He paused a minute, thinking about something.

Gavin watched as the old man took a swig of his scotch and scratched at his temple before speaking again. "The original forty-one were meant to be distributed, and now that isn't going to happen. Well. That only leaves the remaining. I'll have Doctor Sutton take a look."

Gavin nodded. Not the answer he wanted, but if Doctor Sutton were to push the idea that The Packet could no longer be seen as workable, they might throw it out. He hoped.

"I'll also have him add the military into the equation."

Gavin was startled by this and spoke before he could stop himself, "Sir?"

Major Sullivan smiled. "Well, we have plenty of boys that can fill those slots. Why not, they can service the needs too."

Gavin was horrified. If the major was going to make alterations to The Packet, how could he do that without ruling The Packet altogether invalid? It should all be thrown out. He didn't have the authority to change it. To add to it!

"Anything else, Captain?"

Gavin collected his thoughts. "We have a girl turning twenty in about a month who has been seen associating with a male resident."

Major Sullivan nodded. "Yes, quite interesting. She should be observed and returned to her own room by curfew. Let Doctor Sutton explain the restrictions and explain the process."

"Yes, Major." Gavin finished off his scotch and set the empty glass on the table.

"Oh and Captain?"

Gavin looked down at the old man with a polite nod.

"Make sure the residents do as they're instructed. I don't want them thinking there are no rules. We can't have order without structure."

"Yes, Major."

"Goodnight, Captain."

"Goodnight, Major." Gavin saluted his major and left.

Gavin returned to his tiny, standard-issue room filled with rage. The major had not seen the obvious fact that The Packet was invalid, unusable. Instead, the major saw an opportunity to alter it based on his opinion, not a scientific one. Talking with Doctor Sutton would be Gavin's next step. If Doctor Sutton could convince the major that the forty-one people missing did, in fact, invalidate The Packet, then perhaps the alterations would stop. The Packet would stop.

Gavin's thoughts turned to Olivia. At least she wasn't close to twenty. Even if she were, he'd fixed that. He had at least prolonged it.

Chapter 9

Watching for random sightings of Gavin had become a sort of hobby for Olivia in the past month. She didn't speak to him, though, not since the night he'd come to her room, when he'd delivered the doctor's note and confirmed that the kiss he'd given her didn't matter. That had been a month ago.

At first, she had been angry at his cold words and determination to achieve permanent distance, but then she'd become sad. A lonely sensation developed in the pit of her stomach that only partially eased when she saw him. Eventually, the slight enjoyment she had at spotting him for a moment was replaced with a quiet yearning. She wanted him to notice her, and she couldn't rationalize it. She wanted it even though she knew it was forbidden.

She'd waited for him during meals in the Grand Hall, the one place she could usually find him, and at first she'd hoped that he would secretly acknowledge her or find some way to communicate, a nod of his head, a slight shift of his eyes, anything that would say *we're in this together*. But he didn't, not once. He always entered alone, usually to join a few of his soldiers for a conversation before quickly departing to his captain assignments, which seemed to keep him overly occupied. Once she'd tried sitting a few tables down from him, catching the tail end of a joke that seemed to throttle his ribs into a euphoric laughing frenzy. He appeared happy in that moment. Olivia had not been.

She stared at the side door to the Grand Hall again, his usual point of entrance, and found the surrounding area unoccupied. He still had not walked in. The room was half-empty, breakfast had been served earlier, and most of the residents had already eaten and left for their assigned duties. Olivia stared at the plate before her that still contained a few crumbs, the only evidence of her two biscuits and eggs. She guessed that today she wouldn't see him, at least for breakfast. She'd give lunch and dinner another try. *Why do I care?* This was a common question she had regularly asked herself for the past month, and which was only answered with a shrug of her shoulders and the familiar flash of her first real kiss—a kiss that had been with him.

She shouldn't remember it. She shouldn't have allowed it to be burned into the foremost thoughts of her mind. It overpowered her and she couldn't help but consider it. She shouldn't, but she inserted him as her Viking Prince when she read and re-read her one and only romance novel, envisioning herself as the princess he loved. She knew that it was probably the wrong thing to do, but when the storyline hit a sensual moment in which Harek the Viking Prince leaned in and grabbed Princess Shana for a gentle yet ravishing kiss of need, Olivia had been unable to stop herself from comparing the same emotions that she had when Gavin kissed her—a foreign emotion—a short flutter of excitement. The Princess, an all-out spoiled brat who'd been completely opposed to Harek until that kiss—a kiss that changed her in some odd, magical way—was the same as Olivia. She couldn't stop thinking about it, about him. It was a shortcoming of which she was fully aware, and like the Princess, she didn't care.

After waiting a few more minutes, Olivia gave up on his arrival. She figured she'd see him at lunch. She collected her plate and utensils and turned them in to the dirty-dishes window where a resident quickly took them with a clanking fumble. The resident was familiar, a black-haired woman in her thirties named Clare who seemed very out of place during her shifts five days a week. Not that taking dirty dishes was an extreme difficulty, but the woman wore large, diamond-studded earrings and an expression on her face that stated *I'm from the upper crust.* She'd also overheard Clare speaking one day to another resident, describing the servants she once had in her marble mansion and how she'd never imagined being stuck in the kitchen. The other resident speaking to Clare had been Sophie, a redhead with a pleasant demeanor and gorgeous smile, who'd said she was just happy to be alive. Clare had grunted at that response with a flick of her hand, a common gesture from Clare whenever she got to talking about anything she disliked, which seemed to be often. Flailing Arms was Olivia's private nickname for the ungrateful women.

Today Olivia paid no attention to Clare's grumblings, instead turning a smile toward Sophie, who was gathering the garbage bin beside her labeled *Food Only*, which was used for composting and later applied to the gardens.

"Hi Olivia," Sophie said as she traded the garbage bin out for an empty one. Her bold red hair caught Olivia's eye, bound up on her head in what could be judged as perfection.

Olivia wanted to ask how she always managed to fix her hair as if it were done by a professional, but she didn't want to interrupt her from her duties. "Hi. Will I see you later?"

Sophie nodded as she began to roll the bin off the floor. "If I get done early you will," she said with a backward glance and smile. Her flaming hair and unusual blue eyes had made her stand out to Olivia when they'd first met as being almost unreal, too perfect, too beautiful. Finding out that Sophie was an authentic person with an uplifting vibe that seemed to radiate right out of her was sort of an oasis for Olivia. She felt at ease and excited to be around her.

Olivia waved goodbye as she took another fast glance around the dining room. No Gavin. She exited the Grand Hall, hoping that Sophie would manage to finish her work early.

Sophie had become a sort of friend, someone to chat with whenever Olivia would see her in the Grand Hall. Sophie, thirty years old and the recent president of a fortune 500 company, had been assigned the duty of kitchen manager, a big step down from running a multi-billion dollar business. Impressively, Sophie didn't harbor any resentment about her current situation. She'd simply said that the job may be different, but managing people and running a smooth operation could be applied to any job, and she didn't mind. Sophie's down-to-earth personality and warm smile had been part of what drew Olivia to her. On occasion, they'd sit next to one another in the movie room, or if Sophie could sneak a minute off work, she'd sit with Olivia in the dining hall.

Olivia liked talking with Sophie about the places she'd been. Sophie had traveled during her twenties, backpacking through most of Europe and Asia. She'd said it was a great opportunity to explore and build on her worldly exposure to different cultures. Olivia especially enjoyed hearing about Italy and the canals of Venice; it seemed like an unreal place as Sophie had described it. Olivia had a sudden realization during one of their talks that not everyone in the vault had been strange or stupid for signing The Packet. Sophie had explained that she'd done it not because she thought it would happen, but because it seemed to be a novel idea to own a room in an underground vault. "Why not?" She'd said, not hiding the reality of it having been a good decision. *An expensive decision*, Olivia had thought, wondering how much money Sophie once had in her other life.

Olivia never brought up the concerns she had about The Packet, though. She didn't feel it was the right time. Gavin's direction of keeping to the rules and not trusting others deterred her from bringing up the subject to anyone. As the weeks had started to go by, however, she wondered why she should even trust Gavin, a person who wouldn't attempt to say hello or even give her a discreet smile. But no matter how many times she wanted to walk up and yell at him for completely disregarding her on a daily basis, she couldn't dispute that she did trust him. He'd saved her life. She had a certain loyalty to him that she couldn't break, no matter how mad he made her.

Olivia shook him from her thoughts as she passed the Exchange, a sort of local store for the residents where clothing, personal hygiene products, and any other needed supplies could be picked up. Everything was issued to residents, there was no form of payment, but there was a cap on the amount of each item that a person could request; the items were rationed out once per month. Mr. Rossi managed the Exchange. Olivia met him for the first time when she'd been directed to pick up a uniform and computer for her new training program.

Mr. Rossi, a tall man in his early thirties, had been very polite and highly detailed. His former life had been as a talented financial executive who had been employed as a consultant through fortune 500 companies, just like Sophie. It was a reoccurring theme that Olivia had heard repeated over and over again, former occupations of the residents took place at the highest caliber of companies, just another requirement in the admission process to the vault.

Mr. Rossi waved at Olivia as they locked eyes. Olivia smiled. After noticing his stare that slowly glided over her, Olivia turned her head, hiding a blush. Mr. Rossi fit the standard of most of the residents—a perfect specimen of good looks and impeccable genetics, another in-your-face, obvious requirement for being accepted into the vault's family. Mr. Rossi reminded Olivia of a dashing Italian without the accent. He'd been born and raised in Burbank, California. His family had been from a small town outside of Florence. He had been Americanized, this is how Sophie described his past to Olivia. Sophie had actually spent several evenings getting to know him and had excitedly relayed the information to her new friend. Though Mr. Rossi, or Albert as Sophie called him, seemed to have an interesting way of looking at Olivia, making her feel like she was under the microscope.

Two soldiers passed Olivia in the hallway, both wearing their standard fatigues. Olivia hadn't gotten to know many soldiers, due to the regulation of no socializing, which every soldier seemed to respect. Most of her days had been checking in with Dillard, the only soldier she was allowed to truly speak to. The rest of the soldiers seemed detached. Olivia sometimes felt invisible to them, as if she were another stranger in a busy crowd. A hilarious joke she'd laughed at in her own mind, realizing that 158 other faces in the vault had become familiar in the past month. Not that she knew every single person, that wasn't possible, not with the divisions and the separate duties, yet when she saw a familiar face she had placed in a hallway or in the food line, she'd started to refer to them as such. In her own secret mind, she'd say, *Oh, there's that Brussels sprouts guy*, about someone who had once commented when standing next to her in the food line: "Did they really have to grow those?" Or that red-eyed girl, the one who'd collided into her, offering a tiny "sorry" as she'd scurried off, her head down in an attempt to hide tears. Olivia could place almost all the faces in the vault now.

Olivia spent more time noticing the red door that read *Restricted Access* in yellow letters. It was a door that she regularly passed on her way to her duties, on her way to meals, on her way back to her division. She had never been allowed through this particular door, not many people were, though she'd seen several people in white coats enter and exit—doctors and scientists, she'd assumed. She had no idea what went on beyond the red door but had made a mental note about most of the people's ages as she saw them coming and going. Many appeared to be in their late forties. *Maybe a few of them are the vault residents near age fifty-two*, she'd thought. Another strange observation she'd made in the past few weeks: Most residents seemed to be in their early thirties or younger, with the exception of the doctors or scientists who came in and out of that door. Olivia wondered what their story might be. Once she had even seen a couple of younger doctors emerge from the mysterious door—trainees, she'd suspected.

Olivia scanned her badge at the next doorway, which opened to the hallway toward general worker rooms, several of which she'd previously been allowed to explore. Most were for replenishing supplies like clothing or repairing equipment. Janet, a twenty-five-year-old black beauty, managed one of the rooms for mending or creating clothing. Janet had been a fashion goddess before the attack, as well as a model. Most of the residents' uniforms seemed rather plain, "A travesty," she'd once confessed to Olivia, and it was one she'd be remedying in the coming months. A few other rooms had been set up for making or altering metals and plastics, so that items could be produced or recycled as needed. Daniel had explained all of this to her throughout the past few weeks.

Daniel was Olivia's boss. Three weeks ago Olivia had been taken off babysitting duties and given a chance to learn engineering from Daniel. He'd mentioned on several occasions that a completely new vault with top-of-the-line equipment didn't really need much maintenance, and the work wasn't coming anytime soon. Without much to do, Daniel had spent most of his days training his new protégé, Olivia, who'd begun learning the components of all of the machines throughout the vault.

Olivia's first day had been filled with excitement, until she'd picked up her new uniform from Mr. Rossi. At least the computer had been a plus, giving her access to resident emailing and chatting capabilities; however it's main function was to perform diagnostic checks on any and all equipment throughout the vault. It was a great tool for any trainee, which seemed to contain unlimited software and tutorials for her learning needs. The uniform had given her the opposite reaction, making her feel like an undervalued car repairman or, on second glance, like a prisoner. She sported a grey jumpsuit that fit snugly against her rear and it didn't excite her or Janet's fashion senses. Janet had promised to work on those when given the chance. Daniel had simply smiled ear to ear when he saw her in it. He'd later agreed to the uncanny comparison to a garage worker but laughed it off by saying that as engineers they sort of were and that it protected them from grime and scratches while repairing equipment.

He'd made fun of her on the first day too. "Did you expect you'd be wearing a dress?" he asked with much amusement.

Olivia ignored his comment and pretended not to be bothered by her clothing. Olivia found out later that Daniel's humor and kidding around were regular events.

Daniel Bandt, a twenty-year-old wiz kid and the vault's lead engineer, didn't allow the stereotype of being an unspoken shy nerd last beyond his specific duties. Professional when needed and brilliant beyond a shadow of doubt, he was, in fact, a charismatic young man. Daniel's fabulously shocking good looks wasn't the only odd detail about this genius, and having a personality that was relaxed with humor was possibly the most surprising.

A giant grin, accompanied by a slight chuckle, had been the grand finale to any of his most successful jokes, while the less impressive resulted in a raise of both his brows, which he followed with a semi-satisfied smirk. The least entertaining attempt at humor would get a shrug and a short grimace that reflected he too understood he'd just bombed. Olivia was acquainted with them all now, considering all the time they'd spent together, the most she'd spent with any other individual inside the vault. Olivia had become accustomed to his infectious humor, though it hadn't always been so. Especially, when they'd first met.

On that day, while reluctantly wearing the tight-fitting, prisoner-like uniform with her computer tucked gently under one arm, she'd gone to check in with her newly assigned boss, Daniel

Bandt. She was excited for the first time since she was brought to the vault. It almost felt like the first day of school; however, her attire didn't boost her confidence. When she arrived at the door of her new workroom, a note stating *Meet me in the garden* had been left on the door. She was unsure if it was intended for her, but upon entering the workroom and finding no boss and no other workers, she decided after an internal debate that she'd at least swing by the garden.

When she entered the garden for the very first time, for a single second she was covered by a tingling sensation of contentment, feeling as if she'd just stepped outside into a sunny day. The awareness that this couldn't be possible was the only reason she paused to search out the heating lamps and overhead lights that confirmed the truth to her doubting mind.

No matter the false reality that beamed throughout the largest room underground, Olivia had welcomed its synthetic offering with a smile. It was the first smile she remembered having since she'd entered the vault, not counting the fake ones she'd given to Dillard or the others. A genuine smile lit up her face in the same way this room had been lit to grow life. She stared at the outstretched room and its magnificence in the form of small and large sprouts taking root and growing underground. The strangeness of it all turned her mind into a pinwheel of thoughts that only enhanced her forgotten emotions as they welled up before her eyes as tomatoes and squash. She'd been so caught up in the sight of so many rows of vegetables tended to by residents and planted by others that she didn't hear the man's voice.

"Excuse me. Did you hear me?" the voice asked.

Olivia turned, sure it wasn't her he was talking to, but a natural need to check made her look anyway. The man stood taller than her, his uniform the same grey jumpsuit that she wore. Then, when he scrunched his brows as if unsure of something, she noticed his eyes—ocean blue—*a strange tint for someone with brown hair*, she thought.

"Are you Olivia?" he asked.

She nodded. His face was covered with several dirty smears, matching the spots on his uniform. She stared at him as she always stared at good-looking guys—lost.

"Good. I need your help. Follow me." He walked away, expecting her to follow.

And she had followed, wondering if he was, like her, another trainee. When he stopped at the wall beside a large vent, he bent down to his knees. Olivia hovered over him, waiting for direction, he didn't give any. Instead, he removed the vent and crawled inside the wall on his hands and knees. Olivia froze for several seconds and stared as he disappeared.

"Are you coming?" he asked from within.

"What?" She asked, not wanting to enter the tiny opening.

"Come on. Follow me."

Olivia looked around as if she could find an excuse not to, and when she didn't, she finally spoke, bending slightly down toward the passage as she stated, "I don't think I'm the right person to help you. I'm supposed to meet Daniel Bandt here. I can find you someone, someone else if you want."

He poked his head out of the vent, causing Olivia to pull back at the sudden closeness. A slight grin formed on his face. "Then look no further. You're my person. Come inside and I'll introduce you."

"Introduce me? In there?" She asked unbelieving.

"Don't like to get dirty, huh?"

"What? No, that's not a problem."

"Then stop standing there. You're keeping Mr. Bandt waiting."

Olivia did as requested, climbing into the tiny vent on all fours just as she'd observed the other trainee do. She didn't want to cause any problems, though she couldn't quite understand why, on her first day, she'd been asked to crawl in a vent shaft.

When she finally caught up to him, they were several feet within the wall, where a small network of pipes connected.

"Hold this," he ordered, as he motioned toward a pipe before him. Olivia scanned the tiny chamber, noticed there was no other person around, and became suspicious.

"Hold this," he instructed again.

Once she grabbed the pipe, he moved to the other side of the chamber. "If it starts to move or there are any leaks, let me know. She watched as he went to the wall, turning several knobs until finally she felt a tiny vibration in the pipe.

"It's moving," she shouted.

"Good. Stay there." A few minutes went by. "What about now?"

"Nothing," she said. "Where is—"

He interrupted. "All fixed."

"What was broken?"

He crawled back to her as if he hadn't heard her question. "You can stop holding this now." He touched her hand and removed it from the pipe.

She quickly took her hand back from his and tried to remember what she'd wanted answered. "What was broken?"

"The water line," he said simply. His warm breath hit her forehead, reminding her of how close he was.

"The water?" she asked, worried.

He stared at her for a moment. "Well, almost. The water to the garden had to be rerouted, it was going to cause a leak."

"Oh, is that what you do?" she asked, shifting her weight.

"Yes. I'm a plumber it seems." He smiled and chuckled. She didn't understand when he shrugged his shoulders. "Seems you will be too."

"Oh no, I'm supposed to learn engineering."

"You are?" He asked with a wry grin.

"Yes."

"From Daniel Bandt?"

"Yes."

"Well. What sort of things do you expect to learn?" He asked, while staring at her in the tiny chamber.

She felt as if they shouldn't be alone inside such a close space. It seemed strange having a conversation within a hidden room that reminded her of a metal tunnel with pipe décor. "Mechanical design and improving structures," she said, as if he should already know this.

"Sounds like engineering."

Olivia felt like he was mocking her, and she didn't like it. "A lot more interesting than being a plumber." She wanted to defend the art of being an engineer, but instead she attacked him. She felt badly and immediately awaited a snide remark, but she didn't get one.

"I wonder who designed this water system. Hmm, I guess I just improved his structure," he said while glancing at the pipes.

Olivia followed his eyes, wondering how he'd missed out on her insult. Before she could process his statement, he spoke again.

"Guess a pretty clever engineer was hired to design these pipes. Even though I'm a mere plumber, do you think I might be considered an engineer? I did just make an adjustment to his design."

Olivia squinted at him while trying to ignore the slight cramp in her legs from sitting on them since they'd started adjusting the pipes. "Uh, I don't think so." She looked around at that moment, wanting to find the way out through the tiny chamber. When her eyes fell on the vent opening, she moved toward it while saying, "If we're done..."

He lifted his hand in a gesture to proceed on toward the exit as he spoke. "But we're far from done. We can finish this lesson back in my office."

Olivia stopped crawling and curved her head back to see his serious expression. She fluttered her eyes in disbelief. "Excuse me. Your office?"

"Yes. Believe it or not they give a plumber an office."

"They do?" she asked.

He smiled and chuckled. "Nah, probably not, but they give the head of engineering one."

It took Olivia a few seconds to get the joke. He wasn't a plumber but the boss, and she'd already insulted him. She felt humiliated and stupid. "You're Mr. Bandt?" she asked in utter disbelief.

He chuckled again, not allowing the huge grin to disappear from his face. "Let me guess, did you expect you'd be wearing a dress?" He'd been overly amused at her embarrassment.

She didn't answer, and instead she quickly scurried out of the tiny tunnel, feeling his full attention on her bottom as she wiggled out of the cramped space and back into the garden. When he finally emerged, Olivia had composed herself, hoping that the red face she thought she had was only in her mind. She was unable to believe that he was the head of engineering. He was so young.

When he rose to his feet and finally made eye contact with Olivia, he returned to a more serious expression, no signs of his earlier laughter. "Hey, let me show you the water filtration system I designed."

"You designed it?" she asked, not knowing why she'd even opened her mouth again because stupid kept coming out.

He nodded. "I did. In fact, I designed most all the systems. You could say I created this vault."

Chapter 10

Daniel Bandt had, in fact, designed the vault system. A child genius and graduate of MIT Engineering programs in Aeronautics and Astronautics, Mechanical, Nuclear and a few others that Olivia couldn't remember because she'd been so shocked and impressed at the same time. Not that Daniel Bandt was one to boast about his achievements, he simply answered the question one day when Olivia asked what college he'd attended. His answer had been given as if one was relaying the local forecast.

He hadn't held the first meeting against her as she'd worried would happen. Olivia blamed his casual sense of humor and laid back attitude for an easy dismissal of her stupidity. He hadn't dwelled on it; instead, he just gave her several assignments to read and study before going over the vault's mechanics, or at least what he was cleared to teach her, and she appreciated it. Coming to work everyday had become a welcomed distraction from her current situation.

He asked her to call him Daniel. Even if he had several degrees, including a PhD, he didn't ask for formalities. If anything, Olivia fell into his good humor and called him Doctor if she was feeling daring, which he would take in stride. A few times she'd sworn that she'd seen a glimmer of pride, but he wasn't the type to show any such thing. He could easily be mistaken for a young man of twenty who seemed relaxed and without worry, but that's only if one didn't already know about his brilliant mind.

Olivia had never met a whiz kid until Daniel. She had never pictured one being so funny. She'd held an image of a quiet and reserved person in such a category. Daniel was pretty open with such a stereotype, saying that he'd already tried the whole locked-in-a-room-by-myself thing in his early childhood. If anyone mentioned his humor, he'd say he had a soft spot for standup comedy. Everything else was a mystery. He didn't talk about his life in the days before the vault or about his family. He only mentioned once that he'd agreed to design the vault and that being one of the residents was part of his payment.

Olivia arrived at the familiar doorway. Next to it, in tiny black letters, was a sign that read *Engineering*. There was a little sign like this attached to each non-residential room throughout the vault. Olivia found that it reminded her of when she would go to a doctor's office and the name of each physician would be on the outside of each doorway. The only difference within the vault was that each of these rooms was labeled with a generic meaning of what each department did rather than with a specific number or a person's name. She'd found that when looking for a certain worker's room, she would have to ask directions. Instead of being given a room number, directions were given in the form of several twists and turns, followed by a warning that if she'd gone past some room or another, that she'd gone too far. It didn't really matter though, because within a few days she'd learned most of the room locations. The vault wasn't a large office building; it didn't need numbers to address the location of various rooms.

Olivia entered the Engineering Room. It reminded her of a

cross between a junk drawer and a mad scientist's lab, with plenty of tools and extra pieces of machinery that were ready for creation or repairing. Olivia passed through the prep room and made her way to the back, toward Daniel's office. He was there, staring down at several pieces of paper as he casually scribbled on them. He wasn't wearing his normal grey jumpsuit. He had on a plain white T-shirt. As he looked up, Olivia locked eyes with him.

He smiled. "Hey." His blue eyes always seemed to surprise her.

She waved her finger at him. "What's with the shirt?"

Daniel looked down at his shirt. "Uh, it's a shirt."

Olivia smirked. Even though he was the boss, he wasn't much older than her and she felt comfortable. "I know it's a shirt. Where's your uniform?"

He shrugged. "I find it too conforming. Don't need it while sitting at a desk."

"Huh. Does that mean I don't have to wear mine either?"

He shook his head. "Nice try."

Olivia exhaled deeply. "I don't see why."

Daniel looked down at one of the papers he'd scribbled on, as if distracted.

"Hey," Olivia said as if he'd just turned and walked away from her.

Daniel shook his head. "Hey what?" He didn't take his eyes off his desk.

"What's up, Doc?" Olivia giggled.

That caught his attention. "Ha ha."

"I try."

He shook his head, a small smile forming as his bright blue eyes locked once again with hers. "Are you finished with your assignment?"

"Yes." She had finished it yesterday without a problem.

"Well, finish reading about the computer interface."

"I've done that."

"Then move on to the mechanical part."

"We've already covered that."

"Yeah. Um. Go into the system and review the mechanics of the machines and the computer codes to run them."

Olivia tilted her head. "We aren't going to review?"

"Not today. You can take off and review that on your own."

"Trying to get rid of me?"

He chuckled. "Sort of," he said with guilt. "I have a few problems that I have to work out on my own.

Olivia shrugged her shoulders. "Okay." She stared down at his handwriting, numbers in tight fitting equations, written small and confusingly to the average mind. "I don't mind having a day off," she said with a hint of excitement in her voice.

He squinted at her. "I'll quiz you tomorrow," he added, not letting her off the hook without doing some reading.

"Thanks," she said, wishing she'd not mentioned it.

He smiled. "You're welcome."

She smiled tightly back.

He dropped his head and continued scanning his papers. He nodded to himself and began scribbling more formulas.

"Bye," Olivia said as she waited for a response.

For a moment he continued to work on his problems, still writing away. His actions triggered an intense image in Olivia's mind. She saw Daniel as a mad scientist before her, writing in haste, then stopping to think about it, then scribbling something, then beginning all over again—all the while making several different faces that clearly said he was frustrated, then excited, then intrigued. When Olivia was about to give up being acknowledged, he whirled his hand in the air, still keeping his eyes on the paper, and said, "See you tomorrow."

Olivia laughed inside as she exited Daniel's office, realizing that he'd heard her but needed to finish processing his current thought before being sidetracked. That was Daniel, a very focused person.

Olivia retraced her path, walking past several of the worker rooms before getting to the main entryway. Along the way she debated if she should stop by the Grand Hall for a quick glance, checking to see if one person might be taking his breakfast late. She was in deep thought, considering a lame attempt at spying and wondering what she would do for the rest of the day once her reading was complete. She almost didn't notice the two soldiers waiting outside the red door.

She looked at their faces, noticing that they seemed familiar, one with blond hair, the other brown, but she couldn't place them. She guessed that she'd never been formally introduced. She considered for an instant if she should ask them about what went on behind the red door. She glanced both ways, making sure no one else was in the hallway as she casually slowed her pace. She didn't think it would hurt to ask. Asking a simple question wouldn't be considered socializing, would it? She slowed to a stop as she came directly in front of the red door that stood behind their backs.

They noticed her as she turned to face them, meeting one another's eyes, as if silently speaking. Olivia smiled nervously as she gathered her question in her mind, trying to find words that would sound casual. As both soldiers' eyes came to rest on her, she opened her mouth to speak, but before she could get anything out the red door opened, revealing a young girl standing in the doorway.

The brown-haired soldier quickly turned toward the young girl. She appeared to be hunching slightly, her black head of hair dangling in mid-air. Olivia tried to strain her neck to look inside the doorway and for a brief moment saw that a second door had been left open. Beyond it glowed a white haze of lights, and her eyes focused on several large machines that appeared to be medical scanners, like ones she'd seen on television shows, but before she could make them out the door closed, and two physicians she'd not seen earlier stood before her, one on each side of the hunching girl.

Suddenly, without turning, the blond soldier took a step toward

Olivia and stretched out his hand as he spoke, "Move back." He raised his voice a notch when Olivia didn't do as directed, "Now! Move back now!"

Olivia, surprised at his forceful tone, took a step back while nodding her head. She continued to watch the young girl as she was assisted into the hallway.

"Take her back to her room," one of the physicians directed the brown-haired soldier, who hesitated. "Take her," the physician ordered as he raised the girl's arm for the solider to take. The soldier grabbed her arm as the other two physicians went back inside the mysterious room. The red door closed.

"Let's go," the brown-haired soldier remarked to his fellow soldier. Suddenly, the girl's legs went out beneath her and she began to fall, but the brown-haired soldier quickly grabbed her by the waist, holding her up. Her head fell to the side, exposing a youthful face that reminded Olivia of a porcelain doll with flawless skin. Her features indicated she was of Asian decent. Olivia felt a sort of panic in her gut as she stared at the weak girl before her, debating if she should go to her for help, but the blond soldier still stood in front of her. She decided not to press her luck.

The soldier yelled, "Move back," and it frightened her for a brief second.

She found her voice, though, and asked, "Is she okay?" in a tiny murmur.

Apparently it was loud enough for the blond solider to hear, because he answered. "She's fine, move along. Now," he barked in what Olivia could only believe to be his most annoyed tone.

Olivia nodded slowly, taking a few steps back toward her original path, passing the brown-haired soldier who held the girl. When she was directly in front of the two, she dared to slightly turn her head and caught a look at the girl opening her eyes. Powerful green eyes stared back into Olivia's own, with a glimmer of what she knew without doubt was fear.

"Keep moving," the blond soldier shouted out toward Olivia,

who tried to swallow down the gut-wrenching feeling that suddenly struck her. She continued walking straight to her room.

Olivia couldn't shake the image of the girl's face from her mind. A million thoughts rattled in her head at once as she tried to convince herself that everything was fine, the girl was fine, that maybe she had become ill and the red door was the doctor's room. The doctors had tried to heal her, and she needed assistance back to her room because she was so sick. Maybe she had food poisoning. The food didn't taste bad, but you couldn't always tell that way. Maybe she had caught the flu. Did the flu exist underground? Of course it did, why wouldn't it? Yet, no matter how many reasonable excuses she tried to come up with for the incident she'd been witness to, she kept remembering two things: The red door didn't have any signage stating what type of workroom it was, which meant it was a secret, and then there were those green eyes—unusual green eyes that had harbored fear.

By the time Olivia made it down Division Four's hallway, she'd calmed down, believing that she had seen nothing but a sick girl being escorted back to her room. It had to be the most logical of reasons. She tried to put the encounter out of her thoughts, reminding herself that she had plenty of reading to complete if she was to free up her afternoon. As she turned the corner, she caught a glimpse of Gavin emerging from a doorway. Her doorway. Her stomach flipped and her heart rate quickened so fast that she could feel the thumping in her throat. He'd come to visit her, finally! She wanted to jump up and down, but instead she held it all in, only allowing a huge grin to form. Then, suddenly her smile deflated as she witnessed Dillard emerge from the same doorway. Olivia quickly counted the doors and found that she had in fact been wrong. They had both come out of Dillard's room. Dillard's doorway! Gavin and Dillard?

Quickly, Olivia ducked back around the corner, hoping that neither one of them had seen her, at the same time wishing she'd taken an extra second to notice more, like if Gavin was smiling at

Dillard or if she was smiling at him. Anything that would indicate that their visiting one another in Dillard's room was not what she feared it could be. What was Gavin doing with Dillard? Olivia answered her own question. He was her superior. Dillard was a soldier. Why was she thinking the worst? Then, another fact popped into her mind. Dillard wasn't at breakfast either. They'd been together.

Olivia heard the approaching footsteps. She wanted to flee in the other direction, but they'd see her. She swallowed hard and did the only thing she could think of. She lowered her eyes to the ground and began walking around the corner toward her room.

She could have sworn that when he first saw her, she'd heard a break in his sturdy step. She held her breath and picked up her pace. When she spotted his legs from the corner of her eyes, she could feel a flush of heat on her cheeks.

"Morning Miss Parker," Dillard said in her usual military tone.

Olivia cursed silently, keeping her eyes on the ground as she said, "Morning," and then it was over. They'd passed her by, and she hadn't heard a peep out of Gavin. She glanced back in just enough time to see their backs as they cut around the corner. They both were wearing their standard fatigues, nothing out of the ordinary, just two soldiers walking down a hall.

Chapter 11

Olivia spent the rest of the day in her room attempting to learn the vast amount of computer codes. Her wondering thoughts, however, continued to interrupt her attempts to memorize anything. The strange green-eyed Asian girl made her curious and caused outlandish theories to run wild, while thoughts of Gavin with Dillard made her suddenly ill. How could he? And why should she care? He made it clear that she was nothing more than another duty on his list. She fought through her assignment, finally giving up when she figured she reached a stopping point. The funny thing was that it took her twice as long to finish, due to the thoughts that seemed to take over all on their own. She'd even worked straight through lunch without leaving her room.

Olivia looked at the computer clock and noticed that dinner would be served soon. If she wanted anything to appease her grumbling tummy before attending the movie in the entertainment room, she'd best go. Part of her wanted to stay hidden, but she had told Sophie she'd be at the movie and didn't want to make her wait.

Disappointing her friend wasn't something she was eager to do. Sophie was thirteen years older, yet somehow that didn't seem to matter. Their conversations had been some of the most interesting because Sophie knew way more about life. She'd lived it. Olivia wondered if she could tell Sophie what happened today with the Asian girl and Gavin. Would she dare? Sophie would have an older insight, but then she'd know about Gavin and that would be bad. Olivia decided that if she brought up anything, it would be in a tactful manner.

Olivia had mixed feelings about the vegetable stew that had been prepared for dinner with a side of cornbread. It wasn't very filling and most whispers around her agreed. The lack of meat in most meals had been a surprise to most residents, but Olivia didn't know why the residents were surprised. Did they truly expect to have livestock underground? She'd heard from Sophie that they had frozen meat in a freezer, but it was put back for rare and special occasions. Olivia thought Thanksgiving would be the next holiday where meat would be appropriate, but she didn't bring it up, wondering if tradition would go on inside the vault. Would they still be in here for holidays? She hoped the whole stay in the vault would be brief. Olivia dreamed of spending the holidays with her mother and brother. The thought of staying inside the vault during a special occasion would not give her anything to be thankful for.

Olivia finished the last bite of her stew while staring at the empty chair across from her. Olivia entered the Grand Hall at a busy time, toward the end of the evening. Most of the room had been filled when she'd first arrived, but more than half had cleared out by the time she took her seat. She found herself scanning the room, not because she wanted to but because it had become her habit. At that very moment, she was repulsed by her actions and for her effort, and then she saw him.

Olivia couldn't stop watching him as he stood in the food line only a few feet from her table as he reached for a piece of cornbread. His back was to her. He didn't seem at all embarrassed or guilty for his earlier behavior. He seemed, as usual, in his strict military posture, even while reaching for a second piece of cornbread, despite the sign above his hand clearly stating that only one was allowed. Olivia grunted at his ability to look the other way when taking something he wanted. "Just like him," she mumbled to herself.

He turned on cue as if he'd heard her tiny whisper and needed to defend his actions, and their eyes met. She released a tiny gasp as he took a step toward her. Instantly, her heart fluttered as he took another step in her direction. Was he going to acknowledge her? Here, in front of everyone? She felt like a statue, locked in her own body as he moved toward her, no ability to move, no thoughts, she waited for him to come to her and when she thought she'd stopped breathing, a voice broke in reminding her that she wasn't made of stone.

A sudden red blur blocked her view of Gavin. "Olivia, did you hear me?"

Olivia blinked as she noticed Sophie had taken the chair in front of her. Quickly, she glanced to the left of Sophie's head and noticed that Gavin had turned away from her and was almost at the soldiers' table, his usual spot. Olivia let out a heavy sigh as she watched his back for the second time that day.

"Is something wrong?" Sophie asked as she started to turn her head to follow Olivia's gaze.

Olivia couldn't allow Sophie to see him. "Sophie," Olivia squeaked, causing Sophie to turn back. Olivia rushed her words in an attempt to sidetrack Sophie's curiosity. "Uh, no. All's well," Olivia said quickly.

Sophie didn't appear convinced as she scanned Olivia's face for the truth. "Don't tell me you're not coming tonight?"

Olivia shook her head. "No, I'm coming."

Sophie tilted her head to the side. "You seem pretty zoned out."

Olivia smiled and forced a laugh. "I do that sometimes." She wondered if Sophie had noticed exactly who made her zone out.

Sophie shrugged her shoulders. "Who doesn't? Well, I didn't mean to interrupt your meal."

Olivia glanced down at her empty bowl. "I'm pretty much finished," she said with a shrug.

Sophie peeked down toward the empty bowl. "Very tasty today."

Olivia sighed, content at the moment, but really wishing for more. "Yeah, especially the cornbread."

"I know. It was the best part of the meal."

Olivia glanced quickly toward Gavin, who at that very moment was taking a bite of his own cornbread, nodding in agreement to something the soldier next to him said. "Wish I could have had a second one," Olivia said with a sigh.

"Portions are rough," Sophie stated. "Especially on the heavier-set residents."

Olivia turned her eyes back to Sophie. "I haven't seen any overweight residents."

"Not overweight," Sophie corrected her. "Just those accustomed to larger portions. The residents who are maybe ten to fifteen pounds above their optimal weight."

Olivia gave a look of disapproval. "As if that matters down here."

Sophie nodded. "It shouldn't, but it does, especially when you have to feed a certain number of people with a small portion of food that must be grown underground. Everyone gets their needed amount, but the enjoyment of food is not a luxury here, and it's harder on most people who used to eat more."

Olivia nodded in agreement as she understood that Sophie was responsible for managing the portions and that her complaint wasn't the first. Olivia also knew that Sophie always meant well and that she was doing her best with what she had. "Oh, I know it's all planned out. I'm just saying it would be nice to indulge every now and then."

Sophie smiled, reminding Olivia of how sweet and perfect she appeared with her red hair and flawless skin. "Well, perhaps I can arrange something in the future."

"Now that's something I would look forward to." Both girls smiled at each other. "Can you make sure it contains chocolate?" Both girls laughed, then sighed in unison at the mention of chocolate.

"It has to last," Sophie said simply, reminding Olivia that time was against them for keeping unique items. How long would those things last down here?

Olivia pushed her chair out and reached for her tray. "Oh, well. Guess we'd better hurry and get you changed if we want to make it for the show."

Sophie agreed and both girls exited the Grand Hall, but not before Olivia took another glance toward Gavin, who seemed unfazed by her departure.

Sophie escorted Olivia for the first time to her room in Division Six, where thirty to thirty-four year olds lived. It appeared to be exactly the same as her own division, the hallways, doorways, and rooms were an exact duplicate, if you didn't count Sophie's unique decorating style.

Olivia had sometimes forgotten how others had been well prepared to travel into the vault. Sophie was a planner and so it shouldn't have been a shock to see a standard room upgraded with personal items, yet Olivia was shocked. She'd been so surprised that when Sophie entered her room, she'd stayed in the doorway examining the rich fabrics that had been used to bring some color into the room. Purple scarves covered each of the lamps, one on each side of the bed, casting a purplish tint around the room. A red comforter and matching pillows had been impeccably arranged on the bed. On the desk were framed pictures of people, Sophie's family perhaps, and on the two chairs in the room were orange cushions. The cement walls had been covered with different sized pictures and prints, one had various landscapes around the world and another was filled with famous prints that she'd seen in her art history class.

Olivia was overwhelmed with a warm sense of comfort as she thought how cozy Sophie had made the room.

"Well, come inside," Sophie prompted Olivia.

Olivia smiled, noting how silly she must look with a big grin covering her face. "Sorry," she said as she entered the room and closed the door. "Your room is so neat."

Sophie chuckled. "It's the same as yours." She walked to her closet opening it and began shuffling through her items.

"Oh no. Mine is boring and yours, well, yours is alive."

Sophie stopped shuffling for a moment, pulling out one yellow dress. "What? My junk?"

Olivia took a seat on the bed, allowing her hand to graze over the red silk material in the comforter. "Not junk. You have your own things. Gosh, I can't believe how I missed not having my own things."

Sophie pulled a blue dress out of the closet. "I'm sure you brought some things."

"Not much. My purse and the clothes on my back."

Sophie turned her head to Olivia. "Really? You didn't pack a bag?"

"You did?"

"Well, yeah, my emergency bag for here," Sophie said as if it was something everyone did.

"I didn't."

Holding both dresses in her hand Sophie turned around to face Olivia. "You don't have anything?"

Olivia shook her head. "My purse had some make-up and the clothes I was wearing." Olivia recognized sympathy on Sophie's face and didn't like it a bit. "No big deal," she said trying to sound unaffected by such a demeaning fact.

Sophie held both dresses up. "Well, which do you like?"

Olivia smiled when her eyes landed on the yellow dress. It's brilliant color and delicate material seemed to be fit only for a princesses. "Wow, those are fancy."

"Not too much," Sophie said with confidence. "I'm going to meet Albert and wanted to look, you know, nice. He's seen me a lot in my horrible uniform." She tugged on her white jacket that had two medium-sized grease stains. "And I want to show him I clean up nicely."

Olivia giggled. "Show him? You look great everyday."

Sophie gave her a cynical expression. "Come on, which one?"

Olivia studied the blue dress's material that layered over each other, giving the dress a rather textured appearance, still beautiful, just not Olivia's choice. "The yellow one. It's gorgeous."

"Really?" Sophie said with doubt.

"Really," Olivia said her eyes beaming with envy.

"Fine, the blue one it is," Sophie stated.

"Uh," Olivia moaned.

"I don't really look good in yellow. I don't even know why I packed this one," she said casually as she laid it on the bed. "Blue is really my color." She walked over to a long mirror on the bathroom door that was partially hiding behind an orange cloth that acted as a room divider. "You know what, you should wear it."

Olivia instantly wanted to say yes but knew that would be too much, and before she could stop herself she said, "I couldn't," but truly wished that she could.

"No really. Yellow doesn't look good on me, but it would look great on you. Actually, you can have it," she said as she began to undress.

Olivia turned away, giving Sophie privacy to change. "That's too much, Sophie."

Sophie made two clicking noises with her tongue. "Don't be silly. I'm giving it to you as a gift. You're my friend, are you not? I'd like you to have it. Don't say no again."

Olivia laughed as she reached out for the dress and gathered it in her hands. The material felt as nice at it appeared. "All right," she mumbled.

"What?"

"I said thank you, I love it." Olivia couldn't help imagining herself in such a wonderful dress, and then she remembered where they were going, a small room that projected movies. *Would this not be overly dressy*, she thought?

"Put it on," Sophie said.

"Oh, Sophie, tonight?"

"Yes."

"But you have a rendezvous of sorts, and I'd rather save it for a special occasion."

"Well, if you haven't found out yet, those occasions should be enjoyed daily."

"I agree, but I don't have any shoes." She didn't want to wear the dress tonight. She felt as if she'd look dumb, in fact, dressed up for a movie.

"You can have some of mine."

"That's too much. Besides, I doubt they'll fit."

"What size are you?"

"Seven and a half."

Sophie laughed. "Me too, you sure are lucky."

Olivia shook her head and couldn't help but laugh. "So it seems."

Thirty minutes later, Olivia stared at her image in the mirror. She'd been transformed, thanks to Sophie's taste in wardrobe, talent in make-up application, and ability to master any kind of hair. Olivia stared at the yellow dress that flowed just past her knees. The material reminded her of what a ballet dancer might wear to enhance her turns. At that thought, Olivia turned in a full circle, watching the dress in the mirror as it floated up in the air. She giggled as she noticed her hair, swooped halfway up, allowing tiny ringlets to flow down. She smiled, thinking this is what she might have looked like if she'd gone to prom. She pushed the thought away.

"Looking good," Sophie said as she slipped on her own shoes.

"Thanks to you," Olivia said with another turn in the mirror. She'd never felt so pretty before. Dressing up for family events had been one thing, but this was more adult, more womanly. Her smile widened as she observed the nice shade of red lipstick on her lips that Sophie had chosen, called Divine, and so she thought she appeared as such as she gazed upon her reflection. "I wish we were in the same division."

"That would be nice," Sophie responded from the other side of the room, looking more beautiful than Olivia thought was possible. Her hair was down for the first time, spilling past her shoulders and giving her an unreal presence, as if she had stepped off the cover of a fashion magazine. The blue dress she'd picked out only amplified her blue eyes, bold red hair, and cameo skin. Olivia couldn't believe she was her friend.

Olivia giggled. "You could teach me how you fixed my hair."

Sophie smoothed out the bottom of her dress. "I can show you anytime. It's not hard."

"It looks hard." Olivia looked up to see Sophie in the mirror, standing behind her with a sisterly smile. Olivia couldn't wish for a better sister. "Why do you think they have divisions based on age range?"

Sophie adjusted Olivia's hair, pinning down a loose curl. "Well, it sort of reminds me of when I was in college and the freshmen were bunked with other freshmen."

Olivia stared at Sophie in the mirror. "So people can meet each other."

"In a way, I think, a support method in theory. Thirty year olds know thirty year olds and teenagers understand other teenagers; they have comparable experiences and equal understanding of, well, that time in one's life."

Olivia shrugged. "It isn't the same, though."

"What do you mean?"

"Well, we're all in the same experience now."

Sophie frowned as a loose hair popped out again. "Maybe so, but difference in age is basically being on a different wavelength." She pinned the loose hair with a smile.

Olivia frowned. "You're not bunked in the kids' division."

"You're in the age range of the division."

"Well, yeah, but I'm not a kid."

"No one said you were. I'm not thirty-four or near it, but that age range is in this division too."

"Yeah, but."

Sophie cut Olivia off with an unconvinced glance. "So what? Where else would you like to be, surrounded with boring adults who look at you as a kid or with others who share your views because they too are on the same wavelength?"

Olivia sighed. "I'm just tired of being called a kid."

Sophie laughed. "You're far from a kid. However, you shouldn't want to grow up too fast. By the time you do, you'll wish you'd taken my advice and enjoyed what youth has to offer."

Olivia grunted. "What does it have to offer now?"

Sophie cast her eyes down as if that comment had burned. "Huh. Perhaps you have a point, things will never be the same, but you have your youth, as my mother would always say. Youth is something you can't buy and you should enjoy it."

Olivia shrugged her shoulders. "Youth is limiting."

Sophie laughed. "I suppose it is in certain instances."

Suddenly, a loud knock rendered both girls silent.

Sophie gave Olivia an equally surprised expression in the mirror before gliding over to answer the door. In the doorway stood Albert Rossi, the manager of the Exchange and Sophie's date for the evening. Before Sophie could greet him, he stepped in and closed the door behind him in one quick movement. "Albert," Sophie said, shocked at his sudden appearance.

"Sophie," Albert said with urgency. "Oh, Sophie," he sighed, noticing her appearance, and before Sophie could respond, he said, "You have to listen fast, before… if you don't I won't be able to tell you again, and I don't know if I'll ever get to," he said, running his words together in a fast, breathless manner.

"What is it?" Sophie asked, grabbing his shoulders as if that would calm him.

His face twisted in agony as he turned from her, noticing Olivia peeking out behind the orange divider.

Olivia gave him a nervous smile.

"Oh, I, I didn't know you had company," Albert said in apology.

"We were just getting ready to meet you," Sophie said as she scanned his face. "What's wrong?"

"Oh, nothing, nothing's wrong," he said, keeping his eyes on Olivia.

"Well, something is, you were just saying that you had to tell me something?" Sophie asked, confused.

"I, I can't," he said as he gestured to Olivia with a sideway tilt of his head.

"Because of Olivia?" Sophie said, not backing down.

"Yes," he said simply. "I shouldn't be here anyway," he said.

"I don't understand, Albert," Sophie said.

Albert sighed as he stared at Sophie's sad expression. "I guess it can't do anymore harm. He glanced once more at Olivia before he explained. "I don't have time, so here it is." He turned to Sophie. "I've been instructed to stop seeing you. I was told to not give you any other reason than that I wasn't interested."

Sophie frowned. "Instructed? But why?"

"I don't know, I mean I was given a silly reason, but…" He drifted off and began to pace with his hands in tight fists. He stopped and turned to Sophie, grabbing her arm with one hand and pulling her close to him. "Oh, I don't want to stop seeing you. How can they do this? How can they tell us what to do in such a personal matter?" He touched her face gently with his other hand.

Sophie shook her head as if she hadn't understood anything he'd just said.

"I can't stop thinking of you and I won't," he said tenderly.

Sophie stared at him.

In one movement, he pulled her against him and kissed her deeply. When he pulled back he said, "I'll never stop thinking of you, I promise."

"They? Why?" Sophie said between sobs.

"You know who, they've ordered it, and they're in charge," he said.

Just then, another knock on the door interrupted them.

"Open up!" a male voice shouted from the other side of the door.

No one moved, not even Olivia, who'd been silently watching the entire scene from the other side of the room. She watched as the door busted open and two soldiers emerged. Albert turned around, shoving Sophie protectively behind his back. Both soldiers grabbed Albert, one on each side of him. Sophie screamed, and Olivia covered her mouth with her hand, staying hidden behind the orange divider.

Albert resisted their grasp, stating with authority, "I did nothing wrong. I was breaking my date with her. She can tell you. I did nothing wrong."

"Quiet," one of the soldiers shouted as he shoved Albert to his knees.

"Don't hurt him," Sophie shrieked.

"I did nothing wrong," Albert yelled.

"Let him go," Sophie pleaded as the soldiers began to fight Albert's resistance, holding him down toward the floor with force.

"Halt," another voice shouted in a military tone. Captain Gavin Grant walked through the door. "No need to bruise him," he said in a casual manner.

Olivia's mouth dropped open at the sight of Gavin and his obvious approval of the situation.

"I didn't do anything," Albert said.

"You didn't. Then why are you here and not in your own room?"

Gavin asked, staring down at Albert.

"I was breaking my date with Sophie. I didn't want to leave her waiting," Albert said.

"Is this true?" Gavin looked to Sophie, who quickly nodded. Gavin stared at her for a long moment before addressing Albert, "How can I be sure that you didn't go against protocol?"

"I don't understand what he's done. What he just told you is the truth. Why is he being interrogated?" Sophie covered her mouth as she asked the question, as if realizing that she shouldn't have questioned them.

Gavin looked at her. "He has broken protocol and is a danger. Information that he might have shared could put you in danger as well."

"Why is that?" Sophie asked.

"What did he tell you?" Gavin asked.

"He told me nothing. I have no idea what danger he poses. I hardly know him and you tell me I know too much. I know nothing. It's true. He came by to break our date," Sophie said.

"It sounds like a lie," another soldier stated.

"It's the truth," Olivia announced as she stepped out of her hidden spot and right into everyone's view.

Gavin's obvious surprise momentarily covered his face. He stared at her for a lengthy time before gaining control again. "How long have you been here?" Gavin asked in his military tone.

"For the past half hour," Olivia said staring straight back into his dark blue eyes.

"Is what she said true?" he asked simply.

"It is. Exactly as she said it," Olivia said softly.

"Why are you here?" he asked.

"We were getting ready for the movie tonight. Sophie for her date with," Olivia gestured to Albert.

"You do not have clearance to be in Division Six."

Olivia couldn't believe she needed clearance to be there. "To visit?"

"You must have clearance. No resident is allowed in other residents' rooms without clearance."

Sophie and Olivia looked at each other confused.

"Neither of us were aware of such a rule," Sophie said to Gavin.

"You are now. This man is not allowed to associate with you from this point on," Gavin said to Sophie.

Sophie gasped. "But..."

Gavin cut her off. "...I can't say anymore. It's important that you follow the vault regulations. Do you understand me?" Gavin asked.

Sophie closed her mouth and nodded.

"Take him away," Gavin ordered.

His soldiers yanked Albert up to his feet and led him out of the room.

"And you," Gavin looked at Olivia. "Come. You're to be taken back to your division."

"No."

Gavin clenched his teeth.

"Olivia," Sophie said with fear. "Go, go on back. I'm, I'm not feeling so good. We can see a movie another night."

Olivia stared at Sophie's face and knew she couldn't cause her more grief. She quickly walked over to Sophie and gave her a hug. Sophie gratefully hugged her back. "Okay," Olivia said softly, "I'll see you tomorrow."

Sophie let her arms drop from Olivia and took a step back. "Tomorrow."

Olivia forced a smile and turned to face Gavin.

Chapter 12

Wanting to speak the words that you feel and actually finding the courage do so seemed to be the internal war Olivia faced as she walked next to Captain Gavin Grant, the stranger she'd witnessed interrogating her friend Sophie. He'd not shown one shred of being *her* Gavin, not during his strict delivery of military protocol or even as he walked beside her down Division Six's corridor.

Olivia had been utterly surprised by Gavin's sudden appearance, and she'd not been able to stand by quietly as her friend was grilled about Albert's actions, which Sophie had no control over. Olivia still wasn't sure what had caused the entire drama to unfold. Albert's comments about being kept away from Sophie because the military said so was strange. It didn't make sense, yet the way the soldiers had burst into the room and wrestled Albert to the floor had seemed serious enough. It all happened so fast. Olivia didn't know what to believe. Had Albert done something wrong, or had Olivia never met Captain Gavin Grant until today? He hadn't seemed like the same charming guy from LAX so long ago. She almost thought that maybe that person didn't exist, and the one she'd witnessed standing outside of Dillard's room and in Sophie's was the *real* Gavin.

Since Olivia was wearing a new pair of high heels from Sophie that she wasn't yet accustomed to, she accidentally brushed against Gavin's arm as they walked. When she tried to yank away from him, she slipped. Gavin's natural reaction was to grab her arm, but not in a gentle manner, causing Olivia to yelp out in pain.

"Let go!" she yelled, not holding back her anger.

He dropped her hand as instructed. "If you can't walk in them, you shouldn't wear them," he stated as he glanced down at the black heels she wore.

"I can walk in them fine." She rubbed her arm where he'd left a red mark. "If you hadn't run into me, I wouldn't have tripped."

He grunted, turning his head from her. "I didn't run into you. You tripped over your own feet, wearing shoes that are too much for you."

"What's that supposed to mean?" Olivia continued to rub her arm while staring up at his unreadable profile.

He turned to face her, his blue eyes scanning her for a lengthy moment before he turned away and began to walk again. "It means you're going to hurt yourself wearing those things."

Olivia took several fast steps to catch up to him. "The only reason I got hurt was because you grabbed my arm like a brute and nearly tore it off," she said.

He peeked down at her with a sideways glance and saw her face vibrating with rage. He exhaled heavily. "I only meant to stop you from falling," he said softly, a hint of an apology attached.

Olivia didn't take it. "Well, now I'm going to have a big bruise on my arm," she complained sourly.

"Better than falling on your face," he stated with amusement as he turned a corner.

Olivia huffed at his response while keeping up with his pace.

"If you dressed appropriately, you'd be able to walk without needing assistance," he said smugly.

Olivia swallowed down the urge to growl. "Appropriately?" she asked as her brows crinkled in defense. She wanted to scream at him for his insult. Did he not see what she saw in the mirror? What did he see? "I, I don't understand?"

He stopped and turned abruptly toward her, grabbing her by the bruised arm and causing her to stop mid-pace. She fought the urge to cry as he held the delicate spot. He glanced over her again, suddenly revealing a slight annoyance in his stare. Olivia could swear she thought she saw anger in those blue eyes of his. "You should not dress like this." He swallowed deeply as he connected his eyes with hers. She could feel the heat of his breath quicken against her face as he leaned in. She held still, staring back at the face, the eyes she'd fantasized about so many times. He opened his mouth and she held her breath, but he didn't do what she expected, what she really wanted him to do. Instead, he said, "It will get you into trouble."

Olivia blinked in confusion.

"Wear your issued clothing, Olivia." He turned his face as if looking at her was too painful and immediately dropped her arm. "That's an order."

He returned to his pace and Olivia followed in angry silence. She couldn't believe he'd insulted her new dress and had given her yet another order never to wear it again. *Why?* He could ignore her, he could come and go as he pleased, he could bust down doors and give orders and expect them to be obeyed, but she couldn't? She was forbidden to wear a dress! Why?

As he turned out of Division Six, she dared to grab him by his arm, which didn't cause him to stop as he'd so effortlessly done to her. Instead, he stared down at her hand on his arm while still keeping pace, which only fueled Olivia's anger. "Can you stop?" she shouted in annoyance.

He stopped and she breathed out her frustration. "What is it?"

he said staring down at her.

"Why? Why can't I wear a dress, but you can eat two pieces of cornbread when the sign clearly states one per resident. Why is that? Huh?"

He looked silently at her with a slight curve in his lip. "Cornbread?"

"Yes, I saw you take two."

Amusement covered his face in the form of a tight smile that held back a laugh, which only made Olivia angrier.

"And why is it that you can talk to whomever you please in whomever's room you want, but I can't? Why is that?"

The smile quickly disappeared from his face.

"Why is it you ignore me one minute, then give me orders the next?"

He stared.

"Why are you so mean to me that you think it's better to insult me than to simply ask how I've been?"

He stared at her for several minutes before she asked again, "Why?"

He straightened his shoulders as he glanced in both directions, making sure no one was around. They stood very alone and hidden. He stepped closer, causing her to step back into the wall. He took another step, closing the distance between them to a mere inch. He stared down at her with a serious expression.

He whispered for her ears only as he listed off the facts: "Military are allowed a larger portion. Being second in command restricts me from no room and giving orders is what I've been hired to do. As far as ignoring you, that is not the case. I've checked up on you, and you are doing well. My intentions have never been to harm you or insult you. You actually are quite breathtaking in that dress and that is the problem, you need not draw attention to yourself. You are my responsibility and the answer to 'why' will always be *because I have to.*"

She witnessed honesty in his face as he delivered each point and she swallowed as he allowed his face to linger closely to hers. She licked her lips as she felt a sudden quickening in her heart at his close proximity. She wanted to say something, but she didn't dare. He moved first. His hand slowly guided up to her face where it moved softly over her cheek. She felt a rush of heat at the spots he touched, then his fingers grabbed a loose curl, gently pushing it away from her face. His hand wrapped around the back of her neck and she thought at that moment she'd do anything he wanted. His lips parted at the same time his hand guided her toward him and she closed her eyes. She felt his breath on her lips and thought she'd melt, and right when she anticipated the touch of his lips, a loud siren went off.

Her eyes flew open to his reflecting the same alarm, an inch away from hers. He immediately pulled away, letting go of her completely. The terrible noise rattled through the vault, alerting everyone that something was wrong. She grabbed Gavin's hand and he squeezed it back. "It's the system's alarm." She nodded as if she understood, but she didn't. He let go and shouted, "Come on." He opened the access door to the main hallway and motioned for Olivia to follow. When she did, she began to see people flowing out into the main hallway, most of them covering their ears. She noticed Gavin shouting into a small communication device that he held up to his ear. He continued to shout something when suddenly the noise ceased and Gavin's words boomed in the air, "Shut it off!"

Gavin noticed that everyone was looking at him. "Everything's fine. Go back to your rooms and an announcement will be made by your guidance counselor." Everyone stared at him, none hiding their fear.

Gavin didn't wait for the residents to question him. He rushed through the hallway toward the stairwell that would take him to Division One, the military division. Olivia followed. When Gavin entered the stairwell, he stopped and turned to her. "Olivia you need to go back to your room."

"But what happened?"

"Olivia, go back."

"But what if? What if?" she stammered.

Gavin's features softened as he understood. "It's probably nothing. It's okay. I'll come soon."

Olivia nodded. "Okay." She watched as he ascended the stairwell. She walked toward the main hallway, wondering what had just happened between them, but at the same time sensing a new closeness with him. He said everything was okay. Somehow the words seemed true because he spoke them and he would come, soon. As she tried to calm herself from the recent siren, she collided with Daniel.

Her hands tightened on his shoulders as she balanced herself. "I'm sorry," she apologized, not noticing Daniel's shocked face.

"Olivia," Daniel said in surprise, his eyebrow arched in disbelief. He stared her up and down as if he were seeing her for the first time.

"Daniel, I'm sorry," she said, removing her hands from his shoulders. "That alarm has me all messed up. I didn't see you coming and…"

"You look different," he said in utter disbelief.

"What?"

His expression changed to an unfamiliar one. "Your hair and the dress," he said, as if he were figuring out a formula.

She shrugged. "Yeah, I told you a dress wouldn't be a bad uniform." She smiled as if she'd just relayed an old joke.

"No, it wouldn't," he said boldly, staring at her.

"Did you hear the alarm?" she asked, confused by his behavior.

"You're beautiful."

Olivia shrugged again at his remark. "Yeah right. That was pretty loud wasn't it?"

He smiled. "Where were you going?"

"To my room."

"Dressed like that?"

She could feel her face getting red. "Oh, no, I was going to the movie with Sophie, but the alarm..."

"To the movie room dressed like that?"

Olivia felt sort of embarrassed that maybe she'd been right. She'd overdressed. "Yeah, I told Sophie this was too much."

"Too much? No, not at all. Just wasted in a dark room." He smiled.

Olivia chuckled. "Right."

"I've got an idea."

"What?"

"Come with me."

"What? I'm going back to my room."

"Why?"

"The alarm, Daniel. Didn't you hear it? A loud alarm went off and we must all go to our rooms."

"Of course, I heard it. I caused it."

Gavin supervised private Davis as he completed a system check through the vault's main computer. The alarm had been nothing more than a malfunction that Daniel Bandt, the head engineer, had caused while making alterations to the power grid. All residents, including the soldiers, seemed to be rattled by the possibility of some new devastation occurring. The report of an all clear was immediately sent out to all guidance counselors to relay to their own divisions. They were advised to tell everyone to go about their normal evening and that a simple test had been conducted. Normalcy was quickly established.

Gavin had turned a chaotic vault back into its usual evening routine in less than five minutes once he'd arrived in the control center. He fell back on his second-nature ability to remain calm while handling high-stress situations. Every soldier seemed to gleam with admiration at the way he'd handled himself as he entered the room and extinguished the problem.

The major reacted differently, though, becoming irate and overly irritated that he'd not been warned about the probable alarm going off. He shouted that Daniel Bandt needed to get permission if he were going to make serious alterations to the system, even if he was the head engineer. Gavin didn't attempt to rationalize the absurdity of the major's recommendation; instead, he listened and agreed that morale wouldn't be affected from a mere test and that residents would receive reinforced training that would direct them in future instances to their assigned guidance counselor.

After Gavin was satisfied with Davis's report, he finally stepped out of the control center. He had only one more thing to do before checking in on Olivia, he thought. He couldn't believe that he'd almost kissed her a second time, blaming her ridiculous attire for that impulse. He'd had the hardest time keeping a straight face when he'd seen her step out from behind that curtain in that dress. It had taken every ounce of his strength to not drag her out of there. She shouldn't have been in anyone's room, even if it was another female's. Even if she was considered a friend, she was connected with a scumbag like Rossi.

Rossi had been caught embezzling goods from the vault and using them to barter on his own accord. Though it had been witnessed only once, Rossi exchanging a computer for certain foods for his personal use. He had to be disciplined, and that included cutting all his social interactions until it was deemed appropriate again. Besides, the major had already issued an order to not allow dating between residents if it wasn't approved by the Fertility Department.

Gavin had watched Olivia's relationship build with Sophie and had allowed it. Sophie appeared innocent of breaking any rules, and besides, she'd only been on two dates with Rossi and nothing had come of it. That fact was keeping her out of a jail cell. Rossi, however, would spend the next three months incarcerated for his actions and would go on record as the first resident to be held in the vault's prison. Gavin assumed more would follow his lead.

Gavin would have to tell Olivia about Rossi. He couldn't have her thinking he was a brute, the word she called him after witnessing his arrest of Rossi. He wanted to make sure she stayed away from anyone who could get her into trouble. If his past month of monitoring vault interactions had showed him anything, it wouldn't be long before something big happened. He only had to be ahead of it, and so far he'd stopped one major problem before it gave too many people any ideas.

Though he'd tried to keep his mind on monitoring the vault, he'd catch himself watching Olivia, and that disturbed him even more. And then there was the issue of tonight and the kiss he'd almost given her. Had he gone mad? He wouldn't mention it. No. It didn't happen. Nothing happened. He'd only answered her question, and then the alarm had gone off, and then he'd promised to check in on her. Why had he done that? He knew the answer though. He needed to make sure she was okay, but then he'd make sure she understood, they had to go back to their earlier arrangement. He'd do his job and she'd do hers, no socializing, no attempts to speak to one another, never allowing what almost happened to happen.

He would make it clear that tonight was really the last time, and he couldn't visit again. *Just one more time*, he told himself, he'd have to wait until it was late in the night so that no one saw him. He wouldn't put her in danger. He decided to give it an hour, giving him plenty of time to check in on each division, but first and foremost, he needed to have a chat with Daniel Bandt.

Chapter 13

Olivia broke out into a fit of giggles, covering her mouth with one hand and her belly with the other. Just as she began to see a blur of tears, she forced herself to take a deep breath and exhaled one last giggle before she dabbed the corners of her eyes.

Daniel, seated across from Olivia at a small round table, watched Olivia's reaction with amusement playing across his face in the form of a huge grin.

"Oh, Daniel," she said between gasps of air, "I can't remember the last time I laughed so hard." She shook her head as if scolding him.

Daniel chuckled as he leaned back in his chair and began to swirl his Pinot Grigio around his wine glass with two swift, circular motions.

"Can you stop grinning at me like that?" Olivia said with laughter still in her voice.

"Like what?" he asked in defense as he smiled from ear to ear.

Olivia rolled her eyes. "You always do that, you know."

Daniel gave her a skeptical look. "Always do what?" He continued grinning.

"Have this enormous grin, that grin," she said pointing at his face, "every time."

Daniel tilted his head to the side and raised one eyebrow. "Every time, what?"

"Every. Single. Time," she said simply as she picked up her own glass of wine and took a sip.

Daniel struggled to change his grin to a serious expression but failed miserably with a chuckle that caused Olivia to join in. "Every time what?" Daniel asked again.

Olivia stared at him for a brief second, noticing his blue eyes gleaming back at her as she awaited his answer. She couldn't help but smile as she said, "Every time you think you've told a *momentous* joke." She made sure to announce the word momentous in a louder tone.

Daniel jerked his head back as if what she'd said was shocking. He looked back down at his glass of wine as if he was considering her statement before finally looking back up with an inquisitive expression. "Do I?" he asked.

Olivia answered with a tilt of her head and a short nod.

He raised one eyebrow. "Momentous is it?"

Olivia shook her head. "I didn't say that."

Daniel smiled at her remark. "Then tell me if it is true, that I just grinned as you say I do, after telling you about the mechanics who I won't mention again, but that you in fact laughed, and may I quote you as saying, 'I can't remember laughing so hard,' which would in fact be proof that I did tell a momentous joke with successful delivery." Daniel stared back at her as if he'd just won a courtroom-drama argument.

Olivia held her lips tightly together and shrugged her shoulders.

Daniel gave her a hurt expression as he grabbed his chest with one hand.

Olivia laughed. "Yes," she said slowly, "I agree, a great delivery and very original."

Daniel winked at Olivia, giving her his famous grin. "I'm glad you enjoyed it."

"I did, thoroughly," she said in her most serious critics voice.

"Thoroughly, huh?" Daniel said while rubbing his chin.

Olivia shook her head in agreement smiling at him. She couldn't believe she'd just said that, told him that he grinned every time he'd made her laugh, but somehow she didn't care. She took another sip of her wine. Pinot Grigio is what Daniel had called it, and he'd been right, it did have an apple-like flavor to it.

She'd been surprised several times by him this evening. First he'd caught her completely off guard in the main hallway when he'd said he'd been the cause of the screeching alarm. He'd quickly explained that a few alterations in the power grid had triggered the vault's alert system, which had been quickly silenced by him. Relief had flooded through her, and she was aware that Daniel had witnessed it and immediately apologized to her for making her or anyone else think something horrible had occurred. She'd been so shocked by his description of diverting one power channel to another one because of an unnecessary power usage that she'd forgotten his earlier compliments of how beautiful she looked until he'd mentioned it again when they entered his office.

Standing there together in the hallway, he asked her to come with him. She tried to tell him she needed to go back to her room, leaving out the part that she expected Gavin to visit her, but Daniel seemed not to hear her. He began to explain the power grid and its different branches, and as he did Olivia found that he was suddenly walking her down the main hallway, past the red door, and right into his office. When she'd said it was probably best she returned to her room, he explained that everything was fine and that he'd just sent a message to Division One letting them know. Again he complimented her, convincing her that she shouldn't waste her evening in her room alone, that if she dressed up for a fun evening he hated that he might be the cause of it being ruined.

He asked her to let him make it special for her. That's when he presented a bottle of wine and two glasses.

"Since I ruined your night, I feel inclined to share this," he said as he showed her the bottle.

Olivia was speechless at the thought of taking a drink of alcohol. She'd never had a drink of wine. She remembered her father allowing her a sip of his beer when she was smaller, but she'd never had a whole drink to herself! She'd thought *no* at first, but when he automatically opened it without an answer from her and asked, "May I?" before pouring it in her very own wine glass, at that moment she felt like an actual adult, and so she'd said, "Yes, you may."

Then, when their glasses were both full, he complimented her again by saying, "To having a beautiful lady share this bottle with me," and proceeded to clank his glass against hers just as she'd seen done in the movies. His compliment made her blush, and she followed his lead; as he took a sip, she did too.

One and a half glasses later, she'd turned into a bumbling and laughing mess. She actually felt happy and relaxed. Then to top it off, Daniel's fun and creative jokes about vault life had actually made her forget about everything else except for the two of them having a conversation, and that was all she wanted to do at that moment, to talk more with Daniel, to try to make him laugh as he'd made her. Presently, she was having a ball.

"Did you know that the dish collector, Clare, used to own a small house of peacocks?" Olivia announced.

"Hmm… that explains her hair," Daniel said.

"Yes, you're right," Olivia said, realizing that her hair, in fact, seemed to be a mock-up of a peacock tail, with the feathers and all. "And she had two of those house monkeys, the ones people get instead of babies."

"I completely see that."

"I wonder why she didn't bring them."

"Well, pet tickets weren't available," Daniel said casually. He picked up the bottle of wine and filled his glass.

"No animals at all?" Olivia reached for her glass, taking the last sip.

"No animals."

"It would have been nice to have a few dogs. I always liked dogs over cats." She sat her glass down on the table.

"I never thought of pets in my design," Daniel said.

Olivia watched as Daniel finished his glass of wine. "Why not?"

Daniel shrugged his shoulders. "I was hired to make a vault for human survival, no one ever mentioned animals." He reached for the wine bottle. "Wish they had."

Olivia watched as he poured another glass of wine for himself and did not offer her any. She leaned in and reached for the bottle. When she placed her hand around the neck, his hand came down on hers. "What do you think you're doing?" he teased.

"Refilling," she said innocently.

He smiled, not pulling his hand away from hers. "Your limit is two and you've finished your second."

"I have a limit?" she asked, narrowing her eyes on him.

He stared back with a gentle expression. "That you do."

Olivia ignored him and began to lift the bottle.

He gently grabbed the bottle with his free hand and pulled it away, while grasping ahold of her hand. "You must be twenty to pour," he teased.

She didn't pull her hand away from his. Instead, she stared at his face for a minute, noticing his blue eyes, the color of the ocean, which were intensely staring at her. She immediately compared them to Gavin's darker blue eyes, realizing both guys had the same color but different shades. She didn't know which ones she liked better and then decided she couldn't possibly like one over the other when both blues were amazing. When his fingers moved under hers, she looked back down at his hand. Heat seemed to form between their touch. Shocked by her body's reaction, she slowly pulled her hand free. When she glanced back up to his eyes, he was still watching her hand. "Why does that matter?" she asked, trying to ignore the strange moment.

He rose from his chair and looked around the room as if he was distracted. "Because you're seventeen, far from twenty."

She scrunched her brows. "That shouldn't be held against me, besides its twenty-one, isn't it?"

He chuckled with a nervous hint as he walked to a shelf on the other side of his office. "I didn't hold it against you. I did give you the wine," he defended, "and it used to be twenty-one, now it's twenty."

Olivia bit her lip while watching him shuffling through the shelf. "Yeah, because you're twenty, huh? Well I'm almost eighteen, and you've cut me off at two."

"Yeah, but I did it for you," he said, picking up a small box and turning around. "I'm guessing this is your first wine." He waited for her to nod, and when she did he went on, "And since it is, two glasses is more than enough."

"Why's that?"

He smiled. "Well, we wouldn't want you having a hangover during your exam."

She frowned at him. "You're not still going to give me an exam."

He plopped back down in his seat with a box in one hand and the wine bottle in the other. "Of course I am."

"Great. Then let me take it now, and then you can give me another glass."

He shook his head. "No, no bargaining."

"So, if I want a third drink I have to be twenty?"

"In my bar you do."

"That doesn't seem fair."

"It doesn't?"

"No, not at all. Considering that the vault makes you work like an adult, be held responsible like an adult, and tells you what you should do when you're not even sure you're ready to do what they want you to do."

Daniel looked at her confused. "What?"

"You know, they make you do things you don't want to do—with your body."

Daniel's eyes softened as if he understood exactly what she meant, but he didn't say so. "I don't think you need to worry, Olivia." He proceeded to pour a small amount of wine in her glass, only enough for one more sip. She watched him in amazement.

"Thought I was cut off?"

He smiled. "You are, but I figured you'd like to taste it with one of these." He placed the box between them and opened the lid, revealing rows of fancy chocolates. Olivia gasped as her eyes scanned the mouth-watering bites.

"Go ahead. Try one," Daniel said.

"Oh, wow," Olivia said, allowing her hand to float over the box. "I can't decide."

"Here, try this one," he said as he picked a tiny square of chocolate out of the box and held it out for her. "It's my favorite. Carmel and nuts, like a Snickers."

Olivia smiled as she took it from him. "Thanks."

"Taste it with the wine," he suggested.

She placed it in her mouth and bit down, and suddenly she thought she'd died and gone to heaven. She moaned contently.

"Good, right?" Daniel smiled as she opened her eyes and nodded with another moan of delight.

She picked up her glass and took a drink of the wine. "Oh! Interesting. Better without chocolate."

"Yeah, next time you'll have to try it with champagne."

"Champagne?" Olivia asked with disbelief. "Yeah right. When will I ever be able to…"

He smiled and raised both hands in a tiny swirling gesture at himself.

"You have a bottle of champagne?"

"That I do."

"Really?"

"Yep."

"I always wanted to try champagne. I've never had any. I've never had any wine before tonight." She stopped herself with a smile, knowing that she'd begun to ramble. "When? When can we try it?" she asked excited.

"Another time."

She pouted.

He pushed the chocolate box toward her. She shook her head. "Oh, I couldn't. You should save them."

"You sure?"

She licked the last bit of chocolate off her fingers as she gazed at one particular white chocolate square. She sighed. "No, not really. I'd love to eat the whole box, but I, well, who knows how long we'll be down here. You might want to make it last."

"Very reasonable of you. Well, when you change your mind, let me know. Of course, I'm not advertising this offer to anyone else. It only stands for you."

"Oh, don't worry. I know that these chocolates could get a man killed."

"More than you know," he said with a smile.

Olivia didn't know if it was the wine or the chocolate that had just finished melting in her mouth, but she felt 100 percent happy, and Daniel had everything to do with it. She couldn't help but stare at him as he got up from the table and replaced the box of chocolates on the shelf, pouring the last of the wine into his glass. She remembered watching him before as he'd worked at his desk, figuring out equations or mechanical problems on paper with a slight crease between his eyes. She thought of the way he'd demonstrated taking apart equipment with ease, as if he were a musician playing his faithful instrument, always sure of his motions, and this is why she picked up on his slight fumble of the box or his almost spill of the wine as he refilled his glass. For some reason, he appeared nervous, and that baffled Olivia.

Olivia yawned. "Do you want me to stay?" she asked.

As she finished the question, he lost hold of the bottle and dropped it on the table. As it began to roll off the edge, Olivia went to grab it, but as he moved to catch it as well, he bumped his glass of wine, causing it to pour out across the table, flowing directly toward Olivia. She decided in that instant to jump up out of her chair in hopes of dodging the liquid, not paying attention to Daniel and bumping right into his face with her head.

Olivia grabbed the top of her head with a grunt. She glanced up to see Daniel holding a busted lip. "Oh no, I'm sorry," Olivia mumbled as she looked at the damage she'd caused.

"It's okay," he said as he took his hand away from his lip. He glanced down at his fingers to see a small amount of blood.

"Are you sure?" she asked in horror. "I'm so sorry," Olivia apologized, stepping toward him so that she could examine the damage better.

"I'm fine," he said, trying to force a smile, but he winced when the action caused a drop of blood to expel from the new cut on his lip.

"Oh, no," Olivia groaned with guilt. "Here," she said, reaching for a small cloth that was on the table.

He took it and pressed it on his lip. "See. That's why you have a limit," he teased.

Olivia couldn't help but laugh. Daniel laughed too but stopped short with a tiny groan. They exchanged glances. "Sit down, let me," she instructed, pulling him down to the chair so that she could kneel down and get a better look at him. He allowed her to do as she wished. Kneeling in front of him, she moved his hand away from his lip and began to examine the damage. "Well, you'll need ice," she said, staring at the tiny cut that was already starting to bruise over. Her hand naturally touched his face, turning it so that she could see it in a better light, then she poked on the spot beside the cut.

"Ow!" he said as she touched his skin. "Is that necessary?"

"Sorry." She glanced up at him. "I can't believe I did this. I feel

129

terrible."

He winked at her. "I'll be fine. It's nothing, but I might retract my offer to drink with you again," he joked.

She smiled, and before she could think what she was doing, she leaned in and gave him a peck on his cheek. When she pulled back, he brought his hands up to her arms to stop her from going away. Olivia looked directly into his ocean-blue eyes, finding his intense stare had returned. She felt suddenly drawn to him and overwhelmed. She'd noted during their first meeting his sexy features but had accepted that he was her boss and didn't think of him as being handsome. Instead of being nervous around him, she'd built up the idea of him being a genius who was more of a teacher to her than anything else, but *educator* wasn't popping into her mind as she looked at him tonight. She felt her face turning red as his hands tightened on her shoulders and was certain of what was about to happen.

Then she heard him. "Hope I'm not interrupting," Gavin said with disdain from behind them.

Olivia glanced up to see Gavin standing in the doorway. His expression was one she'd never really seen before, maybe anger or hurt... no, she couldn't distinguish between the two.

Chapter 14

O livia did not speak, did not move, other than the slight jerk of her eyes that remained locked on Gavin's face. At first sight her heart leapt uncontrollably, but then a slight tightening of his jaw alerted Olivia that he wasn't pleased. Before she could utter one excuse for not being in her room, Daniel dropped his hands from Olivia and turned to see who'd busted into his office without even a knock.

"And why don't I believe you?" Daniel announced as he set eyes on Gavin.

Gavin seemed to check himself before saying something, because he opened his mouth and then closed it again. His eyes went from Olivia to Daniel once more before saying, "I've come for an update on the system's power grid. You never came to Division One for a debriefing…" and just then, Gavin caught sight of two wine glasses, one spilled and the other empty, sitting closely nestled to an empty bottle of wine laying on its side. Gavin narrowed his eyes at Daniel. "Did you get her drunk?" he accused through gritted teeth. Without warning he crossed the room in two fast strides as if he were a bull about to run through his opponent, and Daniel knew what was coming. Daniel leapt to his feet, pulling Olivia up and tucking her safely behind him as he turned just in time to meet Gavin's fist.

Olivia screamed as Daniel crashed into the tiny round table, demolishing it. Olivia covered her mouth with her hands as she stared down. The splintery remains of the table and their wine glasses now shared a spot on the floor with Daniel. Olivia panted as she looked from Gavin to Daniel. "Why'd you do that?" she yelled. Gavin stood by as Olivia dropped down to her knees. "Daniel," she gasped between heavy breaths as she tried to move the table's remains from him.

"Get back," Gavin ordered, grabbing Olivia by the arm and pulling her away from Daniel, who appeared to be fluttering his eyes.

"Ouch, let go of me," Olivia shouted as she tried to pull out of his reach. His grip was too strong on her currently bruised arm. He pulled her beside him when she finally gave up.

Daniel groaned as his hand found the spot of impact on his left cheek.

"Let go!" Olivia shouted again, not hiding her anger.

"It's not what you think, Grant," Daniel mumbled as he got himself up to a sitting position.

Gavin didn't let her go; instead, he stood over Daniel, staring bullets into him. "Getting a seventeen-year-old girl drunk is exactly what it looks like," Gavin rumbled. "Sit over here," Gavin instructed, pushing Olivia down into a chair, "and stay put."

Olivia turned her face from his judging eyes. She had just figured out what he thought he'd walked into, her and Daniel, and she felt ashamed for a brief second. Then she shouted, "I'm not drunk."

Gavin shot her a silencing expression before he turned back to Daniel, who'd managed to get back up to his feet. "The wine is yours?" Gavin asked, already knowing the answer.

"It is," Daniel said simply.

"You gave it to her?" Gavin asked.

"I did."

"Then you will be brought up on charges," Gavin said.

"What?" Olivia yelled as she jumped to her feet. Gavin gave her a hard warning stare to not interfere that forced her to fall right back into the chair. "I wanted it," she mumbled.

"I think you're overreacting," Daniel said calmly. "We shared a few glasses, no one is drunk."

"Your intentions are obvious," Gavin said with a snarl. He took a breath before saying, "You were entertaining an underage girl with alcohol. As her supervisor, you are expected to behave as such," Gavin said.

"You're wrong," Daniel said.

"No, you were wrong," Gavin said stepping toward Daniel as if he meant to hit him again.

Olivia couldn't bear to see Gavin strike him again. "He did nothing wrong," Olivia shouted, in an attempt to save him from another blow, yet Gavin ignored her by grabbing Daniel by the shoulders and pushing him toward the door.

"Stop it. Leave him alone," she pleaded.

Gavin gave Olivia a sideways glance. "Go back to your room, now," he ordered her.

"Leave him alone, he didn't do anything wrong," Olivia pleaded.

Gavin lost his patience and shouted, "Go back to your room, now!" causing Olivia to take a step back as if he'd just scared her.

She'd never seen this side of him, and she didn't know what he was capable of, but she didn't think Daniel deserved this. "Where are you taking him?" she managed to whisper.

"To a cell," Gavin grumbled as he pushed Daniel out the door.

"What?" Olivia said in panic. The image of a prison cell flashed in her mind and she cringed at the thought of Daniel being locked up for giving her a taste of wine!

"Go back to your room, Olivia," Daniel stated.

"But…"

"Listen to him," Daniel interrupted. "Go back to your room," Daniel said softly. Gavin pushed him toward the hallway, not allowing him to get anything else out and giving Olivia no more opportunity to respond.

Olivia wanted to grab Gavin by the arm, she was compelled to do so, but she stopped herself. She didn't understand what had just happened. *What's wrong with Gavin? Why is he overreacting? How can he do this to Daniel? It's only wine!* She took two deep breaths before finding her confidence again. She raced down the hallway until she caught up with them, staying a few steps back as she attempted to hear what was being said.

"I didn't think drinking wine warranted imprisonment. What's the real reason, Grant?"

"Unlike you, my intentions are to follow the rules," Gavin stated.

"Are they?" Daniel asked sarcastically.

"Keep moving," Gavin said as they disappeared from Olivia's vision, entering one of Division One's staircases.

The entire way to the prison block Gavin had to hold himself back from the urge to punch Daniel Bandt in the face a few more times, just until he saw blood. At that moment, Gavin believed Daniel and rotten scumbag to be one and the same. At first, he'd thought he'd walked in on something different and he'd actually been hurt, right to the core, seeing Olivia and him kissing or just finishing. Whatever it was it had caught him off guard, which rarely occurred, but that had done it. He'd tried to go on about his visit being official, but then he'd seen the wine glasses and he'd known the truth: Daniel Bandt had coerced his trainee to drink until she was ready and willing for him to make his move… Gavin was hungry for blood and wished that Daniel would at least put up a fight.

Gavin shoved Daniel into a cell and slammed the door. He

stared at the swollen cheek on Daniel's face, satisfied. "You should really put ice on that," Gavin said, "Oh yeah, no ice issued to prisoners."

Daniel plopped down on the bed, throwing his legs up in a casual manner. "I know your type, Grant. I'd try to reason with you at this point, but it would probably be lost in that thick head of yours."

"Everyone said you were a kid genius, funny that you end up here."

"Well, I designed the vault, not the workers."

"If you think that gives you a free pass to break the rules, then I'm here to remind you, you're gravely mistaken. You may have created the vault, but I run it."

"Do you?" Daniel asked sarcastically.

"We both know you'll be out of here by tomorrow, but don't think I won't be watching."

"Jeez, Grant, I might think you have a crush on me."

Gavin ignored his comment. "Stay away from her," Gavin growled.

"Grant, you really are a moron."

Gavin tightened his fist and imagined laying another on him. "She's only seventeen."

Daniel gave him a smug look. "Almost eighteen, Grant, and I'm just twenty, two years older, hardly makes me a villain."

"Look, you're supposed to train her as an engineer, nothing more. I won't allow it."

Daniel shook his head. "But you will allow her to be impregnated in accordance with the vault's rules? Oh, I see… you, you want it to be you."

Gavin reached out and grabbed one of the bars, imagining it was Daniel's neck. "Say something else. I'm dying to hit you again."

Daniel forced a smile. "I would ask for my lawyer at this particular interval, but it seems we never hired any, so I guess I'll ask for the major."

Gavin released the bar and took a step back. "Of course, in the morning. Sleep tight." Gavin walked away, unsatisfied that he'd not taken another swing at Daniel Bandt's face.

Olivia opened her eyes as she felt a sharp pain in her arm. "Ouch," she mumbled as she looked up to see Gavin staring back.

He shook her bruised arm again.

"Gavin?" she whispered, still half-asleep.

"Are you hurt?" he asked, moving the covers down from her shoulder.

Olivia grabbed her sore arm as she came fully alert to his presence. "Yes, I'm hurt," she said, pulling the cover up with her other hand. "Do you mind?" she asked, not wanting him to see her in her nightgown. She couldn't believe he was there.

"Sorry." He hung his head.

"Why are you here?" she asked, lifting her arm out from under the covers and looking at it. "Ouch."

Gavin sat down beside her, turning on the side lamp and taking her arm gently in his hands to exam it. Upon finding a small bruise on the back of her arm, he removed his hands and said, "Sorry about that."

"Right!" Olivia tossed the covers back over her arm.

He frowned at her. "I am sorry. I didn't mean to grab you so roughly. It wasn't my intention."

She shrugged and proceeded to rub her eyes, and then she remembered Daniel. "Daniel, is he okay? She didn't hide her compassion for him. "What did you do to him?"

Gavin grumbled. "You're concerned about him?" He hadn't wanted to see her react to him in this way.

"Yes, you punched him." She scooted away from him.

He turned his head as if hurt by her gesture. "He's in a cell."

Olivia stared at him with wide eyes. "You put him in a cell for drinking wine?"

Gavin turned his frustration on her. "No, I put him in a cell for getting you drunk. Besides, you have to have permission to have alcohol."

Olivia shook her head as if that would help clear her thoughts. "Permission? He has to have permission to drink his wine? That sounds ridiculous." Olivia saw his face turn rigid.

"The vault has rules, and he broke them."

She hated his excuses and didn't believe that was really enough to warrant time in a cell; besides, Gavin had hit him even though he'd done nothing to deserve it. "Why'd you punch him?"

"He was getting you drunk with certain intentions," he said in defense.

Olivia rolled her eyes at him, wondering how he could think such a thing. Daniel had no bad intentions. "Intentions? He didn't get me drunk, and he didn't force me to drink anything. I did it because I wanted to."

"You don't understand, Olivia. He shouldn't put you in that spot."

She shook her head. *How could he think that?* Daniel had been nothing but nice to her. He was her friend, and she couldn't allow him to get in trouble for sharing his wine with her. Gavin had overreacted, and she had to defend him. "He didn't put me in a spot. He did nothing wrong. If anyone came on to anyone, it was me."

Gavin tightened his jaw. "Did you?"

"Yes," she lied. No one had really come on to anyone, but if Gavin wasn't going to believe anything else, she might as well make him see Daniel as innocent, since he was. Still, the lie stung, and an odd pressure came over her chest.

He swallowed. "Olivia… I," he stammered. He took a deep breath as he ran his hand through his hair.

She curled her knees up against her chest, wanting the entire conversation to end. She wished that she hadn't said yes to his question, but it was too late, she saw exactly what that *yes* had done to him. She wished things were different and that she could say what she really was thinking, but instead she said, "You didn't have to punch him and put him in jail."

He ignored her statement. "You are not to see him unless he's training you for engineering, nothing more."

She jerked upright, allowing her legs to fall back down under the covers, accidently rubbing against his hand. He didn't react. She ignored it too. "What? Why?" Olivia asked.

"It's what's best for you." He suddenly stared down at the cover where her leg had touched him.

Another order, she thought angrily, ignoring where his eyes had fallen. "What's best for me?" she asked bewildered. She defended, "That is not what's best for me. He's my friend."

He looked up at her, his eyes serious. "He's your boss."

"And my friend," she corrected him.

"No, he can't be both."

Olivia averted his eyes and began to fidget with the blanket, picking at it with her fingers as she waited to speak. "Really? But you can be both with Dillard."

"What are you talking about?"

She could feel his eyes on her. Olivia knew she shouldn't go any further, but he'd made her so mad with his orders. She peeked at him from the corner of her eye. "You and Dillard, together, I saw you, did you forget?"

Gavin stared at her. "You saw nothing. We're not together."

Olivia looked back down at her hand fidgeting with the material. "You came out of her room," she said. She bit her lip, unbelieving that she'd just said it out loud to him!

He was silent for what seemed an eternity. "Not that this is any of your business, but she overslept from being ill, and as her supervisor I had to escort her to the doctor for evaluation."

"Oh." She let the information register until the embarrassment of her accusation was too much to bare. She didn't dare look at him, horrified that he would see it on her face.

Gavin stood up as if he couldn't contain himself any longer. "I don't know what rebellious ideas you have going on in your head, but this is not a game, Olivia. You can't behave like this is college. It's not. You're living in an underground vault where most everyone is older than you, and they have the experience to manipulate you."

She felt as if he thought she were dumb. "You think I'm being used?"

"No, but you could. Daniel Bandt is far more than a genius. Strategy and playing people's emotions is nothing to him. He's a master manipulator."

Olivia shook her head. "He didn't do anything?"

"Olivia, I know his life story. He's not an average twenty year old. Your mind is like an infant's compared to his."

"Infant?" she asked insulted.

"No." He ran his hands through his hair again, regretting what he'd just said. He tried to convince her. "But if he wants something, he gets it. He's a genius, and I'd hate to find out what a genius does when he's bored."

The information was too much for her. She'd had one of the best nights with Daniel. He always made her laugh and feel as if this entire new life, vault life, was bearable. Gavin hadn't done what Daniel had done for her. He'd ignored her until she found a friend, a friend that he didn't approve of. He had no right to tell her what to do, she thought. He'd saved her life, but he didn't own it. She didn't want to hear any more criticism from him. Daniel wasn't using her. He wouldn't. She couldn't take anymore. "Get out," Olivia said with venom.

He didn't move.

She raised her face for him to see that she meant it. "You won't talk to me unless it's an emergency, then you tell me not to have certain friends, that I can't trust them. You arrest people and punch them like it's nothing. Maybe you're the dangerous one?"

His eyes flickered with pain, but Olivia took it as insult.

"Everyone is dangerous in here, can't you see that?" he warned.

She shook her head. "I've been getting along fine without your advice for the past month," she reminded him.

He raised both hands as if he'd too had enough. "Fine. Do what you like," he said as he started to leave.

"Gavin?"

He stopped and turned, waiting for her to go on.

"Let Daniel go."

He grumbled in defeat. "In the morning. And Olivia, just remember what I said, and don't forget I do it because I have to. Things in here are not what they seem. Secret groups are starting to form, people are beginning to take things into their own hands that aren't favorable for everyone, and there are thieves like Rossi who try to trade goods that aren't theirs to trade. There's always a struggle for power, and people get hurt. I don't want you to get hurt." He fell silent as he started to leave once again, but before he opened the door he said, "Don't you think I wish I could join you for meals and have conversations with you whenever I wanted? I'm your only friend in here." He opened the door and walked out.

Chapter 15

olidays, had come and gone. There was no celebration, no
decoration, and no mention of them from the major or anyone
in the military. The special meat had yet to be served. The turning
seasons of spring, summer, and fall had been forgotten, surrounded by the same grey cement walls and steel doors. The days had
run together. Time had evaded everyone's attention, it seemed.

Months had gone by without any indication of such. No way
to measure it, not the usual methods, the old ways, not when life
existed underground. No more intruding sun peeking through
the windows at dawn nudging one awake. No more perfectly clear
days that called for flip flops and shorts. No more starlight strolls
in the evening accompanied by annoying crickets or mosquitoes.
No more rain showers to cause floods or humidity. No more
droughts, no more day, no more night. No more of what was once
familiar—nothing usual, nothing desirable. The turning of the
leaves, the harvest moon, and the slight chill in the air that announced a sweater was needed. Nothing to show it's someone's

favorite time of the year. November had arrived and only those who used a calendar knew it, for within the vault at a comfortable 70 degrees, every day seemed just like any other unless you counted The Reviews.

The Reviews, step three in the five-step plan, meant the assigned guidance counselor had to submit reports on each of their division's residents while making adjustments to designated career paths in the most effective way for the vault. This allowed for the enactment of Step Four: *Established*, in which all residents were comfortably adjusted to their daily lifestyles and needs. This third step had become the subject on every single resident's mind because their job or career path might be altered for better or worse, depending on his or her productivity, performance, or bribe. Olivia wasn't any exception, and she knew it.

Olivia held her breath as she stopped in front of Daniel Bandt's office door. She needed to talk with him immediately. She'd let too many days go by without bringing up the subject. She regretted procrastinating or having to even ask him for this one favor. She knew he'd probably say yes, but having to ask, well, made her feel uncomfortable. This feeling of discomfort was a common reaction whenever she had to deal with him ever since the last conversation they'd had about her future. She should have seen it coming. Maybe she did. Maybe she'd wanted it too. Olivia knew exactly when things had changed between them. Olivia had seen things differently ever since the night they drank together in his office, but she'd been wrong.

When Olivia first saw his bruised face the next day, she somehow felt responsible. She went as far as to apologize for getting him into trouble. He simply shrugged off her comment and stated that he had, in fact, overstepped his bounds as her instructor. She was speechless for the first few minutes until he asked her if she was ready to take the exam. That had prompted her to boldly ask why he suddenly felt that way.

His reason was equally as surprising. He told her that he had felt sorry for her the night before, seeing her all dressed up with no place to go, but that giving her alcohol had been the wrong thing to do, that even though life in the vault was far from normal, there were still rules he should have obeyed.

For an instant, she had thought he might be teasing her, half-expecting that large grin and chuckle to emerge at any moment, but it never did. Instead he moved right along, listing off what their agenda would be for the rest of the day. She wanted to push for more of an explanation, but her head had ached since she woke that morning. She assumed a hangover, so she didn't pry, believing that eventually he'd ask her to join him for more chocolates and the champagne he'd mentioned, but he never did.

Things were different after that between Olivia and Daniel. Olivia assumed he was merely having a bad couple of days, and those days turned into weeks and months. He continued to be his intelligent self, instructing her on all the vault's mechanics, all the computer's ins and outs, but he didn't relax around her or make jokes with her as he had before. The fun and games and teasing ceased. His behavior had actually transformed into a level of seriousness she wasn't aware he possessed, and she felt guilty, as if she'd done something wrong. She didn't dare bring it up.

A few months later, Olivia began to feel strange around him. Whenever she turned, he always seemed to be staring, watching her. She wrote it off as him observing her work, but these observations bled over into meaningless tasks on the computer or when she stopped to speak with Janet in their neighboring workroom or even when she'd dine in the Grand Hall; whenever she'd catch him, he'd quickly turn his head.

The Reviews were announced at around this time, and Olivia wondered if they had something to do with the extra surveillance of her working habits. She said nothing, curious like most of the others if she would be able to keep her current position. Tests had been distributed to all of the residents that covered questions on their current duties. Olivia had felt completely prepared for hers thanks to Daniel. He'd given her one exam every week and then a comprehensive exam each month, forcing the information to become second nature instead of just memorized for the moment.

At times, she'd become frustrated with the massive amount of information he expected her to learn, but he'd strictly defended his technique by mentioning the upcoming reviews, which could extract her from her current position if she didn't pass the tests. She'd mentioned once that he was the one who had made the review tests, and he'd said, "I know, and you have a lot to learn if you want to pass them." She considered arguing with him but then decided against it.

She knew that despite his change in behavior, she couldn't argue against Daniel's dedication to teaching her. Plus, she'd spoken to Sophie and a few of the other residents about their upcoming tests, and none of them had any idea what they'd be tested over. That fact had reassured her of her good luck in having Daniel as her boss, so no matter how guilty she felt about making him retract his humorous, laid-back attitude in exchange for the new one that was more serious and reclusive, she was content.

Then, about a month ago, before testing for The Reviews began, Daniel suddenly changed back to his former self. At first, she thought that he'd forgotten who she was when he remarked that he wished to spend a day off of work with her. The idea sounded great, but the sudden shift in his priorities caught Olivia off guard. She hesitated for only a moment before she accepted his invitation. She wasn't going to worry about what Gavin would think. Even though she already knew he would disapprove, she was too curious to find out what Daniel had planned.

Daniel requested that she meet him in the game room before breakfast the next day. When she arrived, he presented her with coffee and muffins. She eagerly accepted, recently becoming addicted to coffee after Daniel had connected a machine in his office. She thanked him and asked, "Why the game room?"

He smiled slyly as he produced a box wrapped with a yellow

satiny material. She stared at him as if he was a stranger trying to shove an unfamiliar object into her hands. He chuckled at her reaction. "I know, I know, but I couldn't resist."

"Resist?" she asked stupidly.

He excitedly pushed the box into her hands, requesting that she open it.

After a few reassuring nods from Daniel, she cautiously unwrapped the material and opened the box. Inside she found yellow shoes, at least that's what they appeared to be until she pulled them out and noticed the four red wheels attached to each one. "Skates?" she asked, unsure of the gift and its meaning. Then it happened, he grinned and laughed just as she remembered.

"I had to get something for your birthday," he said.

Her expression of confusion wasn't lost on him, and in response to her look he asked, "Did I do something wrong?"

She shook her head and laughed again. It was October third, her fake birthday, the one Gavin had made up shortly after sneaking her into the vault. Daniel must have looked it up.

"I love them, but skates?" she asked.

That's when his mischievous grin took form, and he explained, "You mentioned once that the vault's game room wasn't entertaining enough, so here you go. I made them and remembered how pretty yellow looks on you."

She suddenly felt shy and didn't know what to make of him, especially the way he made her feel special. Only a few days before had been her actual birthday, and it had been a disaster. She accepted his gift with delight, letting go of the thought that the day wasn't truly her birthday, enjoying the gift and the company. She didn't understand the sudden shift in his demeanor; however, she didn't care at that moment and chose instead to take in the spontaneity that never happened inside the vault.

She put on the skates and entertained the both of them as she tried to roll around the room without bumping into game tables and couches. She was honored to be given a handmade gift. The rest of the day was filled with laughter as they'd played games, talked about movies, and dreamed of being on a deserted island instead of in a vault. He made a birthday in the vault as perfect as one could.

Why the sudden return to his old behavior? It was not a question Olivia could answer, but she did wonder in the several weeks that followed. Then, other questions began to form. Why did she start to act like a fool whenever she was around him? Why did she feel nervous when he stood closely beside her? Why did she turn red whenever he paid her a compliment? He really stumped her when he asked her where she saw her future.

He'd been smiling at his observation of her one day while she was taking apart an energy cell. She was concentrating on a component when he asked, "Are you happy with your current position?"

She said yes quickly, giving more of her attention to the device in her hand than his question.

"Someone else wants it," he said.

She looked up at him as if he'd said something offensive.

"There's another guy who has a relevant engineering background and who believes he's better suited for the position than you." He had her full attention now, and she defended her knowledge passionately, causing Daniel to stare at her with a satisfied expression. "Of course, you're more qualified. That's why I've been grilling you and training you so hard. So if anything happens to me, you'll be able to take over."

Confusion crept across Olivia's face as he spoke. "What could happen to you?" she asked.

He shrugged it off. "Nothing, but if it did, someone who's honest and uncorrupt should know what I know."

Olivia didn't nag him to explain. She just figured that whoever the other guy was had to be someone Daniel didn't respect. The word uncorrupt did stick with her, but she didn't fully understand how someone who made repairs could be corrupt.

A week later she took the test and passed with flying colors. Daniel was ecstatic. "You can now wear this with pride," he said as he revealed a new grey jumpsuit with the embroidery of her name and underneath it the word *Engineer*.

Olivia matched his excitement, jumping up and wrapping her arms around his neck for a hug. He hugged her back, and when she went to kiss him on the cheek, he turned his head and she accidently planted a peck at the corner of his lips. They both stared at each other for what seemed the most uncomfortable moment before he let go of her and went on with describing the next week's itinerary as if nothing had happened. She spent the remainder of the week uncomfortably dodging any eye contact, feeling like an idiot.

Olivia stared at Daniel's office one more time, summoning up the courage to knock. She had to make the request today, no later. She rapped twice at the door.

"Come in," Daniel said from the other side.

Olivia slowly opened the door.

Daniel looked up. "Hey. I thought you had the day off."

Olivia swallowed. "Yeah, I wanted to ask you something."

"Okay, come in then."

She took the seat in front of his desk. She ran her hand through her hair as she tried to come up with a way to ask her question that didn't sound ungrateful.

Curiosity danced across Daniel's face. "What is it?"

Olivia shifted in her seat. "I have a request."

Daniel smiled. "What kind of request?"

"Work."

"Go on."

She took a deep breath. "I want to transfer to the military division," she said quickly.

Daniel's smile disappeared. "Transfer? You're an engineer. A resident."

Olivia exhaled deeply. "Yes, but I heard that during The Reviews, my guidance counselor has the authority, if my supervisor approves, of course, to transfer me into the military division. I'll still be an engineer, but I'll be trained as a soldier so that they can fill open positions too."

"Wait a second. The military is staffed just fine," Daniel said.

"Maybe so, but residents are given a one-time option to be placed in the military division. I'll still be an engineer, but I won't be considered a resident anymore. I'll be a soldier."

"Who said this?"

"The major. He sent emails out to the qualifying residents."

"And you received one? I haven't heard of this."

"Yes, and I want to do it. I don't want to be a resident."

Daniel shifted uncomfortably in his seat. "Who talked you into this?"

Olivia's voice rose in defense. "No one."

Daniel scanned her face. "Really, no one?"

Olivia stared directly back at him, trying to remember to look in his eyes, knowing that people believed you if you told them something while looking in their eyes, even if it wasn't the truth.

"No one," Olivia said as she stared into his judging eyes and lied. She really hadn't been talked into it, but someone had definitely told her to accept it: Gavin.

As peculiar as Daniel's behavior was during the passing months, Gavin's was just as bizarre. Olivia presumed he'd given up on her the night of the system's alarm. His paranoid comments warning her to trust no one, that secret things were happening, and that he was her only friend had left her in disarray. When she'd encountered Daniel's odd behavior immediately after that, the nightmare of truly being deserted settled in.

Daniel wasn't there to provide the humor she so readily needed. The desire to seek out Gavin on a daily basis to see if he was there had extinguished itself. Even Sophie wasn't available to hang out as often as before, due to her work schedule. Olivia fell into an almost zombie state, with every day feeling the same until Gavin contacted her.

She'd been leaving the Grand Hall after a late dinner when he ushered her into an empty corridor where they could speak privately. She tried to move away from him, still mad that he'd punched Daniel only a few nights ago, but he stood in her way, and just when she thought she'd scream, he apologized. "I'm sorry. I was wrong."

"You should apologize to Daniel," she said.

He grumbled at her remark. "No. I'm sorry for what I did to you," he whispered. "I've been thinking about how I've treated you. How you've been here and what will happen to you, and I can't sit and watch quietly. Not when I've seen... uh. Just listen to me, I'm here for you, but we must be careful. Others can't ever see that we talk."

Olivia nodded silently, dumbfounded, and he'd taken off.

A few days later he flagged her down again, this time when she was on her way to her shift, casually walking up beside her and motioning toward a door that she followed him through. This time he said that he was checking in to see how she was doing, asking if Daniel was treating her well.

She became agitated at the question, revealing that he'd stopped treating her as his friend.

Gavin seemed content with this information, and Olivia was angered by his reaction.

He stated that Daniel should have been behaving as such since the beginning.

Olivia accused Gavin of doing something to their friendship, but he defended himself, saying that whatever was going on between them now wasn't his doing. "If anything," he suggested, "Daniel realized that he wasn't behaving professionally." That meeting had left Olivia in a not-so-happy mood.

A few more days went by again before he followed her into an equipment storage unit, where he asked again how she was doing, then a few days later in the main hallway, then quietly in the breakfast food line. This continued, his visits to her every few days, as if he were a secret agent receiving critical information, though their exchanges were more casual, responses of, "I'm fine," or "I'm tired today, need another cup of coffee," or "What are you reading?" Simple questions and simple responses that kept them connected. The anger she'd directed at him eventually dissolved, and waiting to see how he would contact her next kept Olivia engaged with anticipation.

As the months rolled by, their conversational tactics increased to a stealthy method of short answers to topics they'd started. First dream vacations, favorite foods, favorite type of dog, until they'd reached favorite movies and songs. She once asked him a question in a low whisper as she passed by, "Old Yeller. You cry?" and he responded reluctantly, "A little." Then, he breezed by and said, "Shawshank," and she mumbled, "Sad, but awesome." Later he bumped into her, sliding a note that read, *Listen to track 4 from archive 108*, and she somehow slipped him a note days later with a tactful drop or skillful handoff that read, *Glory of Love," LOL. Sweet but sappy*, in response to their earlier topic of favorite cheesy love songs. He found the right opportunity to slide her another note: *You said no judging*. Back and forth they went with their questions and answers, delivered through notes or careful whispers, and in this way they discovered one another's opinions and personal tastes. Then, to her surprise, he slipped her a note that said, *Expect me at midnight.*

Olivia had conflicting thoughts regarding his purpose, curious to find out what was so important that he wanted to meet her in her room, which he hadn't done since the incident with the system's alarm. She worried something might be wrong, and at the same time she felt a rush of excitement at the thought of actually seeing him again, alone. By the time he slipped into her room that evening, she was unable to contain herself.

Gavin quickly eased her mind with a soft smile she hadn't seen before. "I've got news," he'd said, trying to hide his own eagerness.

Olivia waited for him to take a seat beside her on the bed, but instead he stood at the door with a hand behind his back. "Well, you've figured out how to sneak past Dillard, apparently."

He scrunched his brow at her remark. "It's not easy. She's trained too well," he said with agitation. Then he surprised her by revealing what he was hiding behind his back, a small, chocolate-iced cupcake with an unlit candle.

Olivia gasped in excitement, realizing that he'd remembered her birthday from the day she whispered it to him in the cafeteria line after pining over the tiny chocolate cupcakes that were being given out with dinner. "You remembered," she said softly.

Quickly, he lit the tiny candle with a lighter from his pocket and presented it to her to blow out as he'd said, "Happy eighteenth birthday, Olivia."

She smiled from ear to ear as she stared between the candle and his deep blue eyes, which had become a welcomed sight. "Well, aren't you going to sing?" she teased.

He lifted one dark brow as he said with remorse, "I would wake the neighbors."

She giggled with a nod and blew out the candle with a wish in mind.

"Hope it was a good one," he said.

"It was."

He then instructed her to check her inbox for the news. When she finished reading the email from the major, she looked over to see Gavin smiling next to her. "Does this mean…?" she asked.

"Yes. It means you can be safe," he said.

"Safe? Does it mean we can talk, that we can actually talk

whenever and wherever we like?"

"If you're chosen to be transferred to the military division, it does."

Olivia wrapped her arms around Gavin's neck before she could think better of it and for a moment he sat still beside her, until he too wrapped his arms around her. When she remembered The Reviews she asked, "But my job? My job as an engineer?"

"Can continue. It won't alter your work, only your position, which will get you out of the resident line. Most importantly, you won't be a resident at twenty, you won't have to submit to their rules."

Olivia understood exactly what he meant. She wouldn't be expected to be pregnant at twenty. "But I won't be able to speak to residents," she said sadly. "Sophie, Daniel, the others."

"It's what is best for you, it's the safest. You won't be expected to stop talking to Daniel, no matter how much I wish you couldn't; he's cleared to speak with military, and he's still going to be supervising you as an engineer. As for Sophie, well, give it time, things may change."

Olivia hadn't ever understood his dislike of Daniel, but she ignored it at this point. "How so? I want to, but..."

"But nothing. You'll have me to talk to," he said softly.

"I don't know, I have to think about it," she said.

He became angry at her answer. "You don't get it, still. There's no thinking about it, Olivia. Do it. Apply for the transfer. It's not an accident you received the email. I made certain promises to the major, and if you don't accept it… you're going to accept it." He stood up in the middle of his rant, unable to contain the importance of the decision. "I've got to go. Olivia, if you ever do anything for me, accept it."

He hadn't spoken to her again since the night of her true birthday, and then she'd passed her exam and was so caught up in Daniel's world that she'd procrastinated on the transfer, until now.

Olivia didn't move her eyes, keeping them locked on Daniel's as she said again, "No one."

Daniel didn't give up. "Well, then, you should reconsider."

"I won't," she said.

Daniel scratched his chin. "Trust me, Olivia. You do not want to be isolated in the military division. You won't be able to socialize with residents or attend their events. You'll become an outsider. You know how others see the soldiers."

He was right. Olivia had heard other residents talk poorly of the soldiers over the last few months. There were whispers about their high-and-mighty attitudes, about how they thought they were supreme and were owed respect because of their position. Olivia had found herself thinking the same way about them at times, especially when Dillard would give her a rough time of it, or other soldiers would cut in front of her in the food line or bump into her roughly without apology. The obvious line between military and resident life had been drawn from the first day, but it had grown more apparent as actions and hostility escalated. Just a month ago, one male resident had gotten into a dispute with another male soldier for trying to cut the line in front of him, and when the resident said something about it, the soldier shoved him. The resident lost his temper and after a few kicks in the ribs was hauled off. Some assumed he'd been taken to the infirmary to be seen by the doctor while others said he'd been locked up for two days without food or water. Olivia couldn't believe that Gavin would allow such actions to happen, but he couldn't prevent every small thing, and small things did have a way of slipping through the cracks.

"Yes, I'm aware of the residents' views of the soldiers, and soldiers do seem to think they're entitled, but I'm not going to be like them, so it shouldn't matter."

Daniel shook his head and spoke as if she didn't understand

the seriousness of the matter. "It doesn't matter if you act like a saint, you'll be associated by proxy."

Olivia wanted to know why exactly he was against her transfer. She had thought he wouldn't care, but it was clear he did. "Daniel, you're associated with the military. You work with them and for them. I don't see how you can be against them?"

"I'm not, Olivia. I'm only making sure you see all angles of this choice. Resident life versus military life is very different. I'm not against either one. I'm only trying to help you pick what's a right fit for you."

"Okay. Thank you for your concern, but I've already thought this through, and resident life doesn't suit me."

"Could you tell me why not?"

" Well, the rules for one."

"As a soldier you'll have rules."

"Yes, I'm not trying to get away from all rules… just one in particular."

"Which one?"

Olivia glanced down at her lap, embarrassed with the answer she was going to give. "The turning-twenty rule for girls," she said carefully.

"I see," he said. He cleared his throat. "And what if that rule didn't apply to you. Would you stay a resident?"

She gave him a look of doubt. "I'd consider it."

"Really, just consider? I thought that was the issue."

Olivia stumbled over her words. "I, uh, well it is."

"What if I can get you cleared to be an exception. Seeing as that you're being trained to be my replacement, we wouldn't want anything to happen to you. Childbirth is a little more dangerous in here. I can make sure that particular rule never has to apply to you. And then you'd still be able to come and go as you like as an engineer; you could still associate with your friends, Sophie, Janet."

Olivia sat silently with her mouth open as she tried to come up with a reason she should transfer, but he'd fixed all her problems in a snap, all except for the one that she dared not mention to him: Gavin. She wanted to have freedom to talk with him, to see him… could Daniel fix that?

"Well, then. I'll make sure what I said is done, and I'll send an email to the major letting him know your decision."

Olivia felt like she was suffocating and began to panic as she slowly watched Gavin disappear from her grasp. "No," she said, louder than she meant to. "No, I still want to transfer. This is what I want."

Daniel rubbed his face in frustration. Olivia waited for his response. When he didn't say anything, she rose to her feet.

"No," he said simply. "No, I won't approve the transfer. You are not a solider, Olivia, you're an engineer."

She suddenly saw the rest of her life in the vault pass before her eyes, in which Gavin was but a silent passerby in the background who'd forgotten her. "No, please Daniel. Please approve it. It's what I want."

"Olivia, it's what's best for you. Trust me. I'm also your friend."

She stared back at him as if he'd taken everything away from her. "You take away my choice and say we're friends. If you do this, we won't be friends," she threatened. "I'm eighteen remember. Don't treat me like a child."

Daniel glanced away from her hard stare. "I'll submit your transfer." He stood up and faced her. The serious Daniel stood before her. "But you owe me, friend," he said with a smile.

She smiled back. "Thank You."

Chapter 16

The Reviews had come and gone. Some residents were able to keep their jobs, while others were moved around. The system in which each guidance counselor presented the rationale behind a move or a promotion seemed fair enough. But if you asked those residents who were shifted to a new career path after being labeled poor performers or for scoring too low on the productivity scale, they'd tell you differently. They'd argue that they hadn't bribed sufficiently.

Olivia met all the requirements that allowed her to keep the phantom replacement out of her position, without bribe, but she'd had Daniel on her side. She realized all of this once she grasped the effects of The Reviews.

Sophie hadn't been affected, nor Janet; they both held on to their positions. They'd not seemed worried either, at least not as much as the others, who all seemed to react as if The Reviews were a horrible guest coming to visit. Most of the residents had been on edge, and they'd done their best to be as presentable as possible throughout the entire ordeal. In the days leading up to The Reviews, residents suddenly converted to being polite and courteous people, so nice that Olivia had been shocked. She was especially surprised by Clare's transformation. The dishwasher toned down her hair and radiated a huge smile at each and every meal. Others began to wear their uniforms without wrinkles or flaws. Olivia was floored when she saw that even the gardeners were actually taking the time not to appear dirty. The entire vault gave off a pleasant demeanor on the surface, but the underlying tension was still unmistakable.

As The Reviews came to an end, so did the masquerade. While most seemed content, a few held resentment. Mr. Rossi was shifted from supplies to the garden, and his place was taken by none other than Clare, who'd not once after the switch from dishwasher to supply manager worn her smile. Olivia was surprised to see Clare promoted, as was Sophie, who mentioned quietly to Olivia one day that she'd probably bribed someone. Olivia didn't believe her until she noted that Clare was missing the large diamond earrings everyone had once ogled before her promotion. The man who replaced Clare was the same person who had weeks earlier punched a soldier in rage. His transfer was a demotion from a former position as a facilities manager, and his spot was filled by a general worker from the garden. That was what bothered Olivia, some of the changes didn't make sense, and the newly demoted residents weren't happy. Not that they advertised their opinions about their new situation, but they did grumble quietly to one another.

Olivia couldn't criticize it either, not when she was up for her own transfer. Any hint of insubordination of military protocol might derail her pending classification as a soldier. So when Sophie or Janet would bring up the subject of residents making bribes with food or alcohol, she'd pretend she had somewhere to be. She couldn't risk losing her one chance at becoming free of the restriction placed between her and Gavin.

A few days had gone by since she'd officially applied for her classification transfer. She was nervous when the major asked to meet with her. She'd had no time to ask Gavin his thoughts, since the major requested the meeting take place that very day. Daniel had excused her from work, and she arrived fifteen minutes early. Presently, she waited for him to enter the empty Grand Hall. When he did, she turned to greet him by rising to her feet.

"Miss Parker," the major said in a pleased tone as he extended his hand for a shake. "Please sit," he instructed. When they'd both taken their seats, he continued. "I've heard a lot about you in the past few weeks. All good things of course: Star student, great family background, your uncle was a genius, and you seem to be too, at least that's what Daniel has told me."

Olivia didn't expect Daniel to call her a genius or for her fictional uncle to be mentioned, and suddenly she felt like a fraud.

"Heard you were interested in being a soldier. So, tell me, why would you like to be reclassified?"

Olivia swallowed as she forced a pleasant smile. "Well, I see it in my future. It's what I want," she said with determination.

"Yes, I can see you're eager, but you realize that a resident doesn't have real worries or hard decisions. The military takes on that burden, making sure that life goes on smoothly here in the vault. What I'm getting at is that as a soldier you'll be required to carry out orders, no questions asked. You'll be given access to areas that residents aren't even given. I must make sure you understand that confidentiality and compliance to my rules are to be sustained, no exceptions. Once you agree to this you can't go back, you'll remain a soldier as long as we're in the vault. If you break my rules, you will be punished as a soldier. Do you understand me?"

Olivia nodded, speechless to the restrictions that would be placed on her. She'd known that she'd have new regulations to follow, and she wondered how it could really be any different than what she'd already gone through, but his words had made it official, and it sounded detrimental.

"Good," he said with a smile. "I believe you've made a great choice for your future."

"Thank you, Sir, I truly appreciate this honor."

The major laughed. "I can see why he recommended you. Good choice. Well, I need to be off. You should check in with your guidance counselor today, and they'll arrange the move into Division One. Good day, soldier, and good luck with training. Well, what limited training we can provide here."

Olivia rose as he did. "Thank you, Sir."

He nodded and left.

Recommended me? Gavin, she thought. *He said that he arranged the email.* She feared that in some way she'd let him down. The major scared her. She wondered how soldiers were punished and hoped that she'd never find out. Before her meeting, she thought she would hit the roof with anticipation when the confirmation of her transfer was announced, but after the major's warnings, she'd suddenly been filled with mixed feelings as he'd welcomed her.

She checked in with Dillard, who'd already received word about Olivia's transfer. Her beautiful face didn't reflect a congratulation, instead she snickered at Olivia as she checked in. "Going to be a solider, huh?" she said with an offensive laugh. "Well, best of luck to you. Gather your things, and I'll show you to your new room."

Olivia ignored the cynical tone Dillard delivered so easily as she made way to her room. Olivia had her things packed in no time, considering she had very few personal belongings to begin with. When she walked out of Division Four with Dillard beside her, she noticed a few of her hallmates peeking out of their doors. They were faces she'd never bothered to get to know, faces that were close to the same age as her, but for some reason she'd never connected with them; yet she'd connected with Sophie, Daniel, Janet, and Gavin, all of whom were older than her, all of whom were maturely involved in their current reality of being vault-dwellers, while those youthful faces were not. She wondered if she'd chosen to hang out with residents around her own age if everything would be different for her. Why did she want to grow up so fast? That's what her mom would have asked her, and she would have been unable to answer her. Instead, she probably would have run to her room and shut the door, saying, *Leave me alone, I know what I'm doing.*

When she entered Division One, independence rattled through her bones. She felt a little taller, a little older. As she passed several doors she noticed one—at least she thought it was the one—Gavin's door, Gavin's room, where she'd spent her first night in the vault.

"Here it is," Dillard said, breaking through Olivia's thoughts.

Olivia couldn't be sure, but she thought that her room was directly to the left of his. She didn't allow her eyes to linger on his potential door because Dillard was watching. She walked past Dillard and entered her room. It was the same, the same as Gavin's room, the same as her old room. She dropped her stuff on the bed before turning to Dillard. "My uniform?" Olivia asked.

Dillard chuckled. "I don't think you're getting one," she said snidely.

"Oh," Olivia said, shifting her eyes away from Dillard, thinking her face might turn red. At the same time, she wondered why Dillard addressed her so hatefully. She'd never been a kind guidance counselor, but she'd also never sounded intentionally cruel. When she glanced back up to see Dillard's laser eyes on her, they were interrupted.

"Dillard," a male voice stated in a familiar military fashion.

Dillard turned and Olivia tried to hide her smile as Gavin stood in the doorway.

"Sir," Dillard said with a tiny salute.

"Is the newbie all settled in?" he asked Dillard.

"Yes, I was about to show her around."

"No need. I'm making my evening rounds. You're excused," he said, glancing toward Olivia.

Dillard shot a strange look back at Olivia, "I'm sure you're busy..."

"Not at the moment," he interrupted. "You're excused," he ordered.

Dillard gave Olivia another glance that said she was tempted to say more but was holding herself back with great strength. Olivia stared right back at her, still trying to hide her smile; however, a slight curve of her lip was seen by Dillard, who responded with a jerk of her head toward Gavin. "Good evening then," Dillard said to Gavin, completely ignoring Olivia. Gavin stepped to the side, allowing Dillard to pass.

He held up his hand for Olivia to remain silent as he watched Dillard leave. Once he'd made sure she was gone, he turned back to Olivia wearing a huge grin. "Welcome to Division One, kid."

Olivia's smile disappeared with the word *kid*. "Thanks, old man," she said sarcastically.

"Hey, watch it, or I'll have you peeling potatoes in the kitchen."

"Ha, funny," she said sarcastically. "So, do I really not get a uniform?" she asked with a hint of disappointment. She'd imagined herself several times wearing one.

Gavin chuckled. "Sure, you can have one, but first let me show you around."

Olivia smiled. "What a novelty. You showing me around and talking."

He laughed. "Come on."

Gavin guided Olivia through Division One's hallway, explaining that most soldiers who resided there performed various rotating duties, while the remaining few had a specialized talent. Routine duties consisted of security throughout the vault, including the guarding of sensitive rooms with medical supplies and drugs, supply closets containing valuable equipment or food, the common areas for residents, the garden, and surveillance of Division One's prison, armory, main storage facility, and control center. Soldiers with specialized duties maintained the vault's main computer and operation systems for cameras, air, and water, as well as any attempts of outside communication.

Division One portrayed the epitome of an underground military reservation with all the technological bells and whistles. A handful of soldiers were standing guard over the entryway to the control center and intelligence room. Beyond that lay the armory, and beyond that were several storage rooms and the prison, which could house twenty prisoners, more if needed. A feeling of awkwardness came over Olivia as she laid eyes on the military's *base* as Gavin had put it, because she'd not imagined it to be so surreal. The confounding thought of military life taking place above the residents' heads, of running the entire show, was a new experience to Olivia. She hadn't considered the full impact of her decision until her eyes had seen it for themselves. It made her realize that big brother watching from above was in full effect in the vault.

Gavin stopped outside the control center. "That's Division One. Not as big as you'd thought, huh?"

"Bigger actually," she said, glancing around. Her eyes fell on the soldier inside the control center who sat with his feet propped up on a machine. "He seems bored," Olivia said.

Gavin turned to see what she saw and immediately pounded on the large window, getting the relaxed soldier's attention. The man looked up, trying to hold back a yawn, but when he noticed Gavin was the source of the banging, he quickly pulled his legs off the machine they were occupying and resituated himself to an attentive posture.

"That's Davis," Gavin said. "He's our main control operator. As you can see, the job isn't all that exciting."

"He has plenty of monitors," Olivia said, as she saw four above him and a larger screen on which Davis seemed able to pull up any camera feed he so desired. She watched as he flipped back and forth between the options, finally resting on a live stream of the garden. "Do they watch everyone from here?" Olivia asked, astounded and slightly offended to think she was being watched and hadn't known it.

"As much as they can," Gavin said.

"I've never noticed any cameras. Are they in our rooms too?" Olivia dared to ask, images of what she may have done in front of the cameras popped into her mind, and she began to feel a bit freaked out.

Gavin laughed. "No. We only have a few and those have been moved to critical areas where we don't want restricted residents fooling around, like medical rooms or storage units. I know we have a small community, but valuables need to be guarded."

Relief washed over Olivia's face at the confirmation that her privacy was intact. "Why guard storage units? I thought they were locked up?"

"They can be broken into, and if that happened we'd have it in our database on the camera. Just because we survived the same doesn't mean we *are* the same. People still have bad intentions, even in the vault, and we watch for that."

Olivia nodded, finding it hard to believe that anyone who'd experienced what they'd all survived together would steal, especially when everything was already provided. "I don't know who would do that. I mean everyone knows that we have a limited amount of resources. It would be impossible for them to get away with it."

"Doesn't mean they won't try," Gavin said. "Don't worry about that. You won't have to monitor such things. You'll be mostly trained to understand our protocols and continue your engineering. We might add duties later on, but that would be a long time from now. Come on, let's get you that uniform."

Olivia smiled, just as an alarm in the control center went off.

Gavin bolted through the control center door. "Davis?" He shouted.

Davis pushed a button, turning off the alarm, and then flipped a switch. "Go ahead," he said. No answer.

Olivia rushed into the room. "What was that?"

Gavin put up his hand, signaling for her to be silent. "Davis?"

"I'm trying, Sir," Davis said in a rush. "Go ahead, Adams."

Another panicked male voice accompanied by heavy gasps came over the control-center speakers. "We have a problem," Adams said.

Gavin pointed at Davis to press the intercom button. "Adams, this is Captain Grant. This better be good, considering you set off the vault's general alarm."

Adams' panicked voice returned on the overhead. "Yes Sir. It's bad. It's really bad."

The intensity in his voice made goose bumps suddenly appear on Olivia's arms.

Gavin stared at Davis, then Olivia. "What's bad, Adams?" Gavin asked.

Adams' heavy breath pounded throughout the room like a heavy bass for several moments before he answered. "I think he's dead," Adams mumbled in pain.

The entire room fell silent.

Gavin reacted with a calm and collected expression as he ordered Davis to relay Adams' location to medical and then send over four more soldiers in case of a lockdown. Without another word, Gavin rushed out of Division One and Olivia followed. When he noticed her tagging along, he ordered her to return to Division One. She couldn't argue with him because at the same time two soldiers checked in with him and they all took off in a hurry. Olivia watched as Gavin and the two soldiers disappeared.

When Gavin arrived, Adams stood over several medical doctors while they worked on the body. Gavin leaned in seeing the face of a man. His eyes were closed and trickles of blood had begun to run down his jaw. "He's not dead?" Gavin asked the doctors.

"Almost," the doctor shouted back.

"What happened here?" Gavin asked Adams.

Adams shook his head before he spoke. "I tried to calm him down, Sir. He was hysterical and then he came at me, and I had to."

"You did this?" Gavin asked in horror.

"He wouldn't stop coming. Look, he had a knife," he said, pointing to the ground where a small kitchen knife lay. "I didn't want to hurt him, but he came at me."

Gavin glanced at the two doctors moving around the wounded resident, then back at Adams.

"Why'd he come at you?" Gavin asked.

Adams didn't answer.

"Answer me. Why?" Gavin shouted.

Adams shook his head. "I only hit him because he came at me."

Gavin turned to the nearest soldier. "Lock him up. Now."

The soldier grabbed Adams and escorted him away. Gavin turned to another soldier. "Make sure no one else comes down these halls. See if anyone saw anything. This can't get out. You hear me?"

"Yes, Sir," the soldier said.

Olivia waved as Sophie plopped down in a seat next to her. The Grand Hall was still quite empty, due to it being a few hours before dinner.

"Did you hear that alarm?" Sophie asked as she shifted in her seat.

Olivia's eyes widened. "You heard it?"

"Well, yeah, the entire vault heard it," Sophie said.

"Yeah." Olivia knew she shouldn't tell Sophie what she overheard in the control room. She kept her mouth shut.

Sophie continued. "I wonder what is going on. That's the second time it's gone off since we've been here."

"It's probably nothing again," Olivia lied, reminding herself she can't share this information with her friend. It wasn't allowed.

The major had told her just that morning, and she didn't want to find out how she might be punished. Then an alarming thought crossed her mind, *Someone is actually dead inside the vault.* A dead body lay somewhere inside, and she couldn't say anything about it. She thought she was going to explode when Sophie shrugged her shoulders.

"Guess so. I'm not going to walk all the way back to Division Six just to check. I've got to make sure dinner is ready. It's probably a drill anyhow. Well, if it's a fire, I'll smell it coming."

Olivia jumped on the opportunity to change the subject. "Busy, huh?"

"Yeah, I'm busy," she vented. "David didn't come back from lunch, and I got stuck cleaning dishes. When he gets here, he's going to get an earful from me." Sophie began to nod as if she'd just gotten an idea and then made a pointing gesture into the air. "I'll make him do all the dinner dishes by himself, that's what I'll do," she said in a rush of anger.

"Wow." Olivia was surprised to see her friend agitated.

Sophie exhaled deeply. "Sorry. It's just been a bad day."

"I can tell. You never have bad days," Olivia said.

Sophie wrinkled her brow. "I wish that were true."

"What's wrong? I mean besides David?"

"Nothing. Well." She lowered her voice to a whisper. "It's Albert." She looked around making sure no one else was around. "You remember how he was transferred into the garden and out of supplies?"

Olivia nodded.

"Well, I heard he was giving out things for favors or other items."

Olivia held back the information Gavin had shared that had supported that rumor.

Sophie continued, "And, well, I didn't believe them. I've been seeing him secretly, and I snuck into his room one night." Sophie got nervous and began looking around again. "I shouldn't be telling you this. I don't even know if it's what I think it is."

"It's okay," Olivia said.

"I saw pills. Not just a bottle, but *bottles* of pills. God, Olivia. I think he's been dealing them or something, because I saw a list of names beside the pills. And then, I remembered how he knew so much about certain drugs, recreational drugs. We'd only been talking about them because I'd mentioned college, but he knew so much about them and I'd written it off until last night. God, Olivia, what should I do?"

Olivia shook her head as the information confirmed Gavin's theory on a community that does bad things just because they still can. "Oh, Sophie. That's serious."

"I know." She rubbed her face.

Olivia swallowed. "Look. I can help you if you want. It's why I came here to see you. I was just accepted in a transfer, my job doesn't change, just my classification, and I can help."

Sophie's brow scrunched. "What classification?"

"I'm in Division One now. Moved today."

Sophie's eyes widened. "And I just told you everything," she said slowly as if she'd realized a horrifying secret.

"No. No, it's okay," Olivia defended.

Sophie threw her hands up as if she were warding off a curse. "Olivia. You can't say anything. If they... if anyone finds out! You don't understand. You're a kid. You don't see what can happen if... please, I'm begging you, don't say anything!"

Olivia ignored the kid remark as she saw fear in her friend's eyes. "But Sophie. I can help. You can trust me."

Sophie hissed her next words. "The only thing you can do for me is keep your mouth shut. I was crazy to tell you. Just by knowing, I could be..." She crossed her arms and took a breath. "Oh, God." She exhaled deeply. "Look. I won't see him again. Don't mention me. Please don't mention me," she pleaded.

"I wouldn't. I won't," Olivia promised.

Sophie rose to leave.

"Wait. Let's meet tonight and get your mind off it."

Sophie stared at her as if she'd gone mad. "You realize we can't be friends anymore, don't you?"

Olivia watched as her friend walked away.

Chapter 17

Locking down the vault was one precaution used by the military to sustain safety and control over any dangerous situation that might arise. If a lockdown was ordered, residents would be escorted to their rooms where their guidance counselor would account for each resident until ordered otherwise. The vault had never been locked down, and it was a hard choice for Gavin to make. Considering that a soldier had committed an act of violence on a resident wasn't going to be an easy issue to tackle. Gavin didn't want to draw attention to the occurrence, fearing that a permanent rift between soldiers and residents would be the outcome. He decided against the lockdown, at least until the major stepped in and pushed for it.

The major wasn't reassured when Gavin explained that no witnesses were found and that everything was being dealt with internally. He also wasn't convinced that Adams had done anything wrong. The major had spoken with the soldier, finding that he'd simply defended himself against a hostile resident and that others may be involved, meaning a lockdown was the proper protocol. Gavin explained that he'd conducted several interviews on his own, discovering that the resident in question had punched Adams in a previous scuffle and had been demoted to a position as a kitchen dishwasher soon after because of it. The emotional overload the resident had to be facing didn't satisfy the major, and he'd simply said, "The resident deserved the demotion for attacking a soldier." He then instructed Gavin to use it as an opportunity to search each resident's room, finally getting ahold of the guilty parties who'd been illegally smuggling and dealing drugs.

When Gavin protested that an irrevocable rift would surely happen if the military showed that type of domination over the residents, the major had merely chuckled and said, "That's our role in this, is it not? This will remind them, especially the ones who've thought otherwise. We need to stop the few who think they can go against the rules. This is not a democracy where my orders will be questioned. You will do as ordered by your superior, Captain. I don't have the patience to teach you what you should already know. What I say is the law here, and if you forget it, I can surely take away the favor as fast as I gave it. Remember that you came to me asking me for help in obtaining a certain young lady. Well, I held true to my word, and you swore an oath the day you joined the army. So keep it, or you might find yourself in a cell, and that young lady who you seem to be so fond of, well, she won't be yours as you so requested. She'll be someone else's. I'll make sure of it."

If Gavin could have said no, he would have. Though the thought of standing up to the major crossed his mind with a profound reassurance that it would be the right thing to do, his heart told him differently. He wouldn't be the only one affected by a rash moment of insubordination. No, a lot of other people might also suffer for his actions. The image of Olivia possibly being hurt while he sat in a cell forced him to shut off his anger as he said, "Yes, Sir. Lockdown will commence."

The major appeared satisfied with Gavin's answer, and when he departed he began to whistle a cheery tune.

With a heavy conscience, Gavin ordered a lockdown.

As soon as Sophie left Olivia at the table, a male soldier entered the Grand Hall and announced in a deep voice, "All residents must return to their rooms immediately."

Olivia watched as Sophie faced the soldier. "Dinner is being finished. Surely it can wait?" she asked in haste.

The soldier didn't move from his position as he raised his voice and ordered, "Return to your rooms now."

The three food preps emerged from behind the food line, staring back and forth between one another as they passed Sophie.

"Wait," she said, staring at her workers. They hesitated for a moment, looking at the soldier. "If dinner is going to be ruined, can you at least tell me why?" she asked the soldier.

The soldier showed his impatience by widening his stance as he shifted toward Sophie and her workers as if preparing for an attack. "If you don't go now, I will force you," he threatened.

That got the three workers' attention as they scurried quickly out of the Grand Hall, leaving the soldier to assess Olivia and Sophie. When he took a step toward Sophie, Olivia jumped to her feet and spoke, "I'll escort her," Olivia volunteered, not wanting her friend or ex-friend to get into any trouble.

The soldier focused on Olivia. "You need to return to your room as well."

"My room is in Division One now; I transferred in today. I can take her," she said.

"You. You're the one?" he asked with a strange grin.

The one? Had they heard of her being transferred in? Was anything a secret?

Olivia nodded. "Yes, I'm one of the transfers, but since I'm in

Division One, I'll escort Sophie to her room."

"You're the only one," he corrected her. "Where's your uniform?" the soldier asked.

"I haven't picked it up yet," she said.

"Return to Division One for your orders. I'll make sure she's returned to her room." He moved to grab Sophie, who threw up her hands.

"I don't need to be escorted. I'm going," she yelled, walking toward the exit of the Grand Hall in the direction of Division Six. "You two can go back to your duty," she said, leaving Olivia and the soldier alone.

Rejected by her friend and finding out that she too must return to her room, Olivia did as instructed. What else could she do?

The lockdown was in full effect. All residents had been re-stricted to their own rooms, where they sat awaiting word from their guidance counselors. Residents asked many questions of the soldiers as to what was going on, but a lockdown meant no com-munication. Each soldier's goal was to only get everyone to their room, even if it was by force. Those were the required actions, and that's what occurred. Soldiers herded each and every resident of the vault to their respective rooms. A few residents, irritated by being ordered around, had to be forced. By the time each division was accounted for, injuries were sustained: Two men suffered a blow to the face, another a sprung wrist, another a bloody nose, and yet another two bruised ribs.

When Gavin found out about the harmed men, the soldiers responded with accusations of how those particular residents had refused orders and had become violent; however, Gavin did not see even a single scratch on any of the soldiers. Gavin's hands were tied at that moment. No matter how much he wanted to discipline them for what he believed to be an abuse of power, he understood that the major wouldn't see it that way, so instead he said to each respective soldier who'd conducted their resident confinement with brutal force, "If I find out that you used unnecessary force, I will make sure you spend the next month in a cell." He received the worried expressions he'd hoped for. Even though his thoughts shouted that it wasn't enough, he continued on as he had been ordered by the major.

The guidance counselors searched each room while other soldiers guarded residents in case anyone decided to react poorly to the act of having their privacy invaded. Most residents stood by with a solemn expression, as if they couldn't understand why this was happening, while others lashed out that the personal property of residents was not the soldiers' business. Someone even brought up that they'd paid enough money to keep their room private. Many of the residents had been victims to the search, and Gavin was well aware of it. He knew that the few who'd been breaking the rules would, of course, make it hard on the rest, which always seemed to be the case in life.

By the end of the search, six residents were guilty of having unwarranted items in their possession. One twenty-two-year-old guy who had been assigned to work in the garden had snuck food back to his room, totaling three cases, including alcohol, which he'd probably traded for. This was the usual situation regarding most of the contraband items. Stealing items to have something with which to barter for the other items they wanted seemed to be the most common reason for theft. Another resident caught with contraband was an eighteen-year-old girl who worked as a lab assistant. She'd been lifting several types of narcotics that she seemed to be trading for gourmet desserts, as she was found with far more than she could ever have arrived with. Residents in this position would frequently claim, "That's mine, I brought that in," or "You have no proof it's not mine." Though those arguments may be considered valid for packaged items, the argument would not work for drugs that came from within the vault.

The one resident engaging in illegal activities who didn't come as a big surprise to the soldiers was Albert Rossi. He'd been reassigned to the garden for taking supplies from his previous position. He was found with several bottles of strong pills. He didn't argue, not this time. He, like the others, was immediately sent to a cell. As to how long he'd be staying there, that would be judged by the major himself.

Though the major had been right about using the lockdown to find the residents responsible for the thefts, he'd not been right about the effects on the residents. Gavin saw several unsettling signs of such, just by the way innocent residents now stared at him and his soldiers emptily, as if they had taken something from each and every one of them. Gavin knew exactly what it was. It had actually been taken the first day they stepped inside the vault, only they hadn't realized it until now: Their freedom was nonexistent.

Once the guidance counselors were debriefed, they were instructed to announce the following to the residents: "Several residents have been caught stealing and assaulting other residents. The search is regrettable, but necessary. Please remember we cannot harbor criminals that use our resources for their own personal gain. These resources belong to all of us, not a select few. If you know of anyone else who steals or takes what is not theirs, it is your obligation to report them. If you are found guilty of having access to this knowledge without reporting them, you will receive equal punishment. Your safety is our number one priority."

Once the residents had been instructed as to what had occurred, they were cleared to return to their day. Tension filled the air, and Gavin suspected it wouldn't go away anytime soon.

Olivia stared at the wall in her brand new room located in Division One. *What happened?* she thought. Hit with the sudden realization that death could still occur inside the vault, she'd sat staring at the same wall for what seemed like forever, while heavy thoughts plagued her mind. Was she safe? Was anyone? She had the sudden urge to curl up into a ball, but a knock on the door stopped her impulse.

The door swung open and Gavin came in, shutting the door quickly behind him. He exhaled as he saw her. "Good, you're here."

"Where else would I be?" she asked automatically. "Did you catch him?"

Gavin walked over and took a seat next to Olivia on her bed. "Catch who?"

"The killer."

Gavin shook his head. "There wasn't a killer, no one's dead."

Olivia's eyes widened. "But he said, on the speaker."

"No. The guy's alive. Only bruised up pretty badly."

Olivia sunk down in relief. "What happened?"

Gavin straightened. "Everything's fine. No one's hurt."

Olivia felt like laughing at herself for thinking such dark thoughts. Then she remembered the order that had been given. "But what about everyone being sent to their rooms?"

"It's best you don't know everything. Everyone's out now, the lockdown's over. Things have returned to normal. Wait. How did you know everyone was in their rooms?"

"I was in the Grand Hall and a soldier made an announcement."

"I didn't say you could go there."

Olivia glared at him, offended. "Well, I wish I hadn't. Sophie doesn't ever want to talk to me again."

"Did you tell her what you heard?" he asked, worried.

"No, of course not. I only told her I was transferred, and she freaked out and doesn't want to talk to me anymore."

"Oh."

"Oh, is right. Didn't realize I'd lose my friend."

"It's to be expected. You couldn't stay friends with her anyway. You're not a resident anymore."

Olivia frowned. She wanted to change the subject, scared that she might tell Gavin exactly what Sophie had told her about Albert Rossi. "I know. Well, tell me what happened with the guy who was beat up."

"I can't tell you."

"What? I'm a soldier."

He shook his head. "Doesn't give you clearance."

Olivia bit her lip in frustration. "Great. Well, anything you can tell me?"

"Just that we had to search every resident's room for stolen items and drugs."

"Did you find any?" Olivia asked.

"Yes. We have the thieves in the prison, and the rest of the residents were a bit shaken by the entire experience."

Olivia appeared confused. "Why would that be done after a beating?"

"It was ordered by the major. We've been seeing a lot of items and drugs come up missing, and we've had our suspicions. It actually had nothing to do with the injured dishwasher."

"Dishwasher. David?"

"That's him."

"Did you find out who did it?"

"Yeah. Everything is taken care of. Just don't talk to anyone about this. It's best if you pretend like you don't know anything."

Olivia gave him her lost expression.

He smiled. "Trust me."

"What choice do I have?" she asked with a forced smile.

He resisted the urge to hug her. "Come on. Let's get you that uniform."

A dark grey jacket and matching pants made up her new uniform. In a way it reminded her of her engineering uniform, but this was much more flattering, or so she thought. She'd seen most of the soldiers in this uniform recently; the fatigues seemed to be worn less often. Olivia figured Janet had something to do with that. Olivia didn't know for sure; she'd forgotten to ask Gavin. She'd been more caught up in her thoughts than actually talking with Gavin, and she hated herself for it. Instead of taking the time to enjoy speaking to Gavin with no restrictions placed on them, she'd spent the afternoon in a daze, thinking about the day's events: David being beaten, the residents being searched, and drugs being found. To top it all off, Sophie said they couldn't be friends. Everything seemed to be going wrong.

After Gavin gave her the new uniform, he excused himself as her guide, stating that he had a few things to finish up involving the prisoners before dinner. Olivia hadn't wanted him to go. She'd even tried to inquire about the prisoners, asking if she could accompany him to watch. He'd been quick to say no, that it wasn't going to happen. So she returned to her room and tried on the new uniform, pleased to see that it fit properly on her hips, rear, and thighs. She'd gotten so used to wearing her engineering uniform that she'd forgotten what it felt like to wear different clothes.

She stared into the mirror with her back straight and her feet slightly apart and gave a tiny salute. She felt stupid for doing so and made a funny face. She'd seen the soldiers salute Gavin in such a way, but she didn't feel as if she fit the role even in the uniform, which looked more like a costume to her. Was she really a soldier? She could imagine walking through the Grand Hall wearing her new uniform as people stared at her, thinking, *She's here for our safety*. At least that's what the soldiers repeated on a regular basis to the residents. Would she say it too? She frowned at herself in the mirror. Would she fit in with the other soldiers? She wanted to fit in somewhere. She hadn't fit in with the other residents, not the ones her own age, anyway. She exhaled deeply. This was a new start for her. She would fit in. She had to.

Olivia decided to stop in on Daniel and show him her new

uniform. When she walked into his office unannounced, he was shuffling through several boxes and appeared startled by her. He jumped to his feet with a distorted expression. It quickly vanished as his eyes fell on Olivia's face.

"Olivia," he said in relief.

A half smile crossed her face as she tried to hide her amusement. "Sorry I scared you," she said.

He dropped a small container into the box. "You didn't scare me," he defended. "What are you wearing?"

"My uniform."

He frowned. "You already have one."

"My engineering uniform? I'm a soldier now, and this is what I'm supposed to wear." She raised her arms, modeling it for him.

He shook his head slightly and walked over to his desk, taking a seat. "Well, you work for me, and you'll wear the right uniform."

Olivia frowned. "What? You don't like it?"

He tilted his head. "It's fine if you're a security guard, but you're not, you're an engineer. You don't want the others residents thinking differently."

Olivia didn't understand why he couldn't just say it looked nice on her. If she'd known he'd react this way, she wouldn't have come. "Why? I've been transferred, that's who I am now."

"Is it?"

"What's that supposed to mean?"

He shrugged his shoulders. "You have no idea, do you?"

"Idea? About what?"

"I'm your supervisor, and I say you wear the uniform I issued you. You need to dress based on your job and being a guard is not it. So go change."

Olivia crossed her arms and glared at him. "I'm off duty now. I'll be leaving for the day. It's dinner time."

"Change first," he said in a deep warning voice.

"Sure," she said as she left his office.

Olivia didn't change for two reasons. First, she was completely angry at Daniel's reaction to seeing her in her uniform, and she didn't want to do as he asked, convinced that she wasn't on engineering duty so his wants were meaningless. Second, she was going to sit with Gavin tonight at dinner, and wearing her uniform stated to everyone else that she belonged.

She walked into a busy Grand Hall with her head up and her back straight with one thought in her mind: *Find Gavin.* She saw him immediately in line and walked directly to him, not paying any attention to the irritated stares she received when she greeted him with a short, "Hi," and joined him in line. She wasn't planning on cutting in line, but when she saw the length of it, she realized that if she went to the back she'd probably not get a seat next to Gavin at all. When he motioned for her to go ahead, she decided it was okay. She heard one low grumble from a man two spots behind Gavin, but she ignored it. She felt a slight twinge of guilt, but she wasn't giving up her spot.

Finally, she thought, finally she could stand next to Gavin and not worry that someone might see or that someone might overhear them. Finally she could smile at him and say what was on her mind, mostly. She wasn't going to mention how handsome he looked, even when he didn't smile, even if he seemed lost in serious thought. She picked up her tray and plate and waited to be next for a scoop of carrots. She could sense him standing close to her back and suddenly she felt a flip in her stomach, feeling nervous. She turned her head to the side to peek behind her. He motioned with a nod, signaling her that the line was going on. She spun around and took a scoop of carrots.

She continued down the line, taking one scoop of potatoes and beans. The line began to move faster as she got to the muffins. She took one and reached for a glass of water. When she glanced back to Gavin, she saw him take two muffins and immediately leaned in and whispered, "Two?"

He smiled at her and said, "Here, you can have mine," and placed it on her plate.

She smiled. "I get two as well since I'm a soldier?"

"If you like," he said.

She hesitated as she saw several residents' eyes hatefully staring at her. "Next time I'll get two," she whispered to Gavin.

When she found Gavin's usual seating area with other soldiers, she observed that all their eyes were focused on her. Several soldiers, after seeing her, exchanged a comment between one another, causing a rumble of laughter to explode from the table. She turned to Gavin, who walked past her as if nothing was wrong and told her, "Come on."

Gavin found two empty seats at the end of the table. When Olivia walked up to her seat, a few whistles suddenly exploded from the men. They were quickly silenced when Gavin shot a glare at them. "I'd like you all to meet Olivia Parker, our new recruit. No initiation. I *mean* it."

Olivia gave the soldiers a tiny smile as she took her seat.

No one talked for several minutes. Gavin started eating as if nothing was odd. Olivia began to play with her food, stirring her potatoes with her fork.

"Hey kid, if you don't want those, I'll take them," a male soldier across from her blurted out. Olivia looked up to see a large soldier with blond hair, built like a football player.

"Don't give him any," a black-haired soldier beside him said. Olivia stared at him as he took a bite out of his muffin while his brown eyes stayed on her.

"If she's going to throw it away, she might as well give it to me. That's wasteful," the big, blond soldier said.

"You better eat it up before he takes it," the black-haired soldier said, finishing off the muffin with a second bite.

Olivia peeked over to Gavin, who'd continued to eat his food as if everything was normal.

Olivia slowly took a bite of her potatoes, causing the blond before her to pout.

The black-haired soldier chuckled.

The blond soldier grumbled.

"Take it easy, Eddston. You can have the scraps I don't finish," Gavin said to the blond soldier with a chuckle.

"Mine too," the black-haired soldier laughed. "I'll put it in a brown bag for you and mix it all up, just like old Spot likes."

The blond slammed his fist on the table, causing Olivia to jerk back at the sudden impact.

"Take it easy, Eddston," Gavin instructed to the blond soldier. "Jennings is just jealous he can't gain a pound. Still has a tapeworm," he joked.

Jennings, the black-haired soldier, grunted. "I must," he agreed. "I can't gain any weight in here, especially with these rations."

"Don't you get double?" Olivia spoke without thinking.

Jennings glanced at her. "Yeah, but it's not enough. Not when you have a fast metabolism like me."

"It seems enough for everyone else," Olivia said.

"I'm not everyone else," Jennings said.

"Me neither," Eddston said.

Jennings turned to Eddston, annoyed. "You're a big ogre. You don't have a medical condition that constantly makes you feel like you're starving."

"Medical condition?" Olivia asked.

Gavin jumped in. "Jennings here says he has a fast metabolism, but he's never been diagnosed."

"Because the doctor doesn't believe me," Jennings complained.

"Don't listen to him. He lies about everything," Eddston interjected. "Besides, a fast metabolism isn't a disease, you moron."

"It is too, and I don't lie," Jennings defended.

"You lied about that clothing lady, that tailor."

"Did not, she told me I was cute," Jennings said.

"If you say."

"I do say."

"Ignore them," Gavin said. "They do this every time."

"We do not," Jennings and Eddston said in unison.

"That's why I get here last and leave first, to avoid this," he said with a smile.

Eddston grumbled. "Tell the truth, Grant. It's to avoid him." He pointed to Jennings, "Leaving me here to listen to his woes about the ladies."

"Ladies?" Olivia asked.

"Don't get him started," Gavin said.

"Please don't," Eddston added quickly.

"Thanks, guys," Jennings said. "I always thought you were scared Eddston would steal your tray, Grant."

"That too," Gavin said with a smile.

The three men laughed as Olivia took another bite of her carrots, wondering if these were the great conversations she'd been missing out on. They didn't make any sense to her. Gavin didn't talk to her during the entire meal, instead he shot a few short answers at Jennings or Eddston and mostly ate in silence. Olivia didn't know what to say, not in front of the soldiers, so she listened to their odd conversations, which seemed more like teasing than a full-fledged discussion. When Gavin rose, Olivia quickly followed, even though she'd only finished half her meal. She didn't want to get stuck sitting at that table without him.

"You can stay," he said, staring at her tray.

"Oh, I'm full," she said quickly. "I'll take these for later," she said, shifting her eyes toward her two uneaten muffins.

"Come on then," he said as he walked toward the garbage bins. As Olivia followed, she accidently bumped into another resident, a girl in her early twenties, who, instead of accepting Olivia's apology, shoved her as she hissed, "Stupid, think you're better than us?" A shocked Olivia dropped her entire tray.

Gavin quickly turned. The girl rushed off. "What happened?"

The girl's harsh words replayed in her mind, and she couldn't understand what she'd done to deserve such hatred directed at her. She'd bumped into other residents plenty of times, and no one had ever reacted like that. She hadn't done anything wrong. "I don't know."

"You've lost your muffins," he said.

Olivia shrugged her shoulders, no longer having any kind of appetite for muffins.

Gavin picked up her tray and dropped it off for her while Olivia glanced around the room, noticing several residents staring at her as if she'd done something wrong. A sudden feeling of dread came over her, and all she wanted to do was escape their sight. Just as she began to make her way to the closest exit, she saw Sophie coming out of the kitchen. Olivia stopped mid-pace and smiled. Sophie turned her head and quickly walked in the opposite direction. Olivia bolted out of the Grand Hall, swallowing down the tears that wanted to break through.

Gavin caught up to Olivia. "What's wrong?"

She ignored him as she continued to walk toward Division One.

"You can tell me."

She couldn't, she didn't want to.

He kept pace beside her. "I saw Sophie. Is it because of her?"

Olivia nodded.

"I see. I told you..."

"I know," she interrupted him.

"What did that girl say to you? The one who ran off?"

"Nothing."

"She said something."

"Nothing."

"Okay." He walked with her as she climbed the stairs.

"I'm fine. Need a nap," she said, believing that might make him stop following her, but it didn't.

"Okay. Get one then," he said, while still keeping pace. "I'm going to conduct my rounds."

"Oh."

He smiled. "Hey. I know you're excited about being in a new division, but you know you're not a real soldier."

Olivia rolled her eyes. "I know."

"I think it's best if you don't wear the uniform unless ordered to."

"Why? Then I won't be able to sit with you."

"Sure you can."

"I looked stupid, huh?"

"No. You looked like a soldier, a soldier who ordered everyone in the vault to report to their rooms today and then searched each person's possessions as if they were common thieves. That's what you looked like to them. That's what that uniform will remind them of, and that's the problem."

Olivia didn't argue. She went right to her room without another word.

Chapter 18

A week later Olivia found herself in a restroom, looking at her reflection in the mirror. With a lifted shirt, she touched her belly and imagined it growing big and round. She wondered what it would be like to be pregnant and felt a sudden chill run down her arms as she thought of the girl she'd just seen a few minutes ago, of how it had felt when her right elbow had grazed the girl's belly. It felt more like a firm globe than a stomach. It was kind of creepy, especially when she'd turned around to see what she'd touched and to whom it belonged.

She'd recognized her instantly, right in the ladies bathroom, as the girl who'd emerged months ago from the red door, unable to walk without assistance from two soldiers, the exact same girl who'd looked up with those amazing jade-colored eyes, eyes that Olivia had not forgotten.

It was hard to believe that she'd not seen her since then. How could she have vanished and reappeared six months later? It wasn't quite impossible, not with the way the vault was designed. Olivia had probably only gotten to know about half of the vault's population. Faces seemed familiar, but she hadn't acquainted herself with everyone. The entire interaction of the vault sometimes reminded her of her old neighbors, people she had grown up knowing and politely waving to but never engaging in deep conversations. Small talk in the vault mostly revolved around the topic of food or the lack thereof.

She had, in fact, looked for the Asian girl in the weeks following the afternoon she'd first run into her, and she thought that at least a few times she'd caught a glimpse of her, but she'd been busy with a task or someone had spoken to her, and she'd missed her opportunity. Olivia could have sworn she once saw her in the Grand Hall, but she'd been so far away that she couldn't be sure. To never see her again had seemed statistically unlikely, at least that's what she thought as months went by without a close encounter, but then suddenly she'd appeared, bumping right into her.

Olivia apologized and the girl nodded with downcast eyes. She immediately made the connection and spoke to her. "Hey, I know you. Do you remember me?"

The girl looked up when Olivia started talking and revealed her large green eyes, which was confirmation enough that she was, without a doubt, the girl from the red, restricted-access door.

The Asian girl shook her head, not saying a word.

Olivia was already aware that they were alone before she asked the first question that popped into her mind. "You're pregnant?"

The Asian girl gave her a strange look.

"I mean. Sorry, I only meant that I haven't seen anyone else pregnant here."

The Asian girl stepped to move past Olivia, and Olivia gave the girl ample room to get by with her large belly, but then the girl had suddenly burst into tears. Guilt struck Olivia as she thought she'd somehow upset her, and she promptly apologized as she patted the girl on the back.

The girl's tears ended with a tiny muffled response, "It's not you."

"What is it?" Olivia asked.

The girl wiped her eyes quickly. "This," she said pointing to her own stomach. "It's horrible. I feel horrible."

Olivia's eyes widened as she tried to find something to say, her mind racing with questions. "I, I'm sorry."

The Asian girl turned her red, tearful eyes toward Olivia, who gave her a sympathetic look.

"Not your fault," she said again.

"Oh, I know. I mean. What's wrong?"

The Asian girl shook her head. "Can't talk about it. Please leave me alone."

Olivia removed her hand but decided to still ask the question that had been on her mind for months, "I saw you come out of that red door about six months ago. What did they do to you?"

The Asian girl's mouth dropped open, and she looked stunned from Olivia's comment.

"Please tell me. I can help."

The Asian girl shook her head again. "You can't help me. Look at me. It's too late. They did this to me. They did this!"

"They? Who?"

"The doctors. The…" she broke off, beginning to sob. "And they'll do the same to you," she yelled as she jerked away from Olivia and ran out the door.

Dumbfounded by her comment, Olivia didn't think to follow her, though she immediately wished she had. As she stood in front of the bathroom mirror staring at her own reflection, she knew she should have said more. Olivia had been removed from that worry of being forced to be impregnated when she turned twenty, since she'd transferred to Division One and soldiers weren't held under that obligation. She might not have to go through it, but others would, and that made her sick inside. The reality hit Olivia of what would happen, of what was already happening to the other girls.

She hadn't realized that the vault was already forcing girls to become pregnant. Deep down she'd thought maybe it would never happen, and besides, she thought the five-step plan went according to the steps. The fourth step hadn't been announced, but did it really need to be? Step Four: *Established* stated that within a certain amount of time, all residents will be comfortably adjusted to their daily lifestyles and needs. Hadn't that already happened? Everyone was adjusted, yet were they truly comfortable? Who would decide that?

No, Olivia didn't imagine that step four would be announced. It would be assumed. The hard truth was that step five had been going on right below everyone's radar! Why hadn't she heard about this? Why hadn't anyone heard about this? Could the girls be too ashamed to mention it? Everyone would know soon enough as the girls began to round out. *How can no one know?* Olivia's mind raced. *What did the girl mean when she said 'they,' that the doctors got her pregnant?*

Step Five: *Mature* had started, and Olivia hadn't given it another thought since her transfer. *Mature*, which stated that the vault's residents will be fully ready and prepared for the next generation. Next generation? That was the girls' responsibility? Their burden!

Olivia shoved down her shirt, zipped up her jumpsuit, and began to pace back and forth in the ladies' bathroom. Hollowness in her gut took root as she wondered if Gavin knew and had done nothing. Worse, what if he supported it? *No*, she thought quickly. He'd gotten her out of it. Why hadn't he said anything? *He hasn't said much about the subject at all*, she reminded herself. He'd said that she couldn't know everything. This must be one of those things, and it frightened her to imagine no way out for the other girls. It wasn't fair.

Her first thought was to run to Gavin and demand he tell her what was going on, but he'd probably stop her before she got a word out. She didn't know what to do. What could she do?

She returned to the garden where she'd left her tools after repairing a water valve. Once she'd gathered her things, she decided to return them to the engineering room and end her shift for the day. No other urgent repairs needed her attention, and she figured Daniel would be too busy with his own work that he'd never notice. She thought if she hurried, she might be able to run into Gavin before dinner.

It had only been a week since she'd been given her soldier uniform and then that very day told not to wear it by both Gavin and Daniel. She'd finally done as asked after experiencing several more negative encounters that evening while wearing it, mostly snide remarks said to her by angry residents in light of the search the other soldiers had conducted. Even though she hadn't been involved, she was treated as if she'd been the very one to shake them all down. Additional convincing to return to her engineering wardrobe wasn't needed. Daniel had even worn a smitten look on his face the next day when he'd seen her in her old jumpsuit, and she'd merely ignored it.

Things seemed different since the vault's lockdown a week ago. She'd found out the reason while overhearing one of the soldiers at dinner that a lockdown would probably become a monthly thing. "Get them by surprise," a soldier had said. Gavin had not been there. Olivia had begun to sit regularly with Eddston and Jennings if she beat Gavin to the Grand Hall. She'd gotten up enough courage to join them alone once Jennings had given her a nod one evening as she'd been standing in the middle of the room, searching for Gavin with no luck. They'd made her feel as welcomed as two bickering pals could. She mostly ignored them or added a few sarcastic comments to Jennings' uncensored remarks that usually pertained to Eddston being a large, clumsy ox. She wasn't as clever as they were, so she mostly bombed by chiding, "That isn't nice." They'd snicker at her for her feminine compassion; apparently being rude to each other was the point.

The biggest change she'd noticed was mostly of a feeling of

tension. The pressure that followed the lockdown had not gone away. Some residents seemed on edge or nervous, while others seemed tightly wound up, casting strange glances at soldiers. Jennings brought it up one night at dinner, describing the odd looks he'd started to receive, which reminded him of his tour in Iraq and the people there. Gavin had settled the men by saying, "This is why it's important for the residents to be reminded that we're here for their safety, that all encounters with them should be careful and not harmful." Olivia had tried to put on a smile after that toward the other residents, but they'd already associated her with the soldiers and so she was given the cold shoulder treatment too.

Sophie still wouldn't talk to her. Olivia had even gone so far as to ask Daniel if he would give her a chocolate, which he'd not cared for. He relented, but when Olivia presented it to Sophie as a peace offering, she'd only stared at her as if she'd gone mad and whispered, "Go away, please." Then she looked around to make sure no one saw their exchange and jetted off as if Olivia had a highly contagious disease.

The only reason Olivia hadn't broken down in tears that week was because of the small moments she was able to spend with Gavin. He was just as busy as she was during the days, not really having time to get into a deep conversation about what was happening inside the vault, and a small part of Olivia didn't want to know anyway. She had a bad feeling the entire week and hoped it would go away. When it didn't, she began to ignore it. The comfort of sitting next to Gavin for meals or sometimes seeing him in the Division One hallway reassured her that he'd be there if she needed him. She'd even been right about his room. He was directly beside hers, so when she would go to sleep at night or wake up from a nightmare, she would stare at the wall that now separated them and somehow feel secure.

One important conversation she hadn't yet worked up the courage to engage Gavin in was on the topic of her feelings, or at least letting him know finally that she'd never meant those harsh words so long ago. Somehow she thought if she were to apologize for acting like a child, he might not see her as one anymore. If she showed him that she'd changed, he'd see her as an adult instead of the kid. That was one large obstacle she was still trying to figure out, because he continued to treat her and speak to her as if she were his sister.

At one point, she'd suspected that Gavin punched Daniel in the face because he perhaps did like her as more than a friend. His angered expression when she'd told him that she had been the one to come on to Daniel, even though she hadn't, seemed to support her hunch. Yet his recent treatment of her suggested otherwise. Did he have the same feelings? She'd been trying to think of a plan that would help her discover the truth until today, when she'd seen the Asian girl's pregnancy. All she could think about now was finding out what Gavin knew about it. She cringed at the thought of him allowing it, but he'd said in the past that he had to follow orders, that if he didn't, he'd be just like those residents in the vault's prison.

The residents who'd been searched and found guilty of stealing would remain in their cells until the major decided each one's punishment. At dinner throughout the week, Olivia had heard rumors about them remaining in those cells for months or years, while others said they'd be given a lower-grade job during the day but spend their nights locked up since the vault still needed workers. While on duty, she'd even overheard a few residents gossiping about the prisoners, insisting that they deserved to get punished because they'd ruined everyone's freedom with their actions and they'd been wasting resources. The most interesting comment she'd heard, though, was this: "People will act out when they're confined and ordered around, we just happen not to be those few."

Olivia placed the box of tools onto a counter in the office, deciding that she'd probably need them the next day. As she began to exit, she heard Daniel. "Where are you going?"

She groaned internally at having been caught. "Leaving."

"Done for the day then?" he said, suspiciously looking at the toolbox she'd laid down.

"Since nothing else is on the list." She smiled awkwardly.

He shrugged his shoulders. "Sure, why not?"

"Thanks," she said passing him for the door.

"But you have to do me a favor first," he said, causing her to turn around.

"Favor?"

"I was going to ask you tomorrow, but since you owe me, I'm assuming you'll say yes."

"Great. So I have no choice."

"Of course you have a choice. Everyone has a choice."

"What is it?"

"It hasn't been announced yet, but since it's almost Thanksgiving, the major is going to be holding a banquet. The full spread, meat mostly. I think he's trying to lighten the mood, at least since the raids. Everyone has been on tiptoes. A nice attempt, I'll give him that. Anyway, it's probably going to be the event of the year, and I'd like you to accompany me. You'll finally have somewhere to go in that yellow dress of yours."

Olivia hesitated in answering him as she allowed his question to run through her mind a second time. "Accompany you?"

He smiled. "Yes."

"On a date?"

He raised a brow. "If you'd like it to be." Olivia's blank stare prompted him to continue. "I hope I haven't made you feel uncomfortable."

What do I say, she thought as she watched his smile start to disappear. In that instant, she realized this was it, this was the perfect plan she'd been waiting for. "Yes," she said, "I'll go. Sounds fun."

His blue eyes lit up and his smile returned to a large grin as he said, "Great! Well, enjoy the rest of your day then."

As Olivia squeezed past Daniel to leave, she forced a smile and waved goodbye.

Back in her room, after speculating as to why Daniel had asked her to the first big event in the vault, she'd come up with two possible reasons: One, they were friends, and he wanted to do something nice for her, or two, he liked her romantically. The second thought had to be untrue. He'd even said that he was her boss and must behave as one. She decided that probably he just wanted to show her a fun time. He'd even mentioned the yellow dress that she'd never worn since that night the alarm had gone off and Daniel had given her wine. On several occasions, she'd complained to Daniel about how there was nothing to do in the vault, nowhere to go and dress up. He knew that she had no real friends either. He knew that no one else would ask her. In the end, she figured that he'd asked her out of friendship. Luckily, he had asked at the perfect time to serve an ulterior purpose as well. She needed his help, and Daniel was the only one who could improve her adult image. She needed to prove that she wasn't a kid anymore, and this was going to be a great, in-your-face show that Gavin wouldn't miss.

Olivia still hadn't found Gavin as she arrived for dinner at the Grand Hall, and she winced at the thought of enduring another battle of testosterone at the soldiers' table. Last night Eddston had vowed to show Jennings just how strong of a man he was, and Olivia wasn't interested in seeing how that would play out. So when she saw Daniel cutting across the dining hall, she seized the opportunity to escape their usual brutish conversations and find out what the Thanksgiving event was all about.

She crossed the Grand Hall as casually as possible as she descended upon the table at which Daniel sat. She stopped directly in front of him. "Can I join you?"

Daniel looked up. The left corner of his lip rose slightly. "Of course." He glanced at the empty chair beside him.

She pulled out the chair with one hand while setting her tray down on the table with the other. She plopped down in the seat. When she looked back up, she met Daniel's ocean-blue eyes and smiled. For some reason, he suddenly made her nervous, and she struggled to quickly find a topic. She knew immediately that he would be wondering why she joined him for dinner. She never had before, not when she'd been considered a resident and not since she'd transferred to the military division, as she'd dined with the other soldiers every night. "So," she quickly blurted out, "how'd the rest of your day go?"

He chuckled. "I was swamped. Shouldn't have let you go, but the favor was worth it I suppose." He shrugged as he continued to stare at her.

She shifted in her seat and reached for her glass of water. "Somehow I don't believe you." She took a sip, ignoring his obvious gazing.

He smiled. "You don't? I'll have to prove it then."

Olivia stared at the biscuit on her plate. "How? By unfixing everything you fixed?" she asked sarcastically.

He leaned back in his chair and crossed his arms, still keeping his eyes on her.

Olivia glanced up when he didn't answer her question, noticing that he hadn't taken a bite out of his food.

He smiled. "I didn't mean that."

"Huh?"

"The favor. Its worth will be proven."

"How do you prove a favor?" she asked.

He laughed. "Guess you'll find out."

Olivia shook her head, not understanding what he meant in the least. At first she assumed that he'd made an attempt at a joke, but as she took a bite out of her biscuit, she didn't see any grimace that would indicate he'd bombed or a shrug of his shoulders that relayed a less successful delivery of humor. Instead, a giant grin covered his face, and she decided that whatever it was must have gone over her head, so she simply ignored it.

When he began to eat, Olivia relaxed as if they were back in their workroom taking a machine apart and were simply having a conversation while drinking their coffee. She went right into her questions of what the Thanksgiving event would be like. Though he didn't have much information, he assured her that she'd have a wonderful time and that she should treat it like another prom. That comment had suddenly made her sad, but she'd pushed it aside, finding a new question to ask him.

"What was your prom like?" she asked.

"Never had one." He took a bite of his mashed potatoes.

She quickly recalled that he'd attended MIT in his early teens, remembering that although he was only two years older than her, he'd lived his college life already—the college life she should be living. She knew that his mind was way beyond hers, but socially they were the same. He'd missed many of the same things as her, and she felt a sudden bond. "I never had a prom either." She hadn't ever told him she'd been in high school at the time of the disaster. She never talked about it. They never talked about life before the vault. They acted as if nothing of interest occurred before the doors sealed.

"You didn't?" he asked surprised. "I would have assumed you went with the quarterback."

She laughed as she thought of being asked by Jonathan Bran, the hottest guy in her class, who she'd fantasized about more than once as the lead character in her mother's romance novels. She continued to laugh at the image she got of Jonathan, whose mere smile would turn her into a zombie who could only nod or shake her head whenever he asked whether she'd finished her homework or if she'd be at the game.

Daniel's interest peaked with a raise of his brow and a smirk on his face. "Was he one ugly guy then?"

Olivia shook her head.

He leaned in to encourage her to go on.

When she finally caught her breath, she spoke, "No. I mean. Uh. Nevermind." She shifted in her seat nervously.

He tried to hide his smile behind tight lips, but failed miserably. "Oh, no. Was he as funny as I am?"

She shook her head. "No one could be as funny as you," she said with a sarcastic note.

He winked at her. "You'd better mean that." Even though he obviously knew he'd walked right into it. He coaxed her to go on with her story. "Please."

She rolled her eyes. "Fine."

He waited for her to go on.

"I never was asked."

His skeptical expression made her shrug. "Never asked?" he said in disbelief. "That can't be right."

She glanced down at her right hand as she grabbed her glass and turned it around and around. "Never," she said softly. "Not that I expected it."

He watched her fidget with the glass before turning his attention back to her face. "Why wouldn't you expect it?"

She peeked up to see his eyes intensely staring at her, and she quickly redirected her gaze back on the glass she was turning. "Well, I, uh, never, uh, you know..."

He prompted her to go on. "Never?"

"You know," she hesitated. "Dated."

"Why not?" he asked surprised.

She shrugged. "I don't know." But she did know. She didn't want to get into it, the fact that she thought she needed to focus solely on school and her future, not on boys who merely saw her as another notch on their belts. Now, those reasons seemed silly, childish almost. It made her sad to think of the things she'd missed out on, would miss out on, because she'd been so focused on one task instead of just living.

Crossing his arms and placing his elbows on the table, he leaned in closer to her. "I know," he said, causing her to look up at his sincere expression, awaiting the answer.

She wanted him to tell her why. Could he see it on her face?

He gently extended his hand and brushed a curl from her cheek. The brief sensation made a sudden heat cross her face. She didn't pull back as he allowed his hand to linger on her a little longer than needed. He continued, "And their loss is my gain." She stared at him as her breath caught in her throat. She wanted to ask him what he knew, but before she could, he withdrew his hand and spoke again, "I'll be your first then." A sideways grin formed on his face.

"My first?" she whispered without thinking.

"Yeah." He tilted his head and narrowed his eyes on her hand that suddenly stopped turning the glass. "If that's okay?" The tone in his voice reflected a hint of worry. "We do have a date, don't we?"

The concern in his voice made her smile. "I guess we do."

He grinned. "See, we both get to attend our first dance together. I'll make sure you don't stop laughing."

She gave him a skeptical look.

He put his hand on hers. "You were too intimidating. That's why they never asked you."

She didn't believe him, but she didn't pull her hand away from his. It actually felt nice. She hid her feelings by sarcastically announcing, "Still not funny."

"That's not a joke," he said seriously. He took his hand away and leaned back in his chair. "I'd probably be just as intimidated. Maybe I was, but…"

His confession made her stomach jump. She heard him say he wasn't joking, but what he'd admitted seemed so out there. "But what?" she asked, leaning in.

He smiled. "But I have a bigger I.Q., at least that's what I'm told."

She didn't laugh. She rested her elbow on the table and leaned her face against her hand as she looked at him. He didn't break out into a chuckle either. She waited. When she saw him open his mouth to speak, a tray slammed down beside her. They both looked up to see two male residents in their late twenties sit down beside them, one giving a slight nod and turning back to his friend as they continued a conversation. Olivia turned her attention back to Daniel, who had risen to his feet.

"See you tomorrow," he said casually.

She wanted to ask him to wait, but she didn't. "Okay. Goodnight."

He smiled. As she watched him walk toward the garbage bins, her eyes connected with Gavin. She felt a sudden pang of guilt and instead of smiling or waving, she quickly averted her eyes, not knowing why.

She left the Grand Hall immediately, returning to her room and wondering why she couldn't stop thinking of that sensation she got when Daniel's fingers grazed her cheek. She hugged herself, confused by the sudden excitement it brought her. His words repeated in her thoughts. He'd said that he'd be her first date. She smiled thinking of having a first with Daniel. Then, the guilt returned. Why should she feel guilty?

She threw herself on her bed and began to think of having a real date. She imagined a gourmet meal served with champagne and chocolates, and Daniel would be there smiling and laughing beside her. Then, the music would start and he'd ask her to dance, and she'd accept because she'd waited her whole life to be asked. She smiled, thankful for having such a wonderful friend.

Suddenly, the door next to her slammed shut. She knew it was Gavin. She jumped out of her bed and peeked out of her own door into the hallway, making sure it was clear. She hurried to Gavin's door and lightly knocked. No answer. Worried that someone might see her hovering outside, she quickly turned the knob, opened the door, rushed inside, and swung it shut. Her eyes fell on Gavin's naked chest.

"I'm so sorry," Olivia shrieked as she flipped back around. "I didn't know you were naked."

He spoke with a growl. "Not quite, but I would have been if you'd waited a few seconds longer to burst into my room without knocking," he complained.

Olivia slowly peeked over her shoulder, noticing that he had told the truth. His shirt was off, and he'd been standing behind a chair that had obstructed her view, making her for the briefest of moments believe he was not clothed. "Sorry," she said, while still staring at his well-defined chest that she couldn't seem to tear her eyes away from.

He pulled a white T-shirt on. "You can't be barging in here like that. What the hell is the emergency?" he demanded.

Olivia's mind had gone blank.

"Well?" His deep blue eyes stared back at her with annoyance.

"I, I didn't mean to. I just wanted to talk," she managed to get out.

"And it couldn't wait?" He grumbled.

She looked at him innocently. "Uh. No."

He exhaled. "Well, next time knock," he scolded.

"Okay," she said without thinking, but then she remembered she had.

He waved his hand in the air. "Go ahead then. I don't have much time."

She nodded and tried to think of what her reason was for coming. She felt flustered as she looked down at her hands and back up at him, while a burst of heat radiated across her face. "I, um. I have something to tell you."

One corner of his lip lifted with amusement as he watched her nervous gestures play out before him. "I'm waiting."

She swallowed. The image of the pregnant Asian girl flashed in her mind, reminding her of the seriousness of her visit. She straightened her back. "I, uh, saw something that had me worried, and I obviously can't ask just anyone, in case, you know, someone is untrustworthy like you told me, so I thought you'd know what to do, and I can't wait around."

He frowned. "Can you possibly be anymore indirect?"

"What?"

"Exactly." He shook his head. "Olivia, just spit it out."

She took a deep breath and forced her eyes to stay off his chest and on his face, but his eyes burned an uncomfortable sensation across her face, so she cast a glance to the floor. She couldn't come out and say it directly, though; instead, she hinted at the subject to see if he'd reveal what he knew first. "What if I told you someone was pregnant?" She peeked up at him.

His mouth fell open and his eyes glazed over as if he'd been shocked by her question. "Someone?" he asked. Just then, a spark of anger ignited in his eyes and he burst into a mad dash for the door, his voice erupting into a roar, "I'm going to kill him!"

After a short delay while she wondered whom he was going to kill, Daniel's bloody face flashed in Olivia's mind.

Gavin had already thrown open the door.

"No, wait!" she shouted, but he didn't hear her or didn't care, because he left her staring at an empty doorway with one thought in her mind: She had to stop him. She shot through the doorway, searching. He was almost to the end of the hallway when she broke into a run. "Gavin, stop!" she shouted. He ignored her as he turned down the corridor that led to the stairwell.

Olivia cursed. She knew if he reached the stairwell she'd never be able to stop him, not in front of the residents. She couldn't allow him to reach Daniel, who'd have no idea why he was even being attacked. *What the hell is wrong with Gavin? Why would he think that?* The image of his face in the Grand Hall flashed in her mind, reminding her of the guilt she'd felt at that moment. *It can't be*, she thought, but as she tore down the hallway after him, she felt excited at the thought that maybe he was jealous after all.

When she saw him about to open the door to the stairwell,

instead of shouting out to him she ducked her head and picked up her speed, on course directly toward him. At that moment he turned, his angered expression washed away by shock as she collided right into him, grabbing hold of his shoulders for balance while he tried to brace himself for the impact, causing them both to tumble down intertwined. He grunted, landing flat on his back, the wind knocked right out of his lungs. His arms tightened around Olivia, who lay directly on top of him.

Olivia felt the jolt of air knocked out of Gavin and immediately tried to shift her weight. She felt his lungs through his chest gasping for air, but his arms stopped her from moving and she lay as still as possible until she felt the normal rise and fall return. Then she lifted her head from his chest, pushing her body up. His arms loosened and his hands came to rest on her lower back. She stared down into his eyes, her hair toppling down around his face as she whispered in a tiny voice, "Sorry."

His warm breath hit her face as he let out a gust of air. "Are you all right?" His deep voice sent a shudder through her. She nodded slowly. "Then get off me," he grumbled. He dropped his hands from her and waited for her to move. She didn't.

Olivia recognized the tiny spark of anger in his eyes return and acted on it by crossing her arms on his chest and continuing to hold her ground. She stared right back at him and said, "No, not until you listen to me."

He grabbed her hips. "Please, get off."

When she felt his hands begin to move her off of him, she dropped her head down to his shoulder, pushed her weight toward him and locked her hands under his shoulder.

"What are you doing?" he asked, half-irritated and half-surprised. He continued to lift her easily.

"I'm not the one who's pregnant," she said from behind gritted teeth into his ear.

Instantly, he dropped her back down and turned his head toward her, their faces but an inch from one another. "You're not?"

he said, his blue eyes searching hers.

"No," she said, hurt. "I saw someone else who was and wanted to talk to you about it," she defended.

His expression immediately softened.

"I haven't even ever been on a date," she whispered, the embarrassment of it all radiating through her voice.

"You haven't?" he softly responded.

She shook her head. His eyes shifted to her lips and hers to his. A pleasant rush flushed through her body where hers pressed against him.

"I… I overreacted then?"

She nodded. The magnetism to move closer overwhelmed her, and when she looked from his lips to his eyes she could have sworn he said yes to her silent question. Just when she thought she'd explode from the anticipation, from behind her a male voice erupted into a cheer, "It's about time!"

Olivia and Gavin looked up to see Eddston and Jennings standing right in the stairwell's doorway, grinning down like a pair of delighted idiots. In one fast motion, Gavin effortlessly lifted Olivia off of him and rose to his feet, assisting Olivia up and quickly letting go when it was clear she had her balance.

"Move along boys," Gavin ordered. "The kid's a klutz," he said annoyed.

Jennings and Eddston looked from Olivia's red face and back to Gavin's unreadable face and snickered. "Sure," Jennings said with a wicked grin.

"Move on," Gavin ordered.

Jennings did as told, glancing back once and turning to Eddston to whisper, "If she's a kid, I'm in diapers myself."

Olivia glanced up to Gavin's face and blushed.

Gavin shook his head. "Go back to your room," he ordered in his military fashion.

Olivia sighed. "You really do think I'm a kid?" she asked, disappointed.

202

"You are a kid, Olivia."

His words stabbed at her heart. "Then why'd you want to kill Daniel when you thought…?"

"Because you're a kid. He has no right," he growled.

"Then who does?"

He didn't say anything.

"He's only two years older than me," she pointed out.

"I knew it," he said.

"Knew what?" she asked slowly.

"That he's overstepping his bounds, again."

Olivia grunted in frustration. "He hasn't, but even if he had, so what? It's my choice."

He stared at her, this time holding back his anger more easily than she'd expected. "I guess you're right, but you are a kid. Can't you see that?"

She shook her head. "No. No, you're the only one who sees that." She couldn't contain her own anger, her voice began to rise with each word. "And if you haven't noticed, the vault is making 'kids' like me pregnant. I saw one today. An Asian girl, and she said she'd been forced. She didn't want it, and they forced her."

"Lower your voice," he ordered. He looked down the hall, making sure no one was around. "She wasn't forced," he whispered. "She came in already pregnant. We just wouldn't give her an abortion. We've had to keep her isolated so she doesn't do herself any harm. No one has been forced to get pregnant," he said. "Not yet," he added softly as if he didn't want to see it happen either.

Olivia stared down at her feet, unable to look at his tortured expression. She could tell in that instant that he was conflicted and felt exactly the same as she on the topic. She also couldn't believe that the girl had been forced to keep the baby due to her own actions. It had been her who had made the decision, who had taken the risk. And how could they let her get rid of it? She answered her own question. *Isn't the vault supposed to save life, not destroy it?* Olivia glanced back up to Gavin. She felt angry and sad and guilty all rolled up into one.

When he turned to leave she said, "I'm not a kid."

He ignored her. When he disappeared into the stairwell, she whispered, "I'll show you I'm not."

Chapter 19

Gavin Grant was finding it hard to be thankful for anything at that particular moment, especially while he watched Daniel Bandt wrap his arms around Olivia. It took every ounce of his strength not to rip the guy apart with his bare hands. He grimaced as Olivia broke into a tiny fit of giggles, Daniel turning her on the dance floor. The entire night had been torture, seeing her all dressed up and happy in his company. It hadn't started that night, either. No, it had started long ago. When he'd first seen the two of them sharing the bottle of wine, when he'd first thought Daniel had wronged her, and when he'd seen them dine together every night thereafter. He could explode!

He'd wanted so many times to slam his fist into Daniel's face, but in the end he had no cause. No matter how much he hated the guy, he hadn't done anything wrong, not yet. *Olivia said it's her choice, and she's right*, he thought. If she wanted to stop eating with the soldiers—with him—she could. Even if that meant she'd chosen to share her meals with Daniel Bandt, he wouldn't interfere, at least until he caught Bandt ignoring his boundaries. When that occurred Gavin would be close by, waiting.

As the weeks passed, Gavin kept a close eye on Olivia and Daniel's interactions. Nothing happened that he could act on, and confronting her about it would only push her away, especially after she chose not to eat meals with him anymore. He saw it in her face that night, when he'd accused her of being pregnant. She'd been embarrassed—humiliated. He couldn't believe he'd done that to her. Why had he jumped to such outlandish thoughts? He'd felt like a complete moron, and to make matters worse, he'd wanted nothing more in that moment than to kiss her. Instead, he'd ruined it by calling her a kid. Truthfully, he didn't really think of her as one, not anymore, but it had been his only way to move Jennings and Eddston along. It didn't even work, considering the dirty comments he received in the days afterward, especially when Olivia stopped joining them for meals. Jennings and Eddston tried to drop a few hints that Gavin needed to pursue her, that's what girls wanted. Gavin ordered them never to mention it again, or they'd spend a month in a prison cell. That stopped all recommendations quickly enough, yet his thoughts continued to nag him.

Gavin assumed that Olivia wanted him to give her space, and so he did. When they passed one another in the halls or accidently came upon each other in the food line, he said hello and asked how she was. Her responses were always short, "I'm great," or "Same old day." He didn't try as hard as he could have, but he thought it was for the best, considering that he'd begun to think of her differently. She meant more to him than he'd realized, and he'd had plenty of time to come to that assumption.

It was hard to pinpoint the exact moment. It might have happened when they'd kissed just after he brought her to the vault. Or it could have been in the days that they passed notes, whispering secret codes. That had made him feel young and lost, daring almost, as if he no longer had the heavy burden of his position, as if he were someone else. He guessed it might have been from the sensation he got when she'd pressed against him on the floor, and her lips had been so close he'd been able to taste her with each breath he'd inhaled. He liked to think it occurred at the very beginning, in the airport store, when she'd stared at him wide eyed as he'd teased her about that romance novel. No matter when, a seed had been planted. It had taken root and slowly grown over time. He knew that's why he'd asked the major to transfer her in. Not only did he want to protect her, but he wanted to be able to talk with her, to be near her.

Unfortunately, that wasn't how it worked out. Not since their last conversation, when she said she'd make her own choices, that she wasn't a kid. He knew, then, that he needed to back off. She did need to make her own choices, and he couldn't force his need upon her. He couldn't trust himself, so he backed off. He wished that he hadn't, but he knew it was for the best, at least for her.

He focused on his duties. The major had given the guilty prisoners their days at work, but he made sure their nights were spent in a cell until their behavior could be reevaluated. David, the man who'd been beaten, healed quickly enough and returned to work after being instructed not to mention what had occurred at risk of being locked away. The soldier wasn't punished, but Gavin made sure to have his own talk with him, ensuring that the soldier would comply in the future.

Once the Thanksgiving celebration was mentioned, spirits rose throughout the vault. Gavin thought it was strange—a holiday that should remind them of their dead families instead inspired joyous spirits. Gavin hadn't been infected. His reality wasn't altered by emotions or need. His family was dead while he played babysitter in an underground vault to a heartless conductor who'd orchestrated the entire Thanksgiving celebration as a way to remind everyone that he controlled the vault, even its holidays. He'd said so to Gavin.

Gavin had been routinely updating the major about the vault's happenings. A few weeks prior, Gavin reported to the major, "The residents have eased up on their attitudes towards the soldiers. I haven't received any negative reports on insubordination. It seems the Thanksgiving event has caused their complaints to cease."

The major chuckled as if the news was no surprise. "It's only natural to take one's mind off the bad when one has something to look forward to. Also, they're aware that if they behave, they'll be rewarded."

Gavin dared to ask, "And when the event is over?"

The major didn't stop grinning. "We'll give them something else to look forward to. Ah, Christmas. Which will be the perfect time to begin with the girls."

"Major?" Gavin said with fear.

The major had been surprised by Gavin's reaction. "Ah, you disagree?"

Gavin said nothing.

The major snarled. "It doesn't matter, you'll do as ordered. And if not, the girl, Olivia, yes, she can be our first to begin step five."

"Sir, she's only eighteen," Gavin warned.

The major smiled. "So she is. But if you ever show signs of an opinion, I'll change that rule fast enough. You keep me happy and I'll keep you."

Gavin forced a nod.

"Oh, and I'd like your blonde soldier to accompany me to the celebration. You can arrange that?"

"Dillard?"

"Is that her name? Notify her that she will accompany me as my date."

Gavin held back his opinion and nodded once again, keeping his thoughts tightly locked up.

Gavin was blown away by the major's choice to impregnate the twenty-year-old girls, and if he stepped out of the major's good graces, Olivia would be used against him! The evil bastard made him cringe with fury. He thought he'd helped Olivia, but he'd only shown the major his weakness. Things got even worse when he was ordered to obtain Dillard for the major as if he was a dating service. He knew that Dillard wasn't going to be happy, and she wasn't. When he told her that she would be accompanying the major, she laughed, then almost cried, trying to hide her reaction behind anger. "I'm not a puppet," she screamed. "Do you realize what you're asking of me?"

"I can't do anything about it."

"Why?" she asked, but he didn't answer.

Several sleepless nights went by after that particular conversation, during which Gavin's mind raced with thoughts of his priorities, his oath, his father, his conscience, and finally Olivia.

He felt his gut churn and knew it was from the choice he was about to make. Looking down at Olivia, that choice would change everything, and there was no turning back.

Olivia giggled as Daniel turned her again, his moves swift and smooth. She felt as if she were gliding with him along the dance floor. They moved with the beat of a familiar club song, but she couldn't place it. When he pulled her in for a short dip, she burst into laughter.

"Even my moves are funny," he said jokingly.

"Apparently they are." She tried to sound serious but came across as amused.

Daniel chuckled. "I promised you'd have a great time," he said as he brought her closer against him.

She smiled. "Thanks for keeping your promise."

His grin widened and he swayed with the beat. She casually scanned the room. The lights were dimmed for a dancing atmosphere. Some of the other residents were still having bites of dessert, but most had already joined them on the dance floor. Olivia couldn't believe she was having so much fun, but when she caught Gavin's eyes on her, she froze and caused Daniel to stumble. He grabbed her and pulled her against his chest to stop them both from falling. She smiled an apology up at him, and when she looked to see if Gavin was still watching, she saw an empty seat.

"What's wrong?" Daniel asked.

Olivia looked up at him while she tried to find the beat of the music again. "Oh nothing, just stepping on my own feet." She stepped back from him and continued to dance.

He grinned down at her, his ocean-blue eyes revealing humor. "So I've seen."

She forced a smile.

She'd hardly spoken to Gavin in weeks. His small greetings confirmed that he wanted nothing more to do with her. She'd begun to eat with Daniel every evening, hoping that Gavin would see, that he'd realize she was an adult instead of a kid. She was making a statement. She had a choice, and she wanted Gavin to see it, to treat her as he saw Daniel treating her, but it had done nothing. He did nothing beyond his obligation to check in every few days to see if she was okay. Maybe it was her fault for not speaking up. Maybe she should have cornered him and demanded he explain his behavior to her, ask why he was ignoring her. Instead she decided she needed to prove to him once and for all that she was more than an obligation to him. She could be so much more. She pressed on with her plan, but she could see now that it had failed. He'd hardly noticed her the entire evening. Her biggest fear had come true—Gavin had never been jealous, and she'd been stupid to think that. He'd simply been protective like a big brother.

Earlier that evening, she fixed her hair and makeup as Sophie had taught her. She wore the yellow dress, the black heels, and her mother's gold bracelet. She felt as if she'd turned herself into a model, and Gavin hadn't even noticed. Before dinner started, the major said a few words that demonstrated his thankfulness to the community within the vault and their support in helping life continue on as smoothly as possible inside. Olivia missed most of his speech, searching for Gavin and finding his eyes cast down as the major spoke. When the speech ended, he turned his head, and she could have sworn it was on purpose. Moments like that seemed to repeat, and that's when Olivia decided she'd lost him. Her heart sank.

Before dinner started, she excused herself. Running to the closest restroom and forcing herself to breathe, she fought the tears. She lectured herself on wanting something that wasn't there, and when she thought she had no reason to return to the Grand Hall, Daniel popped into her mind. Daniel, who she'd been using day after day as a sorry attempt to drag some kind of emotion out of Gavin, was waiting for her. But it hadn't worked. Gavin had done nothing. He'd said nothing. She wanted off of the roller coaster of torture. She composed herself by thinking of Daniel.

In the previous weeks, each day she got to know Daniel better. She laughed with him and teased him. He shared his dream of traveling, and she confessed the same. That sparked a weekly game of describing a destination that they researched from the archives, pretending that they'd visited. He described Florence and Rome, imagining that he had toured it during a hot summer, not leaving out the beads of sweat he had to wipe from his face while visiting the Coliseum or trying to barter for a trinket. She described London's quaint pubs and narrow buildings, not forgetting to add her own opinion about the cold, rainy weather she encountered. She even claimed to have acquired an accent during her visit and spoke with one as she recounted her journey. He chuckled, de-lighted, and the next week he turned on his own Australian accent, then Chinese, then Hawaiian. Things continued in this way and she looked forward to it. She looked forward to him. So in the bathroom just before dinner, although she thought she'd cry at the realization that her master plan failed, she didn't. Instead she sought out her friend. He was the reason she returned to the Grand Hall that night.

Earlier in the evening, Daniel had knocked on her door to

officially pick her up for their date. She was surprised to see him holding a corsage, a yellow rose, that he'd made out of paper. He explained that guys were supposed to pick up their dates at their door and that he used his clearance to Division One this one time. She couldn't help but feel that it was, in fact, a real date. The way he behaved was perfection.

He said, "You look beautiful tonight," as he put the corsage on her wrist and proceeded to extend his arm to her. She took his arm and they walked down the halls together. As they arrived, he pulled out her chair for her. He made her feel like a princess. She'd laughed and said, "You're not going to behave like this all night, are you?"

He winked at her and said, "Of course I am. I'm your date."

He even made her sit and wait at the table while he got her food, explaining that since they had no waiters, he would improvise. She was embarrassed by his doting behavior until Sophie casually leaned in and whispered in her ear, "I'm glad you have someone. He really cares," and she was gone before Olivia could respond. That small comment from her ex-friend made her feel suddenly happy, even if Sophie didn't realize that Daniel was just playing the role of the date. When Daniel returned with the food, Olivia couldn't help but fall into the role herself, enjoying every minute of it.

As she and Daniel danced, Olivia suddenly felt out of breath. A slow song came on. "Let's sit this one out," she said breathlessly.

Daniel smiled and turned toward their table, but as Olivia took a step to follow, someone grabbed her arm. She looked back to see Gavin holding it and gasped.

"Dance?" he asked softly.

He didn't allow her to respond, instead grabbing her by the waist and pulling her toward him. She saw Daniel out of the corner of her eye take a step toward him, but Gavin put up his hand as if to warn him. Daniel stayed at the edge of the dance floor watching them.

"He's very attentive to you," Gavin stated with a hint of annoyance.

Olivia stared at him speechless.

"Are you going to just stand there?"

She hesitated for a second before placing her hands gently on his shoulders. He started to sway with her, taking one of her hands off of his shoulder and holding it in his hand. Then he pressed his hand gently against her hip to guide her.

"That's it," he encouraged as she began to move with him.

The deep tone in his voice was soft and sweet. Her heart skipped and she had to take a deep breath as she dared to meet his eyes. His lips curved into a charming smile. "You're looking very pretty tonight," he said smoothly. He turned her as Daniel had, but he didn't get the same reaction. She simply stared at him in a daze. "Did you enjoy the meal?" he asked.

She could only nod, shocked that he was even speaking to her, let alone touching her.

He continued to stare at her, his deep blue eyes revealing no emotion. "Bandt hasn't done anything I should know about?"

She couldn't believe he'd ask that and quickly found her voice to defend Daniel. "He's done nothing wrong, if that's what you're asking."

Gavin lifted a brow at finding a red button. "Just friends, huh?"

"Yes. Friends."

"Make sure he knows that," he said, glancing toward Daniel on the sideline.

Olivia exhaled her frustration. "Is that what you wanted?"

"I'm checking on you," he said seriously.

She looked up at him, not hiding her pain. "I don't want you to check on me anymore."

"You don't?"

"No." She didn't want to be a duty for him. She wanted to mean more.

He looked away from her. "If that's what you want."

Her heart sank. Did he just agree to never talk to her again? She tightened her hand on his in response.

A sly grin covered his face. "I won't stop."

"You won't?" she asked softly, hoping that she hadn't heard him wrong.

"No. I'll never stop making sure you're all right."

She stared at him skeptically. "Because I'm a kid?"

He shook his head. "You're not a kid."

"I'm not?" she said, shocked.

He grinned. "No, you're not," his deep voice rattled.

She smiled. Their eyes connected and she didn't hide that she was satisfied with his comment.

"That's a nice smile you have," he said.

She couldn't help but stare at him as if he was a stranger. "It is?" She tilted her head to the side, curiously aware that he'd just paid her another compliment.

He chuckled. "Yes, it is." He pulled her in closer and softly whispered, "trust me." Before she could respond he covered her lips with his own.

The soft kiss suddenly deepened and Olivia thought she'd be devoured right there as he pulled her against him urgently with a violent need. She gripped at his shirt, holding on to him, unable to think, only able to feel him. Then suddenly, she felt jerked as someone pulled her away from Gavin, and before she could say a word Daniel was between the two of them, swinging a punch and nailing Gavin right in the face.

Gavin stood still while the entire room turned its attention to the two of them. Gavin grabbed Daniel in one fast swoop, locking his arms behind his back.

Olivia watched stunned as Gavin yelled for assistance. Two other soldiers busted in and grabbed Daniel.

Gavin appeared unmoved by the entire scene as he ordered, "Lock him up."

Olivia gasped. "No."

"You attacked her," Daniel yelled in defense as he struggled within the two soldiers' grasp.

Gavin turned to Olivia and asked, "Did I?"

Olivia stared at Daniel, then at Gavin, before speaking the truth. "No," she whispered.

Daniel's face sunk as if she'd struck him. She had to look away.

Gavin smiled. "You attacked me, though, I have plenty of witnesses." Gavin addressed his soldiers with an order, "Lock him up."

Olivia looked toward Gavin, not able to believe what he'd just said. "Why?" Olivia asked quietly as she watched the two soldiers haul Daniel away. "Don't!"

Gavin gave her a hard stare. "Stay here," he ordered just before he walked over to the major and whispered something.

The major nodded and Gavin came back to Olivia. "Come with me." Gavin gently grabbed her hand and they exited the Grand Hall together.

Chapter 20

Gavin led Olivia away from the Grand Hall. The music dropped to a low hum until all that could be heard was their footsteps against the concrete. Her heart thumped in her chest as she tried to figure out where they were going and how she was going to convince Gavin to let Daniel go. The entire scene had happened so fast and the only person she could blame was herself. She hadn't expected Daniel to react like that. *Why did Gavin kiss me? Why did Daniel punch him?* Her thoughts raced through her head as if she'd been in an accident and was trying to remember who'd done what.

Olivia stopped abruptly, causing Gavin to swing around. "Come on," he ordered.

"Why'd you do that?" She demanded an answer.

He ignored her. "Come on, now." He grabbed her arm and continued to pull her at a steady pace.

"I'll scream," she threatened.

"Go ahead, but I did say trust me, remember?" He kept his

pace.

She didn't scream. She figured it wouldn't matter if she did. He could easily throw her over his shoulder without losing a step.

When they arrived at Division One, she half-expected him to say, *Go to your room*, but he didn't. He cut down the hall and went through the double doors to the control room. Inside, a soldier greeted him.

"Is everything in order?" Gavin asked a soldier.

"Yes, Sir. We are in position and have eyes."

"Good," Gavin said as he continued past the soldier toward the intelligence room.

Olivia looked around, expecting him to enter it, but he passed it too. She didn't have a clue. When they entered the vault's prison, she looked up at Gavin and couldn't believe he'd brought her here. He was going to lock her up! Then she saw Daniel, and she wiggled out of Gavin's hold and ran up to his cell. Daniel stepped toward the bars to meet her, his eyes darting back and forth between Olivia and Gavin. He was the only prisoner there. All of the others had been allowed to attend the Thanksgiving celebration.

"Are you okay?" Olivia asked, her voice echoing through the empty cells.

Daniel nodded. "I'm fine. Did he hurt you?"

She shook her head, knowing Gavin would never hurt her, but seeing for the first time that Daniel believed he would.

"Why is she here?" Daniel asked Gavin.

Gavin stood by silently.

Daniel continued, "She's done nothing wrong. She shouldn't be in here."

Olivia couldn't understand why Daniel was acting so enraged to see her there. "Daniel, it's okay," Olivia tried to comfort him, grabbing his hand and holding it. He looked at her, but she could see the worry still there.

Gavin stood, silently watching. A twitch in his eye which was his only readable emotion.

Daniel stared at Olivia. "It's not okay, Olivia. Why are you here?"

Olivia didn't know the answer and looked toward Gavin for it.

Gavin took several steps closer. "She's here because I want fast answers. I'm not playing around, and this isn't going to take all night. You're going to tell me exactly which residents are working with you and what your plan is."

Olivia stared at Daniel, trying to understand what was going on.

"I have no idea what you're talking about." Daniel said.

Gavin gritted his teeth. "Let's skip this, shall we? I already know you've been secretly meeting with residents, gathering them and making plans—plans that will end with many fatalities and that is supposed to be happening tonight."

Daniel narrowed his eyes at Gavin. "You have a huge imagination."

"What are you talking about?" Olivia asked Gavin.

Daniel walked as close as he could toward Gavin until the bars stopped him. "Tell her that you want me here so that I'll be out of your way. Isn't that the truth, Grant? Everyone knows the only reason she was allowed to transfer was because you told the major you wanted her."

Gavin shrugged his shoulders. "And I'll have her, right here in this cell, and you'll watch."

Olivia's eyes widened at Gavin's remark.

"Don't you touch her," Daniel yelled.

Gavin grabbed Olivia by the arm and pulled her away from the cell. Olivia looked up toward Gavin for an explanation, but he kept his eyes hard on Daniel.

"Let her go," Daniel yelled.

Gavin opened the door to the cell next to Daniel's and pulled Olivia in with him.

Daniel roared with anger. "You're an animal. You let her go.

218

Let her go now!"

Olivia could only look back and forth between Daniel and Gavin. When Gavin shoved her onto the tiny cot, she watched Daniel jump to the door, trying to force it open. It was locked, yet his passion to get through it didn't stop him from trying.

"Stop. Stop!" Daniel yelled.

Gavin threw a heated glance at him. "What did you order?"

"Can't you stop, just stop and think what you're doing! You're hurting a girl because you think I'm someone I'm not. Punch me. Beat me up. Just let her go. She hasn't done anything wrong," Daniel begged.

Olivia shot Gavin a warning glance. This had gone far enough.

"Though I'd like to beat you, I'll enjoy doing this more," Gavin said, pushing Olivia down and climbing on top of her.

She broke her silence. "Stop it! What are you—" but before she could finish, Gavin roughly kissed her. She tried to shove him away, but his weight was too much. For the first time, she began to panic.

Daniel rushed to be closer, pressing his body against the steel prison.

When Gavin pulled his face back for a millisecond, Olivia screamed, filling the entire prison block with her voice.

Daniel roared. "No! Get off her!" His hands extended wildly through the bars, tearing at the air, missing mere inches from Gavin's back. "I'll tell you! I'll tell you!" he pleaded.

Gavin looked up, giving Olivia enough room to wiggle away to the corner of the cot where Daniel's gentle fingers rushed to embrace her shoulders.

"Well, let's hear it," Gavin ordered.

Daniel's hands fell to his sides, and Olivia trembled as Daniel spoke, "I designed the vault and I can destroy it."

"You want to destroy it?" Olivia asked meekly, causing both Daniel and Gavin to stare at her. Her expression held disbelief. She didn't know either of them.

Daniel looked toward Olivia. "No. I want to stop them." He glanced at Gavin. "The military. They've taken over the vault as if they're gods who think this is their world to rule."

"There have to be rules," Gavin said.

"Rules that benefit the few. If things go on as they have, we'll have two classes, the military and their slaves."

"What are you saying, Bandt? That you're doing this for everyone else?"

"No. I was doing it for everyone else, but now I'm telling you for my own reasons." He looked toward Olivia. "The major ordered evaluations for implantation of sperm next week. He's going to start using residents as lab rats for procreation because of some document that was drawn up by another man—a man who was fired from his last two jobs because his ideas were too radical. This is how the human race is supposed to exist, as an experiment? No. I didn't do this for myself."

Olivia turned to Gavin. "Is this true? Girls are going to be forced."

Gavin nodded. "It's true."

"You can't," Olivia pleaded.

Daniel grabbed her hand through the bars. "He doesn't care Olivia. He's one of them."

Olivia shook her head. "No he's not."

"You have no idea," Daniel said.

"What's the plan?" Gavin asked.

"You're too late. I'm sure."

"Tell me now. I can stop people from getting hurt. There's a way to stop the major and this isn't it."

Daniel didn't believe him. "You don't want to stop him. You're his right hand."

A loud alarm suddenly sounded from above, causing all three of them to cover their ears at the noise.

A solider rushed into the prison with a panicked expression. "Captain, we have a problem."

"What is it?" Gavin asked.

"Braggs reported a massive water leak near the garden. It's locked down but the water is seeping through."

Gavin turned to Daniel. "What have you done?"

Daniel shook his head as if the news was a surprise to him as well. "They wouldn't! I told them not to do it without me."

"What did they do?" Gavin yelled.

"I was going to cause a lockdown which would have allowed us to surprise the soldiers. We were going to take over the vault, but I told them it was tricky, that only I could do it. Oh, God."

"What? What did they do?" Gavin asked in a rush.

"Get me out of here. Hurry!"

"I can't trust you," Gavin said.

"Well, I don't trust you, but if you don't let me out of here, the entire vault is going to be underwater."

Gavin froze.

"Daniel?" Olivia gasped.

Daniel stared at Olivia. "It's Henry, the other engineer, Olivia. He's good, but he doesn't know the vault's system. He won't be able to turn it off if he didn't redirect the power."

"Gavin!" Olivia yelled.

"Stay here," Gavin said, moving to leave.

"No!" Olivia shouted.

Olivia turned to Gavin. "Daniel wouldn't hurt anyone. Trust me! If he says that he'll cut it off, he will. You heard him, he's like us. He doesn't want to see girls tortured. Unless you do?"

Daniel stared at her, surprised by the way she spoke to the captain.

"Of course not. I'm sick of the major. All the soldiers are. We don't want it either, and we weren't going to allow it, but we weren't going to jeopardize lives when we stopped it. Not like him." Gavin stared harshly at Daniel.

"He wouldn't either," Olivia said. "I know him—like I know you. He wouldn't. Trust him."

"I can't. Stay here. You'll be safe."

"Gavin!" He didn't stop, instead rushing out of the room with the other soldier.

Daniel stared at her as if he'd suddenly realized a secret. "You trust him? After he almost..."

Olivia shook her head and grabbed his hands. "He wouldn't have. If you waited, you'd have seen."

"I couldn't wait. I wouldn't have. You're more important to me than any of this. I wanted to do the right thing. I didn't think anyone would get hurt."

"I know," she said.

Daniel looked around. "You have to get me out. If the garden's doors are leaking water that means it won't take long before the pressure busts the doors. Then there won't be anywhere to go."

Olivia scrambled, trying to find anything that might aide in opening a locked jail cell.

"Olivia!" Olivia turned to see Gavin rushing back in. "The garden door's busted open to the preparation room. Those doors are holding, but I can't say for how long. We're going to have to evacuate."

"You can't leave!" Daniel interrupted. "There's radiation above ground."

"So we sit here and wait for the water to stop?"

"It won't stop, there's enough to fill this entire vault five times over."

"Is there no way to drain it?"

Daniel shook his head. "I have to get in there. Trust me. We want the same thing. I won't let Olivia die like this."

"I won't either." Gavin stared at Daniel and for the first time noted the fear covering his face. Not fear for himself, but for Olivia as he'd said. Gavin didn't hesitate. He walked over and unlocked the door.

Chapter 21

By the time Olivia, Gavin, and Daniel made it to the outer hallway that led to the garden, the major had arrived with four soldiers. They directed their sights down the hall and to the door that had been sealed as an emergency precaution. Tiny streams of water were already emerging from the seams of the door. The major shouted an order to two soldiers, telling them to make sure the residents were taken to their rooms and told nothing.

Gavin tried to speak, but the major stopped him, directing his attention to Daniel. "What the hell is going on, Bandt? I'm told the garden is completely flooded. We caught two men, and they've already confessed to your plan. Did you really think you'd be able to take me from my position? You have no idea who I am!"

"Sir! Sir!" Gavin shouted, interrupting the old man.

The major turned his attention to Gavin. "And I'm holding you responsible for this too! You better fix this!"

Gavin interrupted him again, but this time with a punch to the face. The major fell hard, right on his rear, while the four soldiers stepped back and watched. Gavin shot a hard glance toward the major as he tried to get back up. "He's the only man here who can fix it, Sir! You might want to shut your mouth and let him save us all from drowning."

The major snarled at him. "I'm going to have you in chains!"

The soldiers looked toward Gavin, who ignored the threat. "Put him in a cell," Gavin ordered.

The soldiers nodded and two of them proceeded to lift the old man up to his feet. He started struggling once he realized they meant to follow Gavin's orders instead of his. A mystified expression formed on his face as they pulled him toward Division One. "Let go of me, now! That's an order!" When the men continued to ignore his words, he lashed out. "I'll have you scrubbing floors for the rest of your life. You hear me?"

As the two soldiers carried the major away, Gavin shouted to all four of his men, "Make sure he's confined and then proceed with the lockdown. We don't need a riot. Keep this hallway clear. No one comes through."

"Yes, Sir!" The soldiers answered with large grins of admiration covering their faces.

As the soldiers departed, Gavin and Olivia ran over to Daniel, who'd already begun to work on opening the first door to the garden. When they reached him, he was entering a code on the keypad to the left of the door. As his fingers quickly pressed the digits like a high-speed typist, he casually spoke to Gavin, "Guess you've lost your job."

Gavin gave a half-hearted grunt. "Yeah, seems so."

They heard a loud double-click. The three of them, now alone in the deserted hallway, stared at the leaky door. Nothing happened. Daniel quickly typed in another series of numbers and waited. The *click click* rang in their ears like a car engine that wouldn't turn over. Daniel grunted. "The system isn't responding. I've released the lock, but we're going to have to pry it open." Daniel quickly got into position to force the door to slide to the left, placing his fingers against the rim as he said, "Grant, could use a little help."

Gavin quickly jumped into action. The two men pried the door open with their bare hands while Olivia watched.

Once the door was cracked enough for one person to squeeze through, the water began to pour out along their feet. "Not too bad," Daniel reassured, the rush of water flowing only below their knees. Daniel nodded beyond the opening, "The security door's still holding. I can see it."

Olivia saw the second door too. It was *triple threat*, that's what Daniel had once called it, referencing the security door being three metal layers thick and unmovable. He'd also said not to be fooled by its appearance of a stainless steel fridge door, and then he'd compared its thickness to that found on a submarine. *Too bad it wasn't designed to hold water like one*, she thought as water sprayed out of its edges like a hose. She knew they wouldn't be able to pry that door open even if they had to. "How are we going to get in there?" Olivia asked.

"You're not going," Both Daniel and Gavin said in unison, causing the two men to look at one another in surprise.

The sudden agreement on their part didn't make Olivia happy. She wasn't going to allow them to order her around, together. "I know the system. I can help you, Daniel," Olivia stated with determination.

He shook his head. "No. I can do this alone."

She wasn't going to let him get away that easily. She could help. "What if you need help with the panels? They're not easy to remove on their own, especially not with pressure behind them."

"I'll go," Gavin volunteered.

Daniel nodded.

Olivia didn't like that she'd been left out and said so. "What about me? What can I do?"

Gavin spoke first. "Stay here and keep watch. If this first door breaks, get word to the other soldiers to start evacuating people."

"Don't worry," Daniel said to Olivia, and before she could get a word in, he turned to the door they'd just pried open and instructed her to stand back.

She did as he said even though she didn't approve of the arrangement.

"We'll have to go above, through the access panel and a vent shaft, to keep the security door shut for as long as possible."

"Wouldn't it be easier to let it out?" Gavin asked.

"We can't take the chance of the water damaging the vault's system. It would force the vault into an automatic shut down. The ventilation for air would be limited, and we'd lose all electricity, maybe even the backup generators. We'd be in complete darkness."

Gavin nodded. "Okay, Bandt. Do it your way."

Daniel smiled.

Gavin ignored it and began to force the door they'd pried opened a few minutes earlier closed behind them.

Olivia watched as Gavin and Daniel started to disappear behind the door, leaving her outside on her own.

Gavin gave Olivia a reassuring smile just as the door sealed. After they'd secured the door, he turned to Daniel. "Now what?"

Daniel pointed to the access panel above their heads.

It only took a few minutes for Daniel to take off the panel cover. He climbed in and motioned for Gavin to follow. They shimmied up toward a vent shaft that led them to another access panel directly above the garden. Daniel took another minute to open it. When he looked down into the garden, he said, "Hope you can swim."

"It can't be that bad," Gavin said, moving over to take a look. He groaned when he saw a giant swimming hole below.

The room was filled halfway with water. The lights on the walls were glowing faintly beneath the surface. Fortunately, the overhead lights were still on. It almost looked like a day at the beach if it wasn't for the floating tools and vegetables.

"We can't go down there," Gavin warned. "We'll be electrocuted."

"No, it's safe, for now," Daniel said.

"For now?"

Daniel ignored his question. "Ever seen lights under a pool? Well, same concept. The electrical wiring behind the garden walls is watersafe. It has to be when you're watering crops." Daniel pointed to the far corner of the garden. "The panel we need is over there. I need you to follow me and help me remove it. Once it's off, I'll do the rest."

"Easy enough," Gavin said.

"For you."

Gavin was just about to ask another question about the electricity when Daniel jumped down into the water, yelling, "Geronimo!" and disappearing in splashes.

Gavin waited until Daniel reappeared. "What about the *for now* part?"

Daniel shouted up to where Gavin was hanging partially out of the ceiling. "When the water reaches the ceiling where the outside garden's electrical breaker is housed or it gets high enough beyond the garden walls, well, then you'll know," Daniel said, waving him on.

Gavin cursed as he jumped from the vent in the ceiling and into the garden's new swimming hole below. The water was not as cold as he'd expected, but it was enough to shock the system. He began swimming through all the debris, mostly gardening supplies and equipment that floated close to his face. When he hit a pole with the side of his head, he jerked back, avoiding any further contact. He ignored the pain and followed Daniel, swimming toward him unfazed. When he caught up, Daniel instructed that they would need to go underwater several feet to reach the panel, where they'd both have to pull up and over to the left to remove it.

Gavin nodded and they each took a deep breath. Daniel went under first. Gavin followed. The panel was easy to find, located along the wall where it met what was once the garden floor. It took only one try for the two of them to get it off. Once they did, both swam back to the top, gasping for air. "That wasn't hard," Gavin said.

Daniel gave him a doubtful look. "Stay here. I'll go see what the damage is."

When he disappeared, Gavin spotted a ladder close by that extended up along the wall a few feet above the water. He swam to it and grabbed on, thankful he could take a break from swimming. He looked around the room, unable to believe that this could happen, that he'd allowed it to. He thought of the months that had gone by without his careful scrutiny, of his carelessness that had allowed the residents to plan such an act, but he didn't really blame them. How could he? The fact of the matter was that he felt as they did. Living in the vault with The Packet to guide them, with only the major to decide their fate, had been too much. If they lived through this, he swore at that moment he'd make sure the major wouldn't spend even another day in charge, and an uprising because of a crazy dictator wouldn't happen again.

His thoughts were redirected as he heard Olivia's voice, "Hey! What's going on?"

"Olivia!" he yelled as he looked across the room and saw her head poking out from the opening in the ceiling. "Get out of here!" he shouted.

"Did he turn it off?" she asked.

"Not yet. Now go back," he ordered. "It's not safe."

Just then, Daniel emerged from the water gasping for air. Olivia and Gavin turned their eyes to him.

Olivia's thoughts turned to concern for Daniel, who appeared barely able to catch his breath. "Daniel! Are you okay?" Olivia shouted.

Daniel rubbed his eyes and looked up to see Olivia peering out from the ceiling. He groaned. "I'm fine."

Gavin turned his attention back to Olivia. "Go back. Now!"

he shouted.

Olivia tightened her grip along the opening's edge. "No, I'm not leaving."

Daniel interrupted them. "Wait!" he shouted urgently. "I can't turn it off."

"What?" Olivia said.

Daniel looked at Olivia. "I need a tool. Olivia, I need my black toolbox." Daniel said.

"I'll get it," Gavin said.

Daniel began to pant as he grew tired from treading water. "You can't. There isn't a ladder that reaches the ceiling. The one you're on is the tallest in the room. The only way we're getting out is if we open the door, and that's not possible."

Gavin looked around the room but found that Daniel was correct, he was on the tallest ladder, and it was still at least twenty feet from reaching the ceiling.

Daniel continued, "She's up there. And she knows where it is." He paused for a second as he assessed the room. "Olivia."

Olivia waited.

"I need you to cut the power. We need more time. I didn't want to risk it, but this isn't going to be a fast repair."

"In the control room?" Olivia asked.

Daniel spit out a mouthful of water as he shook his head. "No, remember the backup I tested you on? The wires in the ceiling? That one," he waited for her to nod before he went on. "It needs to be shut down. Now go, Olivia, and hurry."

Olivia nodded again as she watched Daniel struggling. "Okay, I'll get it."

"And some flashlights, we'll need to see," Daniel said with a joking tone.

She didn't laugh, and she didn't wait for Gavin to stop her. She immediately took off, crawling back down the vent shaft, the sound of metal popping under her knees, until she reached the access panel they'd entered through. She climbed down to where *triple threat* was still oozing water. When she dropped into the hallway, she was met with a splash in the face. She looked down to see that the water was now waist-high. She needed to hurry. She struggled to walk down the corridor toward the first door she'd hardly been able to open only minutes earlier. It was like walking through quicksand, and she felt the burn all through her thighs. When she made it to the door she looked down toward the floor. Under the water, she knew, lay the crowbar she'd found earlier to get through the door and her high-heels that she'd stripped off and abandoned.

She rushed, quickly searching with her hands, grabbing the crow bar and prying the door back open. The water from the corridor poured out into the hallway, the same as it had when she'd first opened the door by herself on her way in. She squeezed through the tiny opening she made, fighting with the water, as it too wanted to pass through. She slid the door back as best she could, but she didn't have the strength to close it all the way, and she didn't want to waste the time. Without a second thought, she decided to let it go, leaving the water to spill out through a six-inch gap. She ran down the long hallway, trying to visualize where the black toolbox was. *Right beside his desk, to the right*, she told herself. She didn't want to waste a second. The water was still pouring in, and she knew she had to be fast.

She found the box easily, and the flashlights too—three of them, large and waterproof, right next to the box. She couldn't believe her luck. Holding on to one flashlight and a pair of wire cutters, she threw everything else in a bag and slung it over her shoulder. It was heavy against her back, but it worked.

Promptly, she began to think of her next task: Cutting the backup wire that ran electricity to the garden. Daniel had quizzed her on the circuits and electrical wiring that ran throughout the vault. She'd memorized their colors, and she was confident she could pick out the wire providing backup power. What he'd told her in confidence was that they could all be disconnected in various sections throughout the vault if needed. The wire was near *triple threat*, but she decided to cut the hallway as well, just to be safe. It was easy enough. As soon as she stepped back into the hallway, she found an access panel in the ceiling and a chair to reach it. Remembering the quiz she'd aced, she pictured the diagram Daniel had drawn for her. Hidden in a second compartment deeper in the panel were the wires. There was a blue one and a white one— she knew it was the blue. When she cut it, everything went black.

An eerie sensation came over her instantly. *This is what a blind person feels like*, she thought. The silence was strange. Using her fingers to find the opening in her bag, she dropped the wire cutters inside and clicked on her flashlight. She hopped off the chair and took off running toward the garden, her light bouncing from the wall to the floor and back again. The cold concrete against her bare feet combined with the bottom-half of her soaked dress rubbing harshly against her thighs were two sensations she ignored. Focused, she thought of her next task—*get through the door, climb through the access panel, get inside the vent, and use it to reach the wires, then get to...* A sharp noise interrupted her thoughts. It sounded like a metal bowl being dropped. Abruptly she stopped, finding herself looking at the red door. It was open! She pointed her flashlight into the room. Beyond it, she'd seen something move. She hesitated, staring at the wide opening and wondering who would have left it like this. Her gut told her to move on, that she didn't have time. She gave up the thought of having a quick peek when a figure appeared in the opening, standing directly in the beam of her light. Before her, dressed entirely in black, stood Albert Rossi.

He opened his mouth and spoke her name, "Olivia."

She stared at him, frozen, as he took a step toward her. Instinctively, she jerked the flashlight in front of her as if she needed it between them for protection.

"Come here," he softly coaxed. He stood completely still, scanning her as if he was sizing up the situation. Olivia saw a threatening flash in his bloodshot eyes, and before she could even react he was in front of her in two quick steps, blocking her way down the hall. She couldn't move.

What does he want? Thoughts rattled off in her mind as she connected his presence beyond the red door with Sophie's previous confession about him stealing drugs. No one else was around. He must have been using the chaos of the water leak to steal, and she'd caught him. A sudden jerk of his hand notified Olivia that she was right, he meant her harm. Instantly, she reacted. She dodged him, lunging to the right to run past him, toward the garden, but he was quick, blocking faster than she could maneuver around him and grabbing her arm. She struggled against his hold as he flung her toward the dark room he'd just come out of. She swung her flashlight, hitting him in the nose, the force causing her to lose hold of it. He released her with a howl, blood splattered across his face. She had to act fast. Blocked from returning to Gavin and Daniel, she had only one option. She hated herself for not reaching for the flashlight that now lay on the floor just out of reach, and instead she bolted through the open red door at her back, into the darkness.

Inside, she searched for a hiding spot, the farthest place away from him, using her fingers to feel since she couldn't see through the pitch black. She was careful to muffle the sound of the toolbox in her bag, thankful that his yelling had giving her the cover she needed. She found an examination table to hide behind. She focused on the door, where the sole source of light came from her lost flashlight, where she'd left it and him behind. He stood there still, cursing that she'd broken his nose. Her heart began to race as she tried to think of a way to get by him. Her first thought was to cause a distraction and then run, but the room wasn't big enough. She tried to feel for a weapon. She didn't know if she should risk using the toolbox, worried that if she moved now he'd hear the tools shift inside. All she could think of was that she needed to get back to Daniel and Gavin, that the water was rising, and that she couldn't put down the box—she needed it. So she waited, allowing her eyes to adjust.

She watched his silhouette dissolve into the darkness as he stepped into the room and said, "Get out here, now."

She didn't move.

He made a gargling nose in his throat as he walked back to the flashlight and picked it up. "Ready or not," he said angrily.

She heard his footsteps in the opposite direction and peeked out from behind the table. He was checking the other side first. Should she go? His steps sounded like they were coming toward her. The light beam was on the far side of the room, passing over machines and lab tables. She held her breath. The beam of light jetted across the room as Rossi turned his wrist, hovering several feet from her as she stared at where the beam landed. She saw a jar in the spotlight. A small, deformed fetus stared back at her, its twisted body covered with strange bumps that looked like pus balls. She covered her mouth with her hand as she held in a scream. That instant she knew exactly what that room was: The impregnation room.

She heard his next step, closer. Her eyes shot over to where the beam was directed away from her, exposing a lab table covered in beakers and microscopes. She couldn't wait any longer and decided right then to go for it. She jumped up and grabbed the examination table. The toolbox rattled and with it she screamed a warrior scream, causing Rossi to stop mid-stride. She held on to the table and pushed it with all her strength while running straight for him and straight for the light that had found her. He stood still, mostly in confusion, as she mowed him over. His body hit the floor with a loud thump and she didn't check to see the damage; instead, she dug out a new flashlight, secured the bag tightly against her body, and ran out the door, down the hall, and back toward the garden.

When her feet hit the water she sighed with relief, knowing she made it back to the door. She rushed to open it the rest of the way, and just as she did, she heard Rossi hurtling down the hall, screaming, his flashlight beaming in the far distance. Olivia didn't stop to shut the door behind her, there was no time. She could only hope he was far enough away that he wouldn't see what door she went into.

Her bare feet splashed against the floor as she sprinted down the corridor. The water here was at her ankles now. It had drained out into the hallway while she'd been gone. Her mind focused as it began to run through her tasks—the only thing keeping her from screaming hysterically as anyone being chased by a drug-dealing psycho might. She sprang toward the access panel and climbed up to the vent shaft, banging her knees and scraping her leg along the way. The extra burden of the heavy toolbox pounded against her back, a pain she forced herself to endure.

She hadn't forgotten the electric wire. *Cut the wire, cut the wire*, rattled in her thoughts. She flung the bag off and sought out the wire cutters. Pointing her flashlight to where she'd entered at the access panel, she moved like a game show contestant competing for her life. Her adrenaline was kicking, but she controlled her breathing, willing herself to concentrate. She had to hang slightly out of the vent she'd climbed into to find the hidden compartment, and then she knew the wires would be directly above the entrance to the vent. She found the compartment and then the blue wire. *Cut it.* She did. There wasn't a moment of relief as her eye caught the beam of light coming down the corridor.

He'd seen her flashlight, she was sure of it. She turned around in the vent and crawled to her bag, hooking it around her shoulder and pulling it—causing those pops again as her knees hit the metal. Gritting her teeth, she hoped he didn't hear it. Instead, she heard a shower of popping from behind her, and she knew he was coming when she saw the second beam of light.

Her heart pounded in panic. She scurried as fast as a chipmunk might down a hole, dragging the bag and holding the flashlight. When she saw the opening in the access panel, she screamed, "Gavin!"

"Olivia?" Gavin stared up toward the ceiling. A beam of light shot down, straight into the water below. "Wait, I'll come and get it."

"Gavin!" she screamed, just as she felt a hand grab her leg. She turned to see Rossi behind her. His flashlight illuminated a monstrous expression and blood-smeared face. She kicked, hitting his forehead, but his grip tightened. She flipped over and kicked him once again, this time with a scream. He groaned as her foot made contact with his broken nose and more blood came rushing out. He roared with anger and leapt toward her, causing them both to fall. They hit the water together, a huge splash covering them.

Both Gavin and Daniel rushed toward them, Gavin diving in from the ladder and Daniel swimming as hard as he could from across the room.

Olivia came up for air just as Rossi did. The room was pitch black except for the single flashlight floating nearby. Rossi hadn't noticed that he wasn't alone with Olivia and proceeded to drag her down, grabbing her by the shoulders and pushing her head beneath the water. She tried to fight him, throwing her arms and kicking with her feet.

Gavin reached her first, and in one fast motion he slammed his fist into Rossi's face and then proceeded to wrap his arm around his neck, pushing him under the water instead. Olivia struggled to reach the surface, splashing as she tried to breathe and cough out the water that had gone into her lungs. A hand grabbed her arm, keeping her afloat without effort. She turned with a panicked expression toward the owner. "I've got you," Gavin assured her gently. She nodded between gasps. He wiped away her hair from her face as he held her steady. "You're okay. Just relax and breathe."

She continued to gasp for air as she placed her hand on his shoulder and felt relieved that he'd been there, that he'd saved her.

"Olivia! Is she all right?" Daniel said as he reached them.

"She's fine."

Daniel touched her face as her eyes tried to focus on him, but it was too dark. The one flashlight was bobbing in the direction of her unconscious attacker, facedown in the spotlight, his body casting a creepy shadow among the other debris. "Who the hell was that?" he asked.

She nodded. "I'm fine. Rossi. He chased me."

"I took care of him," Gavin said. "If he tries anything else, I'm drowning him."

They looked at the man in the water. Gavin flipped him on his back and left him floating on some debris. He appeared to be unconscious.

"Olivia," Daniel said with concern. "Did you get the box?"

Olivia nodded. She tried to speak through gasps. "Down there, in a work bag," she motioned toward the bottom of the garden, a few feet away from where she and Gavin were treading water. "It fell in."

Daniel nodded. "I'll get it. Take her to the ladder."

Gavin handed Daniel the flashlight. Daniel held it for them while Gavin led Olivia toward the ladder. When they made it, Daniel took a deep breath and went under the water.

Gavin helped Olivia reach the ladder, where she held on for a minute to catch her breath before climbing up. A small shiver rattled through her as she looked down to see their sole source of light still floating in the water with Daniel underneath, reminding her of a lighthouse as it swayed. When Daniel resurfaced, he had the bag.

"Are you okay?" Daniel asked her once he reached them.

She looked toward Daniel who held the flashlight. "Yes, I'm fine. Can it be fixed?"

"I think so, but there's a lot of damage."

"There's a second flashlight in the bag," Olivia offered, "I had a third but..." She looked around the water as if she'd be able to find the one Rossi had taken, but the room's darkness was evidence that it wasn't there.

"We'll make do," Daniel said, and he motioned for Gavin who'd been resting on the ladder beside Olivia. "Hold this," he said as he handed Gavin the toolbox and flashlight, wincing for a second as the light hit his eyes. Daniel pulled the second flashlight out of the waterlogged bag. He discarded the drenched material and clicked on the light. Together, all three huddled against one another in a sort of lit bubble, using the ladder as their table and chair.

Daniel opened the toolbox and took a quick inventory of the items within. "Good, it's all here," he announced, closing the toolbox and taking it from Gavin. "I'm going to go back in. The vent opens to a bigger chamber behind the wall just past the plumbing tunnel. It's high enough that I'll be able to come up there for air, it shouldn't be underwater yet. I can access the valve I need from there."

She remembered the tunnel he was talking about. It was the same tunnel they'd crawled through when they'd first met. It wasn't that long, but pipes were knotted throughout, and they hadn't gone deep enough in for her to have seen the chamber. "I can help," Olivia panted.

"No," Daniel said in a hard tone. "Get your breath, and I'll come get you."

She'd rarely heard him be so direct. Between the intensity of his order and the pain in her lungs, she agreed. "Okay, be careful."

He winked at her in the narrow beam of the light. "Aren't I always?" After a sideways grin and a deep breath, he went back under.

Olivia and Gavin waited for what seemed like ten minutes. He held on to the ladder as she rested on the edge of a step, both looking back at one another as time continued to pass. "He's been in there too long," Olivia said, worried.

Gavin tried to ease her concern. "He said he had an air pocket."

They stared at each other for another few minutes until bubbles started to emerge along the surface of the water above where the panel was.

"What's that?" Olivia asked, pointing.

Gavin turned the flashlight toward the area and stared, unsure of what it could be. "I'll see." He jumped in the water and disappeared. The glow of his light danced under the water. When he came back up, he shook his head. "Some kind of machinery shifted down there, must have caused those bubbles. Now the opening's partially blocked. I tried to get in, but I couldn't."

"Daniel!" Olivia exclaimed.

"I didn't see him, that tunnel is longer than I thought. He must be at the end inside that chamber." Gavin said.

Olivia jumped into the water.

"Olivia!" Gavin shouted. When she emerged from the water for a breath, he tried to stop her. "You can't go down there. I'll try to move it."

"Let me help you."

"You stay here," he ordered.

"I'm not going to stay here while Daniel is trapped. What if he needs our help and he can't get through. We can't leave him down there alone. You let me help you, or I'll do it myself!" Olivia yelled.

They both took a deep breath and dove under the water. When they came to the piece of machinery, Olivia noticed it was a large hauling device that was used to move supplies. It had somehow shifted as the water level rose. Olivia could feel a pressure stream in the water as they swam near the source of the leak. They both tried to push and pull at the device, but it didn't budge. They resurfaced for air, gasping.

"It won't move," Olivia cried.

"It's too heavy," Gavin said. He glanced around, trying to keep his head above the rising water. "That pole. It might help." Gavin swam and retrieved the same pole that had hit him earlier in the head.

Together they both dove back down and tried again. The light was limiting, but they were able to work by Olivia holding the light as Gavin placed the pole under the machine and tried to use his weight as a lever to shift it away from the panel's entry. It worked for an instant but then wouldn't lift any further. Olivia swam over to the partial opening of the panel's entry. It was small, almost too small for her to fit, but she knew she could squeeze through it. Before she could try, Gavin grabbed her by the arm and pulled her back to the surface. She tried to pull free.

Gavin tightened his grip on her arm, pulling her closer to him. She splashed him in the face as she struggled to free herself.

"It's not big enough," Gavin warned.

Olivia stopped struggling, and he let her go. She wasn't going to let Gavin stop her. "I, I can fit," she said through gasps of air.

"No, you'll get stuck," he warned.

Olivia glared at him while trying to stay afloat. She defended herself through heavy breaths. "This is my choice... I'm going in there... I'm going to help him."

"I can't let you do that," Gavin said.

Olivia's arms were starting to tire. "If he doesn't stop the water," she took a deep breath, "we're all going to die anyway. I can help him. I can help everyone. This is what I do."

Gavin stared at her as he tightened his jaw. "I don't want anything to happen to you. I need you."

"You do?"

"Just hurry. The water's still rising."

Her eyes said thank you as she grabbed the flashlight from him.

He held himself back from stopping her. Instead, he gave her a reassuring grin as he watched her take a deep breath and disappear under the water. With one large gulp of air, he followed. Opening his eyes under the water, he found her quickly, submerged in a pitch-black sea; the glow of her light was a beacon. He kicked his legs, forcing himself to stay below long enough to make sure that she cleared the machinery and safely made it to the dark tunnel beyond. She didn't turn around. She didn't even notice he was there, but when she swam through the tiny opening the sudden urge to vomit hit him. He tried to focus on what lay after, but he couldn't see now that her light was gone. Immediately he panicked. He wanted a way to make sure that she was able to navigate through the tunnel. He hoped she would turn around and come back to him. She didn't return, but he stayed by the opening anyway and he held his breath for as long as he could.

Chapter 22

The sudden jolt of darkness terrified Olivia as her flashlight went out. She fought the impulse to take a breath at that exact moment. She clicked the power button repeatedly. Nothing. She was several feet past the panel's opening now, and her instinct was to turn around, but she didn't. She saw a glow in the distance and swam toward it, kicking hard, dropping the defective light so she could use both hands. She didn't think to feel for objects in the dark, and she rammed directly into a metal pipe.

Simultaneously, a flash of white light sparked in her vision and a stab of pain shot through her head. Her immediate reaction was to scream, causing her to lose most of the air she'd been holding in a silent cry. She swam frantically toward the white glow, using her hands as her eyes to protect herself from running into something else. Still, she felt an urgent need to rush as the pain in her lungs escalated to searing. She needed to breathe.

Fear had nudged her when she'd first entered the hole, once the darkness surrounded her. She continued forward, knowing she had to keep going. Terror consumed her thoughts as pain radiated through her head, and the urge to suck in, to take a deep breath, pulled at her entire being. Growing closer, the light was her air. The light was her life, and she fought for it. She pushed herself through the tangled pipes that crisscrossed the flooded tunnel. Since she'd seen it once before with Daniel she tried to visualize it, but small and narrow was all she could remember. She tried to ignore the way her yellow dress seemed to reach out to the pipes alongside her, holding her back. The thought of dying wasn't her true concern; it was that she wouldn't reach him, and he'd be left to find her body, or that Gavin would find her—they'd both find her dead. It was this thought that kept her from sucking in that water, that made her grip tightly to the next pipe and then the next, pulling herself along, until the light was so bright she thought she'd cry.

She broke the surface of the water with a loud gasp of air. Eyes closed. Arms outstretched. She fought to stay out of the suffocating liquid. She exhaled and took another deep breath, reveling in the sensation she'd never truly appreciated. Breathing was amazing. Her foot touched the floor, allowing her to stand in what appeared to be a large chamber about the same size of her room. It was nearly three-quarters underwater. She broke out into a sob as someone grabbed her.

"Olivia. What the hell are you doing?"

Relief washed over her at hearing the sound of Daniel's voice. She opened her eyes. Anger covered his face, which only made her want to laugh joyfully. She smiled in a half-crazed manner that caused him to survey her more closely.

He touched her head, noticing the blood, and his expression turned grim. "You're hurt," he said.

"Ow," she said, pushing his hand away. "I'm fine."

"You shouldn't be in here. It's not safe." His voice rose. "How did you get through those pipes?"

She sighed. "Barely."

He cursed and grabbed her, giving her a hug. "You could have drowned. I barely made it through and I had a light."

She felt like crying. As she lay her head on his shoulder, she held back, thinking that she couldn't let go now—she'd be ruined. She needed to be strong, so she let him go and said, "What are we doing?"

He shook his head and grinned. "I always knew you were bull-headed."

She rolled her eyes.

"And never takes compliments," he added.

"That's a compliment?" she said, insulted. "I would if they were true," she added with a grin.

He tried not to laugh. "If we don't drown, you're getting nothing but the truth from here on."

She bit her lip as she looked at him. "You mean you never tell me the truth?"

"You're also pretty green," he said.

"That doesn't sound like a compliment."

He shook his head, smiling for a brief moment before a more serious look returned to his face. "I've already assessed the damage and have started to reroute the water's drainage. Whoever did this had a lot of pent up rage. I was almost stumped for once, and you know that never happens."

"Daniel," Olivia said, impatiently waiting for him to get to the end.

He sighed. "Okay, I found a way to strip a few pieces and re-attach them to the damaged joint. I only need to finish the alignment."

"Can I help?" Olivia asked.

"Yeah, actually you can. I was having a problem using both hands and holding a light, so can you?"

Olivia smiled, tight lipped.

Daniel held back a grin. "Light holder isn't what you imagined, huh?"

"No, but I'm happy this is almost over. Let's hurry. Gavin said the water has already doubled."

Daniel nodded. "Okay. You're going to follow me through the water about ten feet over. It might take two to three tries, and then we can start draining."

"You can get rid of it all? How?"

Daniel smirked. "Let's just hope the pressure isn't too strong and there's no need to flush a toilet anytime soon."

"Great… pretty positive."

He flashed her one of his famous, *trust-me* grins, took a deep breath, and dove under. Olivia followed. A few feet in, he stopped. Daniel started attaching a pipe extension to another pipe that had been recently sawed off. Olivia could now see the damage to the other lines in close proximity. Her mind whirled, amazed, as she knew Daniel was the only one who could fix such a mess. If it had been left to her or anyone else, she was sure their fate would have been sealed.

He signaled for her to go back. They both did, surfacing for a large breath of air and then returning to the spot so Daniel could continue working. They did this two more times. When they got air for the third time, they noticed that the water level had risen so high that they could no longer touch the bottom of the chamber. Since they could no longer stand, they were forced to tread water without rest.

"All done. It's fixed," Daniel said between several deep breaths," I still have to turn the valve. Wait here." He took one large gulp of air and went back under.

Olivia waited alone, trying to judge how quickly the space between the water and the ceiling was going to shrink, wondering once he returned if the water would drain fast enough.

When Daniel's head popped out of the water, Olivia sighed thankfully. "Is it done?" she asked.

"Yes," he said. "Let's get out of here."

Olivia looked up from the spot where she was trying to stay

afloat. Her head was only a foot from the ceiling. "It's blocked. The way out is blocked."

Daniel hesitated. "What? But you came through."

Olivia hated telling him the sorrowful truth. "The transporter is blocking the opening. Gavin was able to move it only a little, just enough for me to squeeze through."

Daniel's face dropped. "I'll check. Maybe he's moved it by now."

Olivia didn't argue. She nodded, and he disappeared. She continued to kick her exhausted feet and tired arms as she waited. When he emerged beside her, she saw the answer on his face.

"It's still there," he mumbled.

"Yeah, but the water's draining. It won't be long," she said hopefully.

Daniel's eyes showed his anguish. "I haven't stopped the water completely. It's still coming in. The water's draining, but not fast enough to clear this room."

Olivia's eyes widened in horror. She understood that they only had about thirty minutes before the water would reach the ceiling and they'd be out of air. She shook her head, knowing he would tell her to leave him there to die alone. She didn't want either of them to die. "I'm not going without you," she said, determined to find another way.

"I wish you could. I don't know what happened, but the opening is completely blocked now. The transporter must have shifted." His agony was reflected on his face.

"Blocked?" she struggled to swim, her mouth dropping down into the water.

Daniel pulled her to him and told her to hold on.

She did, thankful for the short break. Straining under the weight of the reality of their situation, she suddenly realized she was pushing on him. "I don't want to weigh you down," she said.

"I'm fine," he assured her.

She wrapped her arms around his shoulders and stared into his familiar, ocean-blue eyes.

"I can almost stand," he said. "There's a pipe below," he forced a smile that in turn triggered her to force one. His warm breath hit her face and she trembled. "Getting cold?" he asked.

She nodded.

"Hold me tighter," he instructed, pulling her closer.

She did as told. Her arms were heavy now from all the swimming, and she found it easier to lay her chin on his shoulder. Several minutes went by as they held each other in silence. Olivia began to shake. It wouldn't be long now.

"You shouldn't have come in here," Daniel said through gritted teeth.

"Who'd have held your light?" she asked seriously.

"I'd have figured something out."

"You would have, but I didn't want you to be alone."

"I've been alone my entire life," he whispered.

She shivered as another chill ran through her. She ignored his statement. "You shouldn't be alone. You're so smart and so… you're quite wonderful. You saved everyone's life," she said with a smile.

"Right, look what I've done. I…" but he stopped himself before he could finish. "How do you feel?" he asked.

"Okay. Cold. I would like to lay down, but this is good." She closed her eyes and leaned her head against his. "This is nice," she sighed.

"Olivia? Olivia!" he said, but she didn't answer. He touched her head and shouted her name again.

She jerked. "Yeah?"

"Don't go to sleep," he warned. "We're going to get out of here. I just have to think."

"I'm so tired," she said.

He touched the gash in her head again and looked at his hand. The blood was thick.

"Olivia, don't sleep, please don't sleep," he said in a rush of panic, glancing around the area.

She groaned in response as he struggled to keep their heads

above water.

Olivia tried to keep her eyes open as a wave of sleepiness hit her. The trembling of her body from the cold helped to keep her alert for only a moment. Daniel searched with his arm until he found a small notch in the ceiling. "Hold this," he instructed Olivia. He directed her hand to the spot and let go of her. "Hold on and stay awake. I'll be right back. I'm getting us out of here."

He disappeared. Olivia struggled to stay awake, her hand sliding several times from the notch that was helping to keep her afloat. Every time her face would hit the water, she'd remember Daniel's words. It felt like an eternity. She didn't think he was coming back. He was gone so long. Surely he couldn't hold his breath that long. She thought of going after him, then everything went black.

A throbbing ache rattled Olivia's head. She wanted to move, but her body wouldn't let her. She shivered, then suddenly felt warmth. The cold water was gone. She was lying on a flat surface.

Daniel pulled Olivia against his bare chest, rubbing his hands up and down her arms. She sighed. She struggled to open her eyes. When she did, she saw his ocean-blue eyes staring right back, relief flooding his face. She continued to stare at him as he held her closely against him, the heat radiating from his bare chest to her flesh. She glanced down to see that her dress was gone, she wore nothing but her wet bra and panties.

He apologized quickly. "I had to get you warm. You were freezing and…"

She interrupted him. "I thought we drowned."

He corrected her softly, "No, not yet."

"Where are we?" she asked, looking around what she thought might be a metal vent shaft.

"I managed to break through another panel and vent duct.

We're above the room we were in. I'm thinking we'll be okay here until the water drains out."

Relief flooded her face, but before she could applaud his rescue she looked down to see that he was wearing only his boxers. "Your clothes?" she asked. She crossed her arms over her wet bra. Where's my clothes?"

"Olivia, that's the least of our worries. You would have died."

She shivered. He pulled her against him. She pushed away for a moment, but gave into him once she felt the warmth of his body on hers.

"I think you have a concussion. You must have hit your head pretty badly in the water. You were going to freeze if I didn't get you warmed up."

She couldn't help the draw to be closer to him, his warmth over her fear of embarrassment easily winning. She dropped her face to his shoulder, closing her eyes and allowing the heat to do as it liked.

"Don't go to sleep," he warned.

"I won't," she mumbled. "How long are we stuck here?"

"It might take a few more hours."

"A few more?"

She shivered again.

"You were out for awhile. You missed my freak out and a wonderful *I'm going to save us speech*. The worst is over. The bleeding on your head stopped and you look like you're warming up, some of your color is back. I just want you to stay awake until we get you to a doctor."

She opened her eyes and saw genuine warmth in his face. She smiled. "So we're alive?"

"So it seems," he grinned down at her.

She closed her eyes again, fully aware of his body against hers, and she felt a blush cover her face. She shifted.

He asked if she was okay, and she shook her head into his chest. He pulled away from her and looked at her beet-red face.

248

A draft of cold air hit her body where he'd vacated. "You don't have to be embarrassed," he said. "I'm not looking or anything."

She mumbled something, and he asked her to repeat herself. "I've never been this naked in front of a guy," she said.

He tried to hide a grin but failed miserably.

She tightened her arms around herself.

"I'm not just a guy," he said.

She stared at him, confused.

"You know me and I know you. I'd drown for you, and you seem to have the same opinion about me. I think seeing each other in basic swimsuit apparel is not going to ruin how we feel about each other. Is it?"

"How we feel?"

"Well, I care about you, enough to strip down and show you my bare chest," he grinned. "You think you're the only one who's shy or embarrassed?"

She smirked at his statement. "You don't have anything to be embarrassed about," she said quickly.

"You do?" he asked, surprised. "You have the best body I've ever laid eyes on."

Her mouth dropped open. "You looked?"

"Just a little."

She scolded him with a teasing squint. "Uh huh."

Daniel shrugged and made a face that screamed sorry.

Olivia went back to his earlier compliment. "The best?"

"The best," he said confidently.

She smiled after a few minutes. "Thanks." She wondered why he'd admitted that.

"Don't overthink it, Olivia. I'd do anything I can for you." His eyes met hers for a lengthy moment that made the room spin for Olivia, and then Daniel broke the tension by saying, "And if you need a blanket, well, I'm more than happy to oblige."

His smirk made her laugh, but his confession of doing anything for her was surprising. She didn't know what to say. "I didn't know..."

"That I could double for a heating blanket?" he interjected before she could finish. "Well, now you do. So, can I help you?"

She allowed his sudden change in topic. Covered in goose bumps and fighting a sudden chill, she accepted his offer. He opened his arms and she climbed in. She nuzzled up against him as his arms wrapped around her. She placed her head on his chest, where she listened to the thudding of his heart for several minutes before she spoke again, "Thanks, for saving me."

"I didn't have a choice," he said softly.

"Everyone has a choice."

"Then mine was easy."

"Easy?"

He chuckled. "Olivia, my choice will always be simple when it comes to you. You might see me as just your boss, or a meal buddy, but I don't think I'm just that. I know I'm not."

She didn't say anything as she listened to his heartbeats increase.

"I mean, I plan on taking you on a second date, if you'll let me?"

The sudden change in his voice notified her that he'd tried to pull off his comment in humor, but she heard the plea in his voice. He'd saved her, he'd saved everyone, and he held her with such care that she knew what he meant. "Yes, but it better be less exciting."

He chuckled.

"And Daniel, you do mean more to me too."

He moved his hand along her back gently.

"You're my best friend," she said.

His hand stopped against her back and she heard him sigh. "As I am yours, always." His hand moved again, rubbing her back, bringing her warmth. He continued to hold her while she fought sleep.

A voice made her jerk awake. Suddenly, Daniel had let go of her and he was pulling on his shirt. He looked at Olivia with a boyish grin. "The rescue party has arrived," he said, handing her the drenched yellow dress. "Shall we?"

Olivia could hear Gavin's voice beneath them, shouting her name. She didn't hesitate, slipping into the dress was a challenge of its own. When she saw Daniel pull on his pants, she shyly turned her head, unbelieving that she was seeing what she was seeing.

Another voice yelled from below and Daniel shouted, "We're fine! We're coming down."

Olivia was assisted from the ceiling panel with Daniel and Gavin's help. Once she touched the floor of the room that still contained a good waist-high level of cold water, Gavin grabbed her, unable to contain his excitement any longer. He celebrated their reunion by picking up Olivia and hugging her. She smiled as he squeezed her, and his voice rattled as he spoke, "You scared me. I thought I'd lost you. I wouldn't have been able to live with myself if..."

Olivia squeezed him as she interrupted, "You didn't. We made it. We all made it." The moment Olivia looked over to see Daniel, he abruptly turned his head, hiding his face. Still, she'd seen him. His eyes had been on her, and his face held an odd stare that she recognized as pain.

Chapter 23

J umping up and down, singing and shouting, celebrating, that's what all the residents *should* have been doing once they found out they'd narrowly escaped death by drowning, but that didn't happen. Instead, the residents were consumed by the likelihood that something like this would occur again, that imminent disaster awaited them, and they all grumbled and complained that someone needed to be punished.

Once Gavin checked and double checked that Olivia's bump was only a minor wound and that she would be fine with plenty of rest and observation in the medical room, he ordered his soldiers to end the lockdown and escort all residents to the Grand Hall, where he explained the near death they'd all escaped.

With the posture of a leader and the set jaw of a man ready for battle, Gavin scanned the faces of the residents and noted how quickly fear had evaporated and been replaced by anger. He hadn't wasted time, explaining that a rebel group had damaged the vault's water system and almost killed them. That's when they began shouting for the traitors to be punished.

"Listen! Listen!" Gavin yelled over the crowd.

The rumbles quieted.

Gavin wished at that moment that Olivia was there. He had courage, but she gave him something more—a way to see things without orders and how choices were important. He took in the sight of the vault's residents and soldiers, the survivors—the future. Gavin chose his words carefully. "Crimes against the vault's residents will be punished, but locking up someone and throwing away the key isn't the wisest method to move this community forward. Every single resident is *safe* and *alive*. The vault is *safe*." Gavin didn't know if the word *safe* really registered by the look of their expressions.

Gavin shifted his gaze to his soldiers. "One man, the major, believed that The Packet was the key to running the vault." As he said those words, his eyes landed on Daniel, who was leaning against the back wall with his arms crossed. "Many disagreed with the major. A few dangerously put everyone's lives in jeopardy for those beliefs tonight."

His last comment ignited an array of negative remarks. The loudest was a man who shouted, "We can't live like this!"

Gavin raised his hand in the air. "Listen. Please," he said with authority. The commotion dropped to a soft murmur.

"The major has abused his power," he said, a note of disgust in his voice. "Using The Packet as an excuse to do as he wished." As Gavin continued, he grabbed each person's full attention. "I believe that *we* can all come together as residents to create a forum for all our concerns, so that every single person will be heard."

"What does that mean?" a man shouted.

Gavin's expression softened. "It means we," he motioned toward everyone with both hands, "all of us can find a better way to make changes together. First, The Packet will cease to exist." A few mouths dropped open, but no one dared to say anything because they wanted to hear the rest. Gavin held his head up, making sure to announce each word with conviction. "I don't believe in The Packet, and I will not allow the major to force anyone to live by it."

Gasps and *oh my gods* rang through the residents. Some people cheered at that exact moment. Others appeared confused and scared.

"For life to continue in a safe way, everyone still needs to abide by a set of rules. Until those have been decided by a group of your peers, these are the temporary rules that will be enforced: First, there will be no acts of violence, and second, no stealing, because every individual has an equal right to everything in this vault."

Gavin ended with a final word. "If we are to survive in the vault together, we all must depend on each other, not on just one person. I stand by you all as we begin this process. It will be a challenge, but we can build our future together. We owe this to ourselves and every person we lost. Let us not undermine their memory and our past. We came from democracy and if it's not broken ... let's make it work."

Overall, the residents were moved by his words, agreeing that things needed to change. As residents mingled, a hint of excitement sounded in a few voices, while others presented a drearier outlook. The atmosphere shifted to one of diplomacy and discussion. Gavin shook hands and spoke to the eager individuals about how it would take time, and that he was open to all ideas. Gavin took leave, wanting to make sure his soldiers understood what would happen next.

Gavin gathered the soldiers together and briefed them about the next few days, making sure they were aware that the major would not be rejoining them. Gavin smiled proudly at his men who stood before him in the most respectful way—backs straight with soldier poise and a snappy salute. They didn't seem too upset over the change in leadership; instead, most of them displayed grins on their faces while a few others kept tight-lipped. Eddston and Jennings were there, side by side, showing their excitement with a fist bump between one another. Dillard stood among them, relief and admiration clearly showing through her bright eyes and wide smile.

Gavin thanked them for their support with his own salute. "At ease." They relaxed their shoulders slightly, but their poise remained strong. "We made the right choice today. Be proud of yourselves," he paused to glance over them. "And we will continue on that path. We must continue to enforce the rules of residents' safety, but soldiers will no longer hold themselves in a higher esteem than the residents. We are all residents here. We are all equal. And that means socializing and becoming friendly should be a top priority. Does anyone have issues with this?"

The majority eagerly agreed, applauding.

Gavin dismissed them.

"I'll socialize," Eddston joked, lifting both brows in a suggestive manner.

The men laughed at his remark, several slapping him on the back.

"What about the major?" a soldier asked, seriously.

"He'll remain in isolation, for now," Gavin said.

That answer seemed to satisfy the asker. The rest of the men were making jokes of their own, agreeing that things looked brighter.

He realized that a few of his men would still need to be carefully monitored in the following days; he would have to find subtle ways to convince them that these changes were in everyone's best interest. At that moment, he wondered if his father, the colonel, would think his actions were warranted. Then he answered his own question—he didn't care, because the dead didn't judge.

The jail wasn't refilled with the previous occupants. Only two men were in cells, Rossi for his theft and attempted murder, as well as the major, who still hadn't cooled down from being stripped of his position. Gavin didn't want to keep the major locked up, but when he'd gone to see if the major understood why he'd done what he had, he received an earful of threats. The major had screamed, "When I get out of here, you'll wish you never made it to the vault. You'll be begging me to cast you out. Radiation is nothing compared to what I have in store for you."

Gavin tried to reason with him about the residents who'd acted out, explaining that The Packet had been too unrealistic and that if things were to continue in this way, they'd all be dead.

The major didn't twitch an eye as he said, "You are weak and you will see. They'll always find a reason to act out. Someone's always going to have more than someone else or want what another has. Don't think you're above it. You've already taken from me." The major rattled on and on about the way of the world, how he was right, threatening each and every soldier if he wasn't let out.

Leaving the major inside the vault's cell for as long as it took him to see that things were different was Gavin's final decision. "The ways of the world have put us here," Gavin responded as he left the old man. Gavin hoped that a few days would surely be enough, and if they weren't, he'd keep him there longer. Eventually he'd allow the major to join in resident lifestyle. As for Rossi, he'd receive therapy for his addiction to drugs and become absolved from stealing, hopefully in short order. Gavin had great hopes for the future, believing that anything had to be better than the plans in The Packet.

After the vault fell into a peaceful slumber, Gavin decided to visit Olivia.

A hand brushed across Olivia's cheek, prompting her to open her eyes.

Daniel stared down at her with an expression that leaked adoration.

"Hey," she mumbled.

"Hey," he said with a slight grin. "Thought I'd check on you.

How are you feeling?"

She sighed. The pounding had stopped eventually, once the doctor gave her some medicine, and now she felt only a slight soreness in her head. "I'm better. Just tired. You look tired too."

He laughed. "I am, but I couldn't end our date with *put your clothes on.*"

She shook her head at him. "Do you always have to try to be funny?"

"Try?" he asked, hurt.

She nodded, causing a wave of dizziness to hit her at the small gesture. She groaned.

"Are you okay?" Daniel asked in a worried tone as he rose to his feet. "Want the doctor?" He glanced around the room.

Olivia grabbed his arm to stop him. "No. I'll be fine."

He looked down at her hand grasping his arm, then turned a skeptical glance her way. "You sure?"

"Yes."

Her hand didn't move, and he glanced down at it again. He smiled as he slowly took a seat next to her on the bed. "If you want, I can stay," he offered.

"No," she said, "You should get some rest too." He struggled to keep his sunken eyes open, and Olivia imagined he wanted to sleep just as badly as she did.

"As long as you let me bring you breakfast, we'll dine right here," he said. When she nodded he spoke again, this time with an Italian accent, "I will bring cakes and cookies," then he shifted to a French accent, "Ah, crepes if mademoiselle prefers."

She laughed. She attempted a French accent but it came out British as she said, "Crepes, Monsieur, if you please."

He chuckled and Olivia loved the sound of it but hated the reason for it. "Darn it, I always sound British."

His smile widened as she bit her lower lip in frustration. "I like your British," he said with a wink.

She gave him an unbelieving glare. Then she remembered

something. "Guess what?" she said excitedly.

"What?"

"Sophie came to visit. I guess she heard I was here and she stopped in. It was only like a minute, but she asked if I was all right and she said we'd talk soon. She also said she was sorry for how she treated me, and I think she was going to stay longer, but the doctor told her I needed to rest. Isn't that great?"

He nodded. "It is. I'm glad for you."

"Do you think we'll go back to being friends?" she asked.

"I think there's a good chance." His voice changed to a serious tone. "Things are going to be better."

"You think?"

He grabbed her hand. "Yes, I think tonight was a good start."

She felt a strange sensation when he held her hand and suddenly remembered his odd expression when he'd seen her and Gavin hug. She wanted to ask him what he'd been thinking, but she hesitated, and he spoke first. "I'll let you rest. Be back tomorrow with breakfast," he said warmly.

"Okay," she whispered, deciding not to broach the subject at that moment.

He rose to his feet, and just when she thought he was about to turn, he bent down instead, kissing her cheek and whispering, "Goodnight, my dear." When he pulled back, her eyes shot to his, and the color of the ocean held her gaze. She was speechless. His lips curved up to a gentle smile and when he turned, her hand instantly shot up to the spot where his lips had left a warm imprint. She watched him leave, wondering why she was suddenly overwhelmed with worry.

Gavin hadn't expected to see Daniel seated beside Olivia, and he stopped himself at the door. When he saw Daniel bend down and kiss Olivia, he clenched his fist. He forced himself to stand still. When Daniel moved to leave, Gavin stepped back into the hallway and waited.

Daniel stopped in his tracks as he saw Gavin standing before him.

Gavin spoke first. "How's she doing?"

Daniel stared at him suspiciously. "She's good. Just needs to sleep."

"Good," his voice rumbled. "Off to bed, then?"

"Yes. It's been a very long day," he answered casually, but then added, "especially for you. That big speech you gave... guess you're going be the one to lead them?" Daniel said with a raised brow.

Gavin considered his statement and said, "Everyone will need to lead together, and I'll be sure to help."

Daniel disregarded his statement. "You're good at it. I can tell. You have a way with words."

"Then you agree with what I had to say?" He surveyed Daniel's reaction, noticing a slight shift in his eyes. "You'll join me in this?"

Daniel grinned. "All you had to do was ask," he said, joking.

Gavin chuckled. "And you'd have given up being a rebel?"

Daniel shook his head. "You were on the wrong side. If I don't help you, well, you might end up looking just as bad as the major."

"I'm not him," Gavin defended.

"They might like the words, but you still wear the colors." Daniel glanced down at Gavin's uniform.

Gavin straightened his back. "I have my work cut out."

Daniel took a step toward Gavin, both of them keeping their eyes centered on the other. "We have our work cut out."

Gavin gave him a courteous nod. "Tomorrow, then. It's been a long evening."

Daniel took one more step as he came shoulder to shoulder with Gavin. "The first step in a new plan?"

Gavin hesitated for a brief second and then spoke sincerely, "Daniel, thanks for taking care of Olivia," he paused, and when he continued his tone became a warning, "but I can take it from here. She means a great deal to me. I'm sure you've noticed. I won't let anything or anyone hurt her."

Daniel's jaw tightened. "Oh, no need to thank me," he said lightly. "I'd have done it whether you wanted me to or not." Daniel grinned at Gavin, giving him an overly content and smug expression.

Gavin's only response was a slight tilt in his head. The silent exchange ended when Gavin turned away. He hesitated for a brief second as if he would say something, but then he changed his mind and opened the door to the medical room.

Olivia turned her head as she heard the footsteps. "Gavin!" She pushed herself up to a sitting position, watching his eyes as they lit up along with a smile.

"Are you feeling better?" he asked.

She chuckled. "Gosh, I should get a bump on the head more often."

He scrunched his brows in confusion.

"It seems to be the only way to get people to visit," she said sarcastically.

"And who has visited?" he asked.

Her eyes lit up. "Sophie! She finally talked to me without running the other way, Daniel, and now you." Olivia could tell he forced a smile. "Well, how is everyone? I know no one was hurt, but what happened with the major and Rossi?" she asked, triggering her memory of being chased and falling into the water, but pushing it away.

Gavin sat down on the bed next to Olivia, the same spot Daniel had used during his visit. The thought angered him. He looked down at her and took a deep breath before answering. "Well, things are going to be a mess for now until everyone adjusts. The major won't admit he was wrong, and Rossi, he's not going to hurt anyone again. It's going to be a challenge getting everyone to agree on the future of the vault."

Olivia looked down at his hand and decided to go for it. She took it in her own. He looked at her curiously and she smiled. "You did the right thing. Everyone will see that. You're good, your intentions are good. I know that and they will too. Life is going to be better in the vault for everyone because of you."

He squeezed her hand gently. "I hope you're right."

"Why wouldn't I be right? You're great at saving people. Look at me. I know I wasn't the most grateful, and I truly apologize for that. I never should have said those terrible things. You don't know how many times I've wanted to say that, to say thank you."

He smiled. "No need. It was the right thing to do."

He looked at her and he saw his choice to save a life. It had been the right one, even if he'd broken his oath to the military. Olivia was right about what he'd done that night. An urge to tell her everything he'd taken on scared the hell out of him, even if he didn't show it. He didn't want to be the leader, but he knew everyone would be coming to him to solve the problems. They would have to go to someone, and he had been the one to give the speech. Though he hated admitting it, Daniel had been right. He looked like a leader now no matter what he said.

He didn't doubt himself, but he worried what he would face, what the residents were capable of. He didn't believe that a utopia was possible, not after what he'd seen in his life—violence, greed, betrayal—all allures that would rise at some point for the residents. He understood that sooner or later, someone or something would challenge his choices and his values. All he had to hold on to was Olivia. She was the reason he fought so hard to do the right thing, and he couldn't forget it.

He stared at the auburn rings that cascaded down her shoulders, and he couldn't fight the desire to touch one. His fingers gently brushed her cheek as they caught a curl. Her green eyes shot to his, and he remembered how he'd first seen them in the airport store, surprised and embarrassed; he'd never forgotten them. He rather enjoyed them now as they captivated his attention, the way they scanned his face looking for a reason as to why he'd suddenly touched her.

She broke his thoughts. "Did you mean what you said?" she asked.

He refocused on her words. "Mean what?"

She exhaled in frustration. He'd said that he didn't want anything to happen to her, but most importantly he'd said he needed her. She hadn't let those words slip away from her memory. She swore she'd get an explanation from him, and she was going to get it. "In the garden, when I went down to find Daniel. You said you needed me. Did you mean that?"

"Every word," he said softly.

She scanned him with her eyes, trying to find more of a reaction, waiting for him to say something else. When he didn't she continued, determined to chisel through his wall. "And the dance, the cell, in front of Daniel?"

He shrugged. "I had to get him thrown into a cell with probable cause. His attacking me was enough." He cast his eyes away before he went on. "And I had to get him to talk to me fast. I shouldn't have." He found her stare penetrating. "I shouldn't have been so rough with you. I'm sorry if I scared you. I should have warned you, but there wasn't any time."

She pushed him to go on. "And you had to kiss me?"

His expression turned to one of guilt as he said, "Yes."

She pried. "You said you'd never kiss me again."

"I know I did."

She tactfully added. "Because you didn't want to?"

An inquisitive expression covered her face and he noticed. "No, I wanted to."

Her mouth dropped open. "You did?"

The corner of his lip lifted to form a half-grin. "I did."

"I thought," she said, looking down at her hand that still held his and looking back at him, "I thought I was a kid to you?"

He shook his head.

She had to control her urge to scream at him. "What does that mean?"

He took his hand from hers. She thought he meant to leave, but he leaned over her and their eyes connected. She gasped as he stopped but two inches from her face and whispered, "I'll never do that again," and then his lips gently touched hers. A tingling sensation erupted throughout her body, and she closed her eyes to the warm rush of his lips moving with hers.

When he pulled away, he brushed his finger along her cheek. "I'll let you get some sleep."

Olivia grabbed his shirt and tugged at it, causing him to stop just above her. "Please, stay... for a little bit."

"Okay," he whispered as he looked around the empty room before he lay down beside her. He didn't expect her to curl up against him, and he smiled as she did.

His arms wrapped around her, and she felt safe. Daniel's face flashed in her mind. She tried not to think of it and finally convinced herself it was because he'd held her exactly the same way only a few hours ago. She shifted in his arms carefully. He pulled her closer to him. She concentrated on the moment that she'd dreamed of, finally Gavin had kissed her and was holding her—what she'd wanted for so long.

When she awoke the next morning, Gavin's sleeping face was there. She stared at him for several minutes, enjoying the sight of him, enjoying his presence. Something she'd never before dared to believe was possible, and just as she thought she'd die from satisfaction, something caught her eye. On the table next to her bed lay a tray holding two omelets, two cookies, and two crepes. Instantly, she knew that Daniel had been there. Her heart sank.

Chapter 24

The vault continued to run as it had before, minus the impending worry of turning twenty, being raided, curfew, and being told who one may or may not associate with. The entire population of the vault slowly began to realize that certain expectations had been removed and other problems occurred in their place—late arrival to shifts, incomplete duties, and a certain air developed of the residents doing what they liked, when they liked. Luckily, Gavin had expected such a reaction and was prepared.

Within weeks of the major's removal from power, Gavin began a board of trustees among the residents, made up of upper-level supervisors who handled different jobs throughout the vault. They'd already implemented a disincentive to keep all residents on the straight and narrow, which was that individuals would lose their job and be demoted if they didn't perform well. That was the vote of the board, and that's what solved the problem.

Other changes occurred as well. The removal of the term *soldier* was agreed upon; instead military members would be considered the vault's security. If anyone needed to report a problem, then they would handle it. No one was above any of the rules. The residents began to work on making sure that everyone agreed on the proper method for handling insubordination on a job or crime that was committed. It was a strange time, for they were making their own rules for their own world.

Overall, the residents began to fall into the idea of having a community that was theirs alone, not one that belonged to an outside party who determined what was right for them. Peacefulness seemed to take over as suggestions for meals changed menus, suggestions for events changed social interactions, suggestions for efficient labor changed jobs, and suggestions for rules changed hostility.

Gavin had taken hold of all problems with an optimistic approach, listening as he'd always done, and administering as the people requested, within reason. Daniel helped, just as he'd offered. His assistance was key in dealing with some of the more sensitive residents who'd been involved with the strategy to overthrow the major, which had led to the flood in the garden. Daniel's dedication was the same as Gavin's, involving himself in all resident discussion and being one of the main speakers to extinguish any uprising problem.

Gavin was suspicious of Daniel at first, but he rose to be one of Gavin's most trusted allies when dealing with the other residents. Gavin was, at times, shocked when Daniel would side with him on debates or figure out a better way of doing something. Gavin didn't argue or ask why he was on board, but he did note the brief glances Daniel sometimes gave to Olivia, and though it bothered him, he said nothing.

Sophie finally approached Olivia in the Grand Hall a few days after the flood. She walked up with a guilty expression and said her name. Olivia was overjoyed to see her old friend, and when she'd offered her a seat beside her, Sophie had taken it eagerly.

Sophie said, "I know I was wrong, and I hope you can forgive me."

Olivia didn't allow her to grovel. Instead, she quickly responded, "It didn't happen, okay? So, are you free for a movie?"

Sophie was.

Olivia returned to work shortly after healing from her injury and was sad to find that Daniel had turned back into a distant boss. She tried to figure him out, though when she asked him about it he wouldn't give her a straight answer.

She first broached the subject with him the day after she saw the tray beside her bed containing the French breakfast he'd promised to share with her. She'd been embarrassed to think he'd seen her sleeping with Gavin and she wondered what he thought. The rest of the day went by and he never came back to visit her, so the next morning she put on her uniform and strolled right into his office looking for an answer.

He had a melancholy glow in his eyes when he looked up. She noted that he tried to hide it as he saw her, quickly forcing a polite grin. "You didn't visit me," she said upon entering.

"I did," he'd said factually, proceeding to turn his attention back to what he was working on. Then he added, "You were busy."

A flash of heat hit her face, and she struggled to defend herself. "I, I wasn't."

His blue eyes glanced up at her and he raised a brow. "You weren't?"

"I was asleep," she said. "You should have woken me."

"And disturb the captain?" he asked, turning back to his paperwork.

She stopped herself from yelling at him and said, "That's…"

"None of my business."

"It is. I want it to be," she said spontaneously.

He looked up at her with a glint of hurt in his eyes. "Why? Why would you?"

She smiled softly. "You're my friend."

He made a noise as if that didn't satisfy him. "Yes, I'm your friend," he said in a manner that seemed to distress him. "I don't feel friendly right now," he warned her in a tone she'd never heard from him. "Try again tomorrow. Okay?"

She wanted to tell him no, that he needed to speak to her, but she noticed tension in his jaw as he spoke, before he turned away as if dismissing her.

She gave him what he asked for. She said, "Okay, I'll see you then," and left.

The next day he acted as if the conversation had never happened, and he instructed her professionally to do what needed her attention in the form of repairs and more quizzes. She waited for him to say something, to mention anything that he might be thinking, but he didn't. Eventually, she stopped trying to drop hints that she wanted to talk to him. She no longer mentioned lunch, and she didn't bring up movies or traveling. He never did ask her on that second date. Their relationship changed overnight, and she couldn't figure out how to repair it.

Gavin changed, too, but for the better. He stopped acting like an official every time Olivia saw him. Instead, his eyes would brighten, a smile would form, and then he'd say her name as if it was his favorite word. She couldn't help but smile too, because it made her happy to finally see him as she'd fantasized. He had finally let her in.

Olivia happily accepted the new Gavin. The first change was that Gavin relieved her from her military position. He simply said, "You're fired," and she laughed when he told her he'd wanted to do that for a long time.

She rolled her eyes and said, "So are you. You're not a captain anymore."

He laughed with her and said, "I guess you're right, what's that make me?"

Olivia shrugged. "A leader of the people, maybe a boyfriend?"

He chuckled as he gave her a huge hug. "You want a boyfriend, huh?"

She'd simply smiled and said, "Yes."

He said, "Let me think about it."

She hit him playfully and he roared with laughter.

Things continued this way. Olivia resumed her engineering duties, assisting Daniel during the day, and then in the evening she hung out with her boyfriend Gavin. Though it nagged at her that Daniel never again mentioned his feelings for her as he had that night they'd both almost drowned, she let it go, believing that it was what he wanted. And so the days went by until finally Christmas arrived.

A knock at the door caught Olivia's attention. She crossed her room and opened the door. Gavin stood there, dressed in a red shirt and black pants, grinning from ear to ear.

"You look great!" he said when he saw her.

Olivia matched his smile and turned, modeling her new red dress for him. "Janet made it for me. She did a great job, didn't she?"

"I'll say." He grabbed her and gave her a kiss on the lips.

She giggled as his whiskers rubbed against her face.

"What?" He touched his face. "Oh no, I forgot to shave."

"That's okay. I like it."

He smiled. "So where's my gift?"

"I was supposed to get a gift?" she asked, worried.

He winced. "That hurt."

She smiled really big. "I got you something."

"Well, let me go first," he said with a wicked grin. He took a blue, square package from behind his back and handed it to her.

She smiled up at him and took it. "What could it be?" she said teasingly.

"Open it," he teased back.

She unwrapped it, tearing the blue paper to shreds. When she finished, she stared at it with a horrified expression. She held a book in her hands that displayed two figures on the cover, a woman and a man grasping each other in a romantic embrace. She looked up at him with a red face. "Romance novel?" she asked with a whimper.

"Thought you'd probably finished that other one," he said casually.

She groaned as his smile widened. She swatted him and said, "Thanks a lot."

"Where's mine?" he asked.

"You don't get a gift."

His mouth dropped open. "Fine, I'll take back the book and enjoy it myself."

She looked at him with a raised brow. "Here," she said, handing him a small box.

He opened it and laughed. "That's what you were up to." He flashed the picture of them she'd had Eddston take several weeks ago. "I love it." He hugged her and kissed her cheek. "Let's go. We don't want to miss anything."

When they arrived at the Grand Hall, everyone seemed full of the Christmas spirit. *Have a Holy Jolly Christmas* rang out over the overhead speakers. The smell of cookies and ham filled the air. People rushed about, completing finishing touches on the food and the decorations. Olivia spotted Sophie giving out a few recommendations about where to place the eggnog. The warm glow of the room reminded Olivia of her family, and she felt a sudden tightness in her throat. She glanced down at her wrist where her mother's bracelet hung.

Gavin noticed. "What's wrong?"

She took a deep breath and glanced up to meet his concerned eyes. "Just thinking of my mom and brother."

His eyes reflected the same hurt. "I was thinking of my family too." He looked around. "It's hard not to."

"I feel guilty, you know, here we are enjoying ourselves, and we should be thinking of them."

He squeezed her arm. "We are thinking of them. We continue for them."

She forced a smile. "You're right. I want to know what happened. If they're…" She broke off unable to finish her sentence.

He comforted her by gently stroking her back. "We will. But don't forget, you have me always."

She hugged him and smiled up, meeting his blue eyes with her green. "You have me too," she purred with content. He smiled that wonderfully gorgeous smile she treasured, and when she thought he'd let her go, he surprised her by bending down and whispering against her lips, "I love you," just before he sealed it with a kiss.

That night almost every one of the 159 people celebrated more than a tradition—they celebrated the ability to celebrate, and they did it with each other. Possibility loomed in the air as the future looked safe and secure, humanity still intact. The residents embraced the cheerfulness of the evening and forgot, at least for the time being, that their future lay within the vault.

to be continued . . .

Olivia's journey continues in *Secrets*, the sequel to *The Vault* and second book in *The Vault Series*.

A New Novel From Jettie Necole

Ruby unites the seductive and sinister actions of the supernatural with the allure and elegance of a Regency romance.

Ruby is the first novel in the *Tree of Blood series* that takes root in exposing the origins of supernatural bloodlines.

A historical romance begins to blossom around Lady Ruby Waterfield, but family secrets and unpredictable suitors expose a world of supernatural creatures—ancient enemies bound by war: vampires and warlocks.

Set in 1811 England, Ruby finally attends her first London Season at the age of eighteen. After departing from her safe, secluded childhood in the country, she quickly discovers that taking her rightful place among the aristocracy is the least of her worries after she becomes the target of a vindictive vampire. Determined to learn the truth about her family bloodlines, this clever debutante must navigate her pursuit while two gentlemen—one, her loyal best friend; the other, a mysteriously handsome stranger—grow increasingly tied to her future. From the dark alleys of Covent Garden to the lavish balls of the high society *ton*, clandestine agendas leave Ruby's heart exposed to a dangerous new world of mystery, magic, and love.

Acknowledgments

~

Lots of love and thanks to my husband for supporting me through this endeavor.

Hugs and kisses to my Mom for always giving me encouragement and guidance when I need it most.

Thank you, Dad, for introducing me to science fiction and most importantly *Star Trek*.

A big thank you to the talented Robby Davis who designed the cover of *The Vault* ~ www.robbydavis.com

Thank you to my editor, K. Clodfelter, for assisting me through the roughest part of writing.

A huge thank you to the readers who enjoyed my story and look forward to the next.

Jettie Necole

is the author of The Vault. She graduated from University of Texas at Austin with a degree in Radio-Television-Film, and she lives with her husband and their fluffy Goldendoodle named Oliver in Kentucky.

Her website is www.jettienecole.com

Made in the USA
Charleston, SC
13 June 2014